SOMETHING WICKED

THE CHRONICLES OF BREED: BOOK THREE

K.T. DAVIES

SCIMITAR MEDIA

Published by Scimitar Media

www.scimitar-media.co.uk

ISBN-13: 978-1999747428

Cover design by Scimitar Media

Original cover art by Michael Gauss

To Raven and Gabe,

the best rum crew a cove could wish for

SOMETHING WICKED

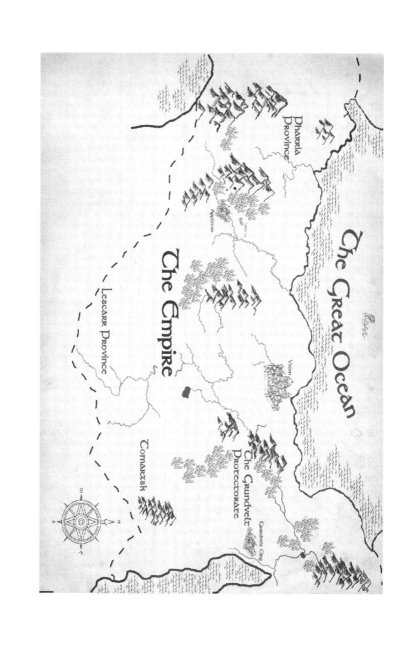

The Great Ocean

Pharria Province

Lescarr Province

The Empire

Appaleon

Comarzsk

Valen

The Grundvelt Protectorate

Grundvelt City

Prologue

"**M**eet Malin, kill Nemann, have dinner with Sceafa." I read the note twice before throwing it in the fire.

"What did you say?" Malin asked. He was lounging on a daybed, swaddled in a fluffy, woolen blanket. A book flapped like a snared bird in his fleshless hands.

"I said you look like a death's head upon a mop stick. You need to eat more. What are you reading?"

"I'm not hungry thank you, *puff guts*. This blasted cough has killed my appetite. I'm reading *The Adventures of Pym the Incredulous*."

I glanced down at my snug, obi-bound midriff. "It's this fabric, it makes me look fatter than I am. And why are you reading that... *novel*. They rot the brain you know."

He grinned, scratched his stubbled chin. For a king, he was a scruffy looking cove. "Everyone's reading it. It's quite the thing."

"It's shit. I didn't even get past the prologue."

He folded his arms like he'd won a point in a game only he was playing. "So, you started reading it?"

"I was curious as to what the fuss was about, but sweet salvation, the prose is pretentious."

His expression became one of mock seriousness. "And we know how you dragon sorcerers hate pretention."

"Oh, please. The so-called 'author' of this ink-spattered dribble bib has an absurdly grandiloquent and hyperbolic turn of phrase that is, quite frankly, unreadable."

"But tell me what you really think."

"Not enough sex or violence, and don't get me started on the use of prologues. Why not just call it, 'Chapter One' and have done?"

Malin laughed, but his amusement was soon ambushed by the cough that had plagued him for weeks. The smell of rot seeped into the air. Our light-hearted conversation was killed by unvoiced worry; unvoiced because there were rules regarding 'the cough' that I dare not break for fear of him getting angry and me being forced to throttle him. The cough was not to be commented on. No mention of the physicker was to be made with regards to the cough, and no show of concern was to be made during or after an attack of coughing. "I've got to go see a man about a rat," I said and headed to the door of the grand bedchamber, built on dragon scale rather than human. Silken drapes that could be opened and closed to partition the room reduced the cavernous echo, but when I turned to sketch a bow it struck me how small the furniture and Malin appeared and how vulnerable he looked, lying there, pretending to read the fucking *Adventures of Pym the Incredulous*.

As though wounded by my stinging criticism the book's pages flapped wildly as he slammed it against the bed. "What are you staring at?" The question was a challenge and a test.

A sick man. "You've got a thing in your hair." I passed the test. The book closed gently.

"Maybe I want it there," he muttered half-heartedly as he brushed the fluff from his greying locks.

I didn't mention the fleck of blood on his cheek. Against my better judgment, I let my head follow my sinking heart and bowed. "Anon, Majesty. Enjoy the book."

***

Garbed in shadows and stuffed full of impotent rage, I apported to Nemann's grand mansion. It was in

Swanscombe; an affluent quarter of new Galewyn. It was an area where over the last forty years the well-off had become the well-heeled— a marked improvement from making their homes out of straw and dung which they shared with the livestock. I designed the quarter myself; modeled the wide sweeping avenues after what I could remember of Valen's fair suburbs. Those who settled in Swanscombe competed for the most opulent manor in the neighborhood. Many attempted this petty feat by building taller-than-the-neighbors' ornamental wind towers. Some commissioned magnificent gardens, and more than one had bankrupted themselves attempting both. The result was quite the confection; a garish, tasteless sprawl of wonders etched in marble that gleamed even on a moonless night. "Mother would have loved it."

"Beg pardon?" A night guard called.

So much for stealth. "Nice night for a stroll."

She sauntered across the cobbled street. "Aye, it is that." She fixed me with a quizzical look. Even in my human-ish guise my scarlet hair and yellow eyes were distinctive. "Are you sure I cannot help you with something?" There followed an uncertain amount of not quite bowing.

"No." This was becoming awkward. I couldn't be seen in the area just before Nemann had a fatal accident. "Thank you."

"Only, if there was anything, anything at all I could help you with…?"

I drew my hood back. "Just fuck off, there's a love— and forget you ever saw me." Her eyes glazed for a moment as the spell of compulsion took hold. A moment later she turned and sauntered away. She'd stop in a few minutes and then continue with her patrol, none the wiser of our encounter. I felt the slightest twinge, which might have been guilt but was equally as likely to have been my back, which was a constant bother to me.

"You use compulsion magic a lot these days."

I didn't turn to look at Tobias. Half the time these days he was no more than a chiding comment, a sneering, judgmental voice in the shadows that daren't show himself. "Oh, you can fuck off too."

"I'm trying to help you, Breed."

"Funny, it sounded like you were warming up to a sermon." I looked up. Perfect rectangles of amber filigree spilled from a ring of windows in Nemann's magnificent wind tower.

"Breed…" I felt the flutter of ghost breath against my neck, or it might have been the wind. Whichever it was I ignored it and apported to the highest chamber of Nemann's tower where I was sure to find the man himself at this hour.

The room was bare save for a desk and chair. A chandelier hung from the ceiling. Nemann was sitting, hunched over the desk. Shock and alarm blazed across his flushed cheeks, caught as he was in hand-to-gland combat. He froze when he saw me.

"Sweet Trinity and all the angels. How dare you!" He rummaged about in his jewel case before straightening his robes as he stood up.

"I would have knocked, but I didn't want to spoil the moment."

"This is an outrage." He stormed from behind the desk and rushed to the door with as much dignity as a man in his position could muster.

I let him almost reach it before apporting in front of him. "Where do you think you're going?"

He leaped back. "You've gone too far this time, sorcerer. The Witnergan will fucking have your guts, and this time the king will not protect you."

"You sure about that, Emmurt? I mean, you of all people shouldn't invoke the name of the Witnergan or the king. Not after what you've been up to, you naughty, little fellow."

He circled back towards his desk, put the huge slab of granite and mahogany between us. He tried to roll up an erotic scroll he'd been using to wake his little dragon, but his hands were shaking so much he couldn't manage it. The vellum was new and kept springing open. I had to laugh.

"Guards! Anyone!"

"No one can hear you, Nemann. Your fucking tower's too tall. What is it that they say about it?"

He swallowed. Nemann was a clever man, and my inference wasn't lost on him. "They say that it is closer to heaven than to earth."

"Aye, that's it. How very apt." I took a step towards his desk.

He started to whimper. He was a big man, but he was a merchant, not a warrior. His bulk was merely decorative. "What do you want?"

"Oh, let me see. I want my eyesight back, because it's fucking terrible these days, much like my sense of smell. I'd also like peace on the border with Glennarn and a really good grape harvest this year. Oh, aye, and you dead. I want that most of all right now."

"I'll give you anything, everything. We can make a deal." His tone was wheedling, his expression imploring and utterly insincere.

"I don't make deals anymore; they've never gone well for me."

His face darkened, and he slammed his meaty fist on the desk. "If I am accused of wrongdoing, I demand a trial. I am a member in good standing of the Merchants' Guild. You cannot deny me my rights."

"You know the rule, Nemann. Fuck's sake, you've played by it long enough."

"Don't get caught."

I applauded. "There's a bright boy."

"But why? Why have *you* come?"

I opened my mouth expecting the reason to fall out and was therefore shocked when it didn't. My mind was entirely blank. I laughed and leaned casually against the doorframe while I frantically tried to remember why I'd written a note to myself telling me to kill Nemann. I knew he was a dirty fucker, but the specific act of fuckery that had caused me to drag my bones over here instead of sending a minion to close his account had momentarily escaped me. "Oh, I think we both know."

He fumbled with the drawer in his desk, pulled out a serviceable looking shiv. "Fuck you, you freakish old bastard. Fuck you and fuck your wretched, sickly king. If disease doesn't finish him, the League will." He clenched his fist and waved it like someone who'd never used it for anything save self-abuse. "And you they will drown in your own blood, with or without my help."

"That's it!" It all came flooding back. "You know, I could have ignored your other misdeeds; trafficking in flesh, selling drugs, burning down your own warehouses to collect over-inflated insurance claims. I might have put that all down to robust entrepreneurship, but then you killed those fishermen, in their own boat and I liked those coves on the *Jacinta*."

He narrowed his eyes. "The what? What are you talking about?"

"The *Jacinta*. It was a small crabber that worked out of Filstock Harbor. Apparently, they wouldn't smuggle for you on account of working for someone else, so you and your fucking League friends decided to make an example of them by burning them to death on their own fucking boat. Do you want to have a guess for whom they were working?" I smiled tightly.

He swallowed hard, licked his fear parched lips. "You... you c... can't prove it."

I raised a finger. "Aha. Hold a moment, would you?" Confused, he didn't move save to wipe sweat from his face while awkwardly brandishing his weapon like it was a warding talisman.

I reached into my haori and took out a box of ashes. I had no real skill with necromancy despite having more than a passing acquaintance with those who did, but I cast the spell and poured the dust into my palm anyway. Nothing happened at first, but then the dust swarmed like a cloud of gnats and took on the recognizable shape of the head of Miralee Penthallow, the captain of the *Jacinta*.

"Good evening, Captain," I said to the ash head floating a few inches above my palm. "Could you tell the court who murdered you and your crew?"

The specter turned first to me then to Nemann who tried to back away through the wall. A cool breeze ruffled the candles and set shadows dancing across the walls. "Emmurt Nemann, Rodris Tuyl, Barish Kerr," the head whispered. My control of the spell wasn't the best as I lacked the cold detachment required to master the art of necromancy. I was thrilled when she started to speak and lost concentration. The head wavered and then dissolved, dusting my hand and the floor in ashes. "Damn it. It took an age dredging the wreck for the bodies."

Nemann sneered. "Like I said, you have no proof. No jury would convict me on evidence gained from a dubious, mage trick."

I cast my gaze to the ceiling dramatically. "My dear Nemann, It doesn't matter what a jury would do. I have all the proof I need."

The look of fear returned, and I could almost hear his brain calculating the odds, trying to decide what he would do, what I would do. "You are not my judge."

I smiled. He didn't. With an inchoate yell, he launched himself over the desk at me like a man fueled entirely by desperation. I waited for him to swing—which he did, clumsily and slowly. I swayed aside, and he cut me. More accurately, he cut my haori, but the bastard got a touch. He came in swinging again. I backed away, unsure as to how the great lump had managed to almost shiv me. He was a fucking bean counter, not a fighter, just what was going on? While I quickly readjusted my assessment, he slashed again, feigning an uppercut before reversing the angle of the blade, and coming in for my face. Just in time, I managed to sweep my cloak around my arm and block.

"Stop!" I commanded. It wasn't a subtle use of sorcery, it was sudden and wrenching and came from a place within me where, until now, I hadn't realized panic resided. His nose began to bleed as did his ears and his eyes, but he stopped fighting. "Drop the knife." He did as I ordered, eyes wild with panic. "Now just get out of the fucking window and keep the noise down, eh? We don't want to scare the neighbors."

He made a strangled animal noise. "Nooo." He shook his head as he marched woodenly to the nearest window and opened the pierced, camphor wood shutters. "Nooo." He sobbed.

"Yeeees," I replied. "Now crack on, Nemann, old fruit. I've got a supper appointment with, er…Sceafa. Yes. Sceafa."

Nemann climbed onto the sill.

"Wait," said Tobias, who had materialized in the corner of the room. Or rather, some of him had. His form was hazy and indistinct, his brown robes a mere smudge of shadow.

"Wait," I said to Nemann. The merchant froze and clung to the window frame like it was a boon companion. The wind ruffled his robes, brushed the tears from his cheeks. "What is it?" I said to Tobias. "Can't you see I'm busy?" I rolled up the erotic scroll and tucked it into my robe. Waste not, want not, after all.

"What are you doing, Breed?"

"I'm saving the gold that would be spent trying this prick in a court of law."

"This isn't you." The shade of my dead friend rubbed his forehead with his stump

I patted myself. "Yes, it is me."

"Please, don't kill me…" Nemann sobbed from the window ledge.

"Shut up." Tobias and I said in unison. Nemann choked back a sob.

"He had an entire ship's crew killed. Good men and women sent to Crabland to teach others a lesson, and that's not all. He's a flesh peddler, a drug trafficker.

He's a bad lot, and Arduin will be better off without him."

"This isn't the right way to do things. Malin wouldn't approve."

"I'm not having this conversation. Just leave me alone. For good."

"I will, I swear." Nemann mistakenly breathed a sigh of relief and sagged against the window frame.

"You don't mean that," said Tobias. "I'm trying to help you."

"Stop bothering me. I have had enough of your self-righteous horse shit. Just fuck off to Deadland and don't come back." Tobias vanished instantly.

Nemann, still under the impression that I had been speaking to him, tentatively put his foot on the floor. "Not you. You can fucking jump now." The merchant's face crumpled, and his eyes became blank stones as the spell compelled him to jump. I didn't watch, I didn't have to. Nemann's wind tower was one of the tallest in the neighborhood. I tucked his dagger in my robe beside the erotic scroll and opened the door leading from the tower and the darkness of the stairwell rose up and swallowed me whole. The darkness erased all trace of Galewyn and replaced it with the furious cold of the Void.

I had been there in the tower that night, and I had compelled Nemann to kill himself, but that had been almost a year ago when Malin was alive. Now he was dead, and I was holding his body while the howling rage of the Void screamed in my face. Together, we hurtled through the cold heart of the heavens. This was how it would end, for Malin, and for me.

They say the best laid plans oft go awry. So I shouldn't have been surprised when something went wrong. As I began to fall into the long, cold sleep of death, an irresistible force seized me and dragged me from the endless arc of our flight. The force began to pull me towards an unknown destination and was so strong that I could only watch helplessly as Malin was torn from my rimed arms and spun away into star scatter of eternity.

Chapter One

"Tis the finest boiled sandroach in the whole of Galewyn," the Master of the Banquet announced. I was sitting in my usual place at the king's table, waiting for the food that had been announced to be served. Tobias was beside me, a knife in one hand, a spoon wrapped in his tentacle.

"What the fuck is that?" I exclaimed too loudly at the sight of the unusual appendage. All eyes in the hall turned to me.

"It's a spoon," said Tobias in that condescending-yet-confused tone of voice most often employed by youths when speaking to their tiresome elders.

"Not the fucking spoon. I know what a spoon is," I hissed as the babble of conversation slowly resumed. "The thing holding the spoon."

"It's a tentacle," he said, again in a tone of voice that invited a punch in the mouth.

"You don't have a tentacle, your father had it cut off when you were born."

Tobias smiled his insufferable smile. "Eat your sandroach before it gets warm."

I looked down to see a sandroach had been set before me on a silver platter. As was the current fashion, the popular delicacy was resting on its shell, which had been boiled pink. Its twelve pairs of legs had been removed and its guts mashed with garlic butter and herbs. It looked so delicious that I just stuck my face into the mash and swallowed. It should have tasted like suckling pig wrapped in fish innards, but whatever was in my mouth tasted more like warm guts and blood with a hint of grass.

It was then that I woke up and discovered that I was face down in a pile of intestines.

I pulled my head out of the hot giblets and spat out the filth I'd swallowed.

A sliver of moon hung in a sky full of strange stars. Wan light illuminated the circle of ancient stones in which I'd appeared. They stood in the rough center of a moorland bog hemmed by hills on one side and woodland on the other. My head was pounding, and I was shivering cold. I got up and wiped gore from my eyes, spat out the taste of grassy gut sausage. It looked like a half-dozen or so sheep had been slaughtered and then thrown into the middle of the ring of stones, although, it was hard to tell exactly how many there were as whoever had done the butchering had gone at it with gusto.

Speaking of whom. Standing about ten feet from the stones was a gore-splattered old fellow and a child. Despite the bloody mess, he looked to be a well-off cove. He was wearing a pair of velvet trousers and a demask waistcoat which was fastened over his slender middle with pearl buttons. A gold chain with an amber drop hung from his waistcoat pocket and was looped around a button. The fellow's starch-collared shirt had, I think, been white once but appeared to have been recently dyed sheep blood red. The child was feral looking with a wild tangle of dark curls and fox bright eyes. She was wearing a green woolen frock, ragged at the hem and patched at the elbows. Nearby, a backpack and walking stick lay next to a cold hearth and a three-legged cooking pot. A long hunting knife lay in the dirt beside the pot.

"Is that it?" the child said with more than a hint of skepticism.

"I jolly well hope so," the old fellow answered, unsure, his gaze darting as though he was expecting unwelcome company.

"It don't look like no guardian," said the child as she gave me the once over while excavating her nose. I guessed she was no older than six, seven at a push.

He smiled at the child. "Looks can be deceiving, my dear. Look at you."

She gave a short stab of laughter. "I dun't know what you mean."

A sound like a firelance being discharged tore through their quiet conversation and roused a murder of crows that were roosting in the woods to cawing anger. Although I didn't see a muzzle flash, when the birds flew, I dropped. Take it from one who knows, lying on a carpet of warm innards is only slightly better than being shot.

The old fellow grabbed the child and pulled her close to him. From somewhere behind them the report of another firelance again shattered the quiet. The child yelped and clung to the old geezer. The dying echo of the second shot came from a different direction to the first. There were at least two culls out there with firelances, and by the sound of it, they weren't far away. My guess was that they were making their way through the trees, which stood some half a mile beyond the angle gate.

"Hush now, Edith," the old fellow whispered. "We don't have much time."

"Er, time for what, pray tell?" Given that the shootists weren't in sight, I stood up rather than lie any longer in the filth. I gestured to the carcasses. "Were you planning on a roast, or is it that you just don't like sheep?"

Looking more nervous than he had a minute before, the old fellow took the child by the hand. He smelled of cologne, brandy, and some kind of magic. But as one cove's turds smell different to another's despite both being made out of shit, his magic didn't smell like my magic.

He cleared his throat. "I have threaded the old, Wild ways, been blessed in the Temple with the willow and the oak. I have anointed the portal with the blood of three ewes and three rams, and I have made libations of bread, mead, and salt. I pray you, accept these, my humble offerings, Guardian of the Gates." He paused as though expecting an answer.

Something dripped out of my hair. "Is that a piece of kidney? For fuck's sake. I've got kidney in my hair."

The child giggled. The old cove appeared less amused. He straightened and stuck out his chin in the time-honored display of confidence. "I, Bennington Cornell, have summoned thee, guardian. I command you to protect this child. I bid thee to protect the Goblin Queen from those who would do her harm, until the Blood Moon has ascended."

I looked behind me in the hope that he was talking to someone else. He wasn't. Behind me were just the ragged silhouettes of unruly tussock grass set against the mirror of cloud-muddied pools of bog water. I scanned beyond the marshy ground, saw bare boned foothills sat upon the land like mounds of rumpled velvet; a fitting pillow for the dark crown of night, glittering with a million stars. He cleared his throat again.

The old fellow coughed politely. I turned. He pointed to a flashing light flickering in the woods behind him. Oblivious to whatever had Cornell on edge, the child knelt down and poked a slow worm with a twig as it slithered past her.

"Sorry, mate," I said. "I forgot you were there. As for all this Guardian guff. I'm afraid you've got the wrong cove. I'm no one's guardian." *Not anymore.* I wiped more giblets from my face and hair. "Urgh. This haori is ruined."

The old fellow's face crumpled. "What do you mean, 'the wrong cove'? You can't be." The child looked up curious.

"I can, and I am— or not, as the case may be."

The wind shifted carrying with it the sound of raised voices. As I'd guessed, they were coming through the woods. The pitch of their voices grew more excited as the drew closer. Five, sulfurous torch lights blazed to life and began weaving through the trees towards us. Whoever they were, they were coming quickly.

"The Pennies are here, Professor. We got to scarper." The child jumped up and tried to drag the old fellow away, but he remained rooted to the spot.

"Please," he implored, but I was already searching the stones for the one that would re-open the gate. "Please— I performed the rite and you arrived. You have to help us."

"No, I really don't and trust me, you don't want my help. It never works out well."

"They will kill her. I—"

The muzzle flash blazed like dragon breath. I ducked an instant before a fist-sized hole was blown in Cornell's chest. The child stared, incredulous as his fingers loosened from around her hand and he pitched into the dirt.

"Well, that was just rude," I said and traced the path of the shot to a shadowy figure some eighty foot away. Moonlight ran silver across his or her shoulders and down the long barrel of a smoking firelance. Feeling a little guilty that the old cove had been jawing with me when he got slotted, I closed one eye and made sure that the angles were right. "Get your head down, girl," I said before unleashing a jagged skein of sorcerous lightning. The gunner might have been a crack shot, but they had no skill at dodging. Their powder bag exploded upon the touch of my fire, turning the stricken cove into a candle. They didn't scream, so much as roar.

I turned to the girl. "If I was you, I'd grab yon shiv and leg it sharpish. Those..." Another firelance roared.

"Down," I said because, for some reason that I cannot fathom, I thought that they were after slotting the brat.

Truly, this was a night for unwelcome surprises.

A searing nova of light exploded in my head closely followed by a blinding, white-hot pain that scorched the inside of my skull. I was knocked off my feet by the brain-rattling impact and then, to add insult to the injury, I hit my already wounded noggin on one of the blasted stones.

The Void opened in my mind, and all sensible thought was drowned in numbing pain. I heard the child yell, and the sound of many feet splashing at speed across the waterlogged ground. I managed to prise my eyes open. Dark shapes and torchlight were approaching from the woods. The smell of sulfur and death wormed their way into the ashen air and mingled with the smell of burning. I pushed myself up on my elbow and tried to focus through the throbbing pain on the left side of my head where the shot had hit me and scored a groove in my skull.

I tried to get up but lacked the ability to coordinate my shaking limbs. My ears were ringing, my vision was blurred. Time fractured, became disjointed as I dipped in and out of consciousness. The next thing I knew I was being punched in the face— an unnecessary act of brutality in my opinion, seeing as I'd just been shot in the head. My nose broke and my head snapped back as another blow landed.

"Steady on, Doc. Remember what Madame said about anything that comes through the gate." Whoever was speaking had a wavering, heavily accented voice compared to the dearly departed Cornell.

"The fucking freak killed Vasquez." This cove had a similar, albeit less refined twang to the professor, save that it was more graveled.

"I thought Cornell done that?" said Wavering.

"He did, I saw him. Fine shot it was too," I think I said although my recollection is hazy. It's possible that I just thought I said it.

"You shut your yap," someone snarled. "And don't be soft, Pavel. When have you seen that old cunt cast a spell like that? All he does is tie fucking ribbons around twigs or stick needles into poppets."

Spells. That reminded me. I tried to bring a spell to mind in order to burn these impertinent culls to ashes. I clawed at the ground, tried to heave myself up. I couldn't exactly see them, but I was sure that if I aimed in their general direction I was bound to hit something.

They had other ideas. One of them— I think it was 'Doc', fell upon me and pinned me to the ground, trapping my arms. Before I could bring so much as a curse to mind, let alone a spell, he lamped me across the chops. It was a tooth-loosening blow which pleased him so much that he did it a few more times.

"All right, Doc, that's enough," said Pavel without particular concern or urgency. "Madame will have our guts if we don't take it back to her alive."

"I'm not scared of Madame."

"Yes, you are, and if you aren't you should be."

The sound of a scuffle off to the left intruded into my pain.

"Let go of me, you stinking crab louse." It was the girl and she was in a raging bad temper.

I would have applauded her spunk if Doc hadn't been kneeling on my hands. Chains rattled, and the weight lifted allowing me to draw a full breath, but my relief was short lived. A moment later, cold, warded bracelets were fastened around my wrists damning me to whatever unhappy fate they had planned for me. When he was done, he dragged me to my feet by the manacle chain.

"I liked Vasquez, she was a nice person. Good singer, liked cats." Doc's face was inches from mine. I opened my right eye and saw the faint trace of an old scar running through a bushy ginger brow and across a nose that had been beaten flat. Mud colored curls framed a pock-scarred face and old copper coins filled the holes where his eyes should have been. I groaned. Doc cracked a smile sprinkled with gold teeth and gave a slow nod. "Oh, yes, fucker. You see me now, don't you?"

It was hard not to as he was close enough to kiss, but I didn't interrupt as I felt a speech coming on.

"It will give me a diamond hard-on to watch Madame suck the life from your freakish bones. And if she doesn't kill you, I'll see you in the pit." His 'breath' was nothing more than the rank and lifeless exhalation of cold lungs that were merely going through the remembered task of breathing. Real breath has warmth, a touch of blood. It is infused with the smell of food, gut juices, and other, muculent spices. Doc's breath was cold, dusty, and smelled faintly of mold, like the bottom of an old chest. *Why are they always fucking dead?* Albeit this one was more adroit than your average, animated corpse. I tried to speak then, but my lips felt like two slabs of raw beef. My brain was also struggling to extract the correct group of syllables in the right order to form the phrase, 'fuck you, piss-pipe' which a part of me very much wanted to say, and part of me was glad that I couldn't. Dejected by my lack of erudition, I slumped, and ironically hung like a dead weight in his hands. Which to my displeasure, he bore with ease. *Dead and strong. Marvelous.*

"Get that little bitch in the cage afore she causes any more mischief." Was the last thing I heard him say before he cast me to the ground and into the pit of darkness waiting to greet me.

Chapter Two

"Is it a demon?"

"No. It doesn't have horns or hooves."

The conversation between Pavel and another of the shroudlings slipped into my bruised unconsciousness.

"It's got claws and scales."

"Dragons have claws and scales. Is it a dragon?"

"Well, no…"

"Right then. Although, whatever it is, it isn't human." I recognized Pavel's drawl. For a dead cove, he seemed a decent sort in comparison to his cadaverous comrades.

"I don't know why Madame uses these freaks. They're disgusting," said the other one.

Pavel laughed. "We're dead, Aba. Most people would consider that we're disgusting."

"We might be dead, but we're still human. This thing is not. Here, d'you think it comes from the same place *she* comes from? I mean, we found it at the stones and they say she came from the stones."

"It doesn't matter where in the nine hells it came from," Doc interjected. "Pick it up and let's get to the rendezvous."

They picked me up by my hands and feet and carried me across the marsh, into the woods, and out the other side. From there it was down a slope which was liberally sprinkled with nettles and brambles. The slope leveled out, and I was dragged through a bank of bracken before being dumped by the side of a dirt track.

Noise echoed wildly around my battered skull, one sound smashed into another. There were voices, the grind of metal, the sound of feet scraping across gravel, and grass rustling in the strong breeze. The child remained brim-full of piss and vinegar and kept up a steady stream of cursing and hissing. I dared a peek. She had been locked in a cage barely big enough for her small self to sit even with her knees drawn up to her chin. The discomfort didn't stop her trying to claw at anyone who came within arm's reach. Call me soft, but I was pleased that they hadn't beaten the fight out of her. Something I wasn't sure I could say for myself.

It had been a long time since I'd been in a fight, and even longer since I'd lost one. I'd forgotten how painful broken ribs were, how acute every drawn breath that caused bones to grate upon themselves. My mangled nose was so thoroughly clogged with dried blood that I doubted I would smell anything ever again until, some twenty minutes after I'd been dropped by the road, my battered olfactories were assaulted by a most unusual, sickly sweet odor. The smell was accompanied by an obnoxiously loud roaring, rattling, shuddering noise, which belonged to a huge, carriage-like conveyance which came rumbling along the road, with two powerful torches set front and foremost upon its chassis and no discernible means of propulsion.

I thought it must have been powered by magic, but as the machine drew closer, I got an excellent look at its workings. It had thick, black wheels and a complicated system of leather belts, strapping, and metal springs beneath the enclosed driver's cabin and the larger, boxed-in wagon in the rear. How it worked was beyond me, but I guessed the strongly sweet, almost intoxicating substance that overpowered every other smell in the area might have something to do with it.

Doc tipped his narrow-brimmed hat back on his head and waved the machine to a halt. I think he looked at me. My vision was slowly clearing in one eye at least, but it was impossible to read any expression in his coin-stuffed sockets. "Get that...*abomination* on its feet."

A pair of penny-eyes instantly complied and hauled me to my feet. "You're calling *me* an abomination? I'm not the dead cunt with coins instead of eyes."

Doc laughed. "No, you're the living cunt I'm going to enjoy seeing get ripped to pieces in the pit— if the boss doesn't do you herself."

Pavel stepped forward and straightened the collar of my blooded haori. The coins in his sockets still had a hint of coppery shine to them. "Now you just hush, you hear? Doc is a proper sweetheart, but he has a wicked temper when it comes to people who murder his friends." He laughed. "Even if she was already dead." He turned to the two culls who had hold of me. "Put our friend in the back."

As I was dragged away, I saw Doc pull an intricate timepiece from his waistcoat, study it, then grunt like it had caused offense. The silver case was old, and tarnished and looked small in his broad, scuff-knuckled hand. "The train's set to leave in an hour, so let's get a shift on." He thrust the timepiece back in his waistcoat pocket and tugged the brim of his hat down over the heavy ridge of his brow, before stomping off to the front of the vehicle. When he turned, I noticed that his jacket was sewn up the back seam with large, looping stitches. He was wearing grave clothes. Now that I looked, I saw that they all were. It was strangely reassuring to know that this gang of undead had an image and a gimmick just like any crew of gutter bloods who wanted to be reckoned with. "Not something I've seen restless dead do before."

"Pipe down," one of my guards ordered as they marched me to the rear of the carriage.

"Bet you don't have driverless carriages where you come from, eh?" said the other of the pair, who had a ring through her nose and blue spirals tattooed on her sunken cheeks. "They're a wonder, they are." She continued the conversation without any assistance from me. "Ours is Germanian. Madame had it imported special. It has the pulling power of six horses. Six! Can you imagine it?" She shook her head to emphasize her wonderment. "Back in my day, such a thing would have been called 'sorcery'." She giggled. "Anyone who came up with such a fanciful notion back then would have been burned with a basket of cats, that's for certain." She sighed. "I do so miss a good witch burning. They don't believe in them nowadays. Not the evil type. They're all 'alchemists' these days, or 'societies of mystics'. It's all rubbish mind, just an excuse for lords and ladies to get naked, fuck, and take drugs." The coins in this cove's eye sockets were misshapen rounds both stamped with a crude depiction of an eagle, or perhaps it was supposed to be a raven. It was hard to tell as the craftsmanship was shoddy to say the least.

As I was hoisted into the back of the conveyance, the pain in my ribs briefly sharpened my focus, but I lacked all desire to fight or even attempt to escape. I told myself that the warded chains were to blame for my apathy; that something in the magic was dulling my naturally feisty nature.

"Now you get some rest, eh?" Spiral Cheeks winked as though we were the best of friends before she hopped down from the wagon. I lay there like a beaten dog unable to even feel sorry for myself, which was enough to tell me that I was in a bad way. Another three of the coin-eyed brutes carried the cage containing the girl to the back of the wagon and heaved it inside. I noticed that even though they were dead and should have been beyond caring about such things, they were all careful to avoid being raked by her clawing fingers as she spat and cursed at them. Once she was inside, the doors were slammed and locked, leaving us alone, in the darkness save for a couple of neat grids of light filtering through the air vents cut into the doors.

"What are you?" she asked me.

"What?"

"If you ain't the bleedin' Guardian, what in blazes are you?"

"Fucked, mostly." I rolled over and tried to smile, but it hurt so I gave up. "My name's Breed. What are you? What's a Goblin Queen when she's at home?"

"She's me. Edith Thorne, but my friends call me Edie." She gave a broad smile. Her tiny eye teeth looked sharp as needles. Her glittering eyes appeared to be entirely black, but that I knew to be a trick of the light as I'd seen her natural peepers earlier. "Professor Cornell, gawd rest 'im, and my Nan, said I've been chosen to keep the Wild alive."

"And dare I ask what the fuck the Wild is?"

"It's like magic, like what you done. But it's different. It's not…" She tilted her chin to the roof of the cage as her child mind sought to put into words that which she knew but could not articulate. "My Nan once took me to the county fair. In the floral marquee, we saw a rare marvel of the vegetable world. It had petals like a purse that were lined with teeth and it ate flies."

"Sounds lovely."

She pouted, irritated by my interruption. "It was like you."

"I don't eat flies. The occasional little girl perhaps, but never flies; I'm not a monster."

She giggled. "Silly. I mean it don't grow here. It's too cold. If you put it outside it would die. It ain't meant to be here, like you and your magic."

"I thought I was supposed to be your guardian."

"The Guardian was supposed to take me away, until after the Blood Moon."

"You're pretty smart for, how old are you? six, seven?"

"*Six*?" She pressed her face to the bars, I assumed so that I could better see her indignation. "I'm nine and three months."

"I beg your pardon. It's just that you're a bit small for a nine-year-old kinchin cove."

"My Nan says, 'you don't get diamonds as big as rocks'."

"And my Mother said, 'poison comes in small doses'." We laughed.

Do not take a liking to this child.

"Professor Cornell came to our house one day and said that the old Goblin King had died in Moon Town, and I was his heir. Nan said she guessed as much, being as how she was a cunning woman. The Professor said he was going to take me to Luan Dun. He said after the Blood Moon had passed I'd become Queen of the Wild." She lowered her voice. "But then these blasted Black Pennies came after us." She shuffled around in the cage until she was able to stick her legs through the bars. She was wearing scuffed brown boots with holes in both soles and threadbare tights. She also had rickets. Both of her skinny legs were as bent as a pair of strung bows. "That's better," she said when she'd finished maneuvering herself into a more comfortable position. "What you looking at? Ain't you never seen anyone with rickets afore?"

"Of course, I have." *Too many, and worse beside.* "I've also seen people with their shoes on the wrong feet— like you."

"Oh." She reached through the bars and rectified the childish error. "I liked the Professor. He talked a lot of nonsense and said a lot of stuff I didn't understand, but he was good to me and Nan." She was a tough little gutter bloom, but she still turned her head to the door, betraying a longing to be with her Nan.

"Do you know where they're taking us?"

She sighed. "To Madame."

"And she is…?"

"Going to kill me."

The power of six horses roared into violent, bone-shaking life and the carriage rolled towards whatever in hell a 'train' was. I should have set about trying to pick the lock on the manacles. I should have tried to console the kinchin cove who was pretending not to cry by hiding her head in her sleeve. I should have done more than lie curled in a ball feeling like death. *Should have.*

But I didn't.

I just lay there, struggling to come to terms with the realization that I'd had the shit kicked out of me and that I couldn't do this anymore.

Chapter Three

Having fallen asleep during the jolting journey to the train, Edie woke with a start when we came to a halt. When the doors were thrown open, I stayed where I was, not as a ruse to lull them into a false sense of security before I made a daring bid for freedom, but because I couldn't be bothered to move.

Being possessed of enough fury to shame a volcano, Edie took up cursing and spitting the instant she laid eyes on the undead crew. Mindful of her tiny claws, they threw a paulin over the cage before unloading her. They left a guard to keep an eye on me. Like the others, this one's eyes had been replaced by coins. He wore a top knot and carried a firelance or 'gun' as I heard them refer to the long-barreled barking irons. I'd never put forward the notion of 'guns' during my time in Arduin. They're graceless things which in my humble opinion all worlds would be better off without. That I was handy with the steels and could wield magic had nothing to do with the omission. I'm sure in the future some clever cove in Arduin would hit upon the murderous advance, but at least I wouldn't be there to see it.

Spiral Cheeks tipped the nod to the guard and jumped into the back of the wagon with dismaying agility. "Bet you've never seen anything like that before, eh?" She chinned at what I took to be the train huffing and steaming behind her, its sleek lines painted in shades of grey in the moonlight. She grabbed the length of chain between the manacles and began to drag me off the wagon. I scrambled to get my feet underneath me before I fell headfirst out of the wagon. My head ached abominably where the shot had grazed my skull. "Yes, I have actually, only where I come from they fly upon wings of silver and gold," I said as tumbled out of the wagon.

"Oh." That took the wind from her sails.

"We also have gigantic, ocean-going leviathans that have scabs on their backs excavated by enslaved sea creatures, in which a warrior caste of crustaceans lie in wait to pray on unwary shipping."

She narrowed her eyes. "You're having a laugh now, eh?" She set off, dragging me stumbling behind her. "That's a good one though. You've got a livid imagination."

"You mean vivid."

"I know what I mean, strangeling."

Spiral dragged me along a graveled cut that ran along side of the train, which was just another mechanical conveyance with dozens of wagons enslaved behind a wheelhouse and firebox. It was all very interesting if you had nothing more important to concern yourself with than modes of transport. I was concerned with not being slotted by these eyeless bastards. Do not mistake me; it wasn't so much dying that was the issue, it was the how and the when and the where that bothered me.

The train was pulled up on the outskirts of a town. Beyond a run of the spiked railing, a crowded jigsaw of rooftops and chimney pots was framed by the eerie, green-white glow of lanterns set upon tall metal poles and spaced at regular intervals along a broad, tree-lined avenue. Something in a locked cargo wagon roared and the carriage rocked violently, but I didn't have long to ponder what rough beast railed against its captivity as Spiral prodded me towards one of the boxes at the tail end of the train.

"This is going to be Madame's most spectacular games yet." She beamed. "She's been pulling in Wildlings from all over the Empire."

"*The Empire?* Where the hell are we?" My heart quickened at the possibility that I might have accidentally found my way back to Edolis.

She gave a quizzical look. "Near Searoburg."

I deflated. "Never heard of it."

She snorted. "I find that hard to believe, even if you did come from the stones."

"Aye, well. I'm sure *for you,* my lack of knowledge with regards to this world ranks up there with other confounding mysteries, like soap, lice combs, and eyeballs."

I should have probably kept that observation to myself as, somewhat piqued, she slammed my head against the side of the train.

***

I woke up in a cell inside of one of the carriages. It was dark and smelled as grim as any pissy, dungeon pit or gallows cart. A child wearing an iron collar stood before me. He offered me a ladle of water. "Who...?"

He put the ladle to my lips and cast a warning glance towards the carriage door where momentarily Doc appeared. "Back in the land of the living are we, outlander?"

"Well, *I* am." I knew I shouldn't goad him, but I just couldn't help myself, it's like a disease.

Doc laughed. "Has life lost its meaning for you, snake-eyes? Because if I didn't know better, I'd say you were trying to get yourself killed." He smiled as he made his way over to the cage. "Don't think you're

the first. I've seen it before; have been there myself..."
The child backed away from Doc as he approached.
Metal groaned, and the carriage lurched as the train
began to move, slowly gathering speed. I occupied the
middle of three cages. My neighbors lurked in the
corners, as far from me and the eyeless jailer as was
possible in the confined space. But I knew that they
were watching.

Doc unlocked the cage. "When I was in the
Celestial Kingdom during their ill-conceived rebellion.
I saw some bad things— did my fair share." He leaned
on the cage, his disconcerting gaze fixed on a point
located somewhere in his bloody past. "I didn't think
nothing of it at the time. You just followed orders, did
what you was told, you know how it is." He shrugged
as though trying to escape the clutching hands of
ghosts. I could have told him he was onto a loser with
that, but I didn't want to stop him mid-flow or hasten
the beating he was working up to deliver. "The
problem started when I got home. I couldn't stop
seeing 'em. The women, the kids, the bloody heads
tied to posts by their hair. The crucified..."

I had a sudden urge to yawn as none of this was as
shocking or revelatory as he evidently thought it was.
Somewhere inside me the desire to live overruled my
instincts and kept my mouth shut. He entered the cage.
My hands were still shackled and tethered to a ring in
the floor, leaving me few options when it came to
defending myself. He crouched before me until we
were eye to coin.

"Them dead bastards never left me alone. Not when I was awake, nor asleep. That's when I met Madame and she gave me the choice: Become a Black Penny; sell my soul to her as many others had done before me. Or just end it and find out if my dead really were waiting for me in hell." He nodded as though he'd seen something in my face that spoke of understanding. In truth, I was still trying to stifle the yawn, which if vented, would undoubtedly earn me a thorough kicking. "You know that choice, don't you? That's why you ran from wherever you left on the other side of that gate. But you can't outrun 'em, my freakish friend. Close your eyes and they're there, ain't they? They won't ever leave you alone, you know? They'll hound you until you're dead." He put his cold hand on my shoulder. "Don't worry, old pal. You'll get the peace folks like you and I crave, one way or another. Either Madame will grant you the gift of death, or she'll hand you over to me and you'll die in service to the arena." He leaned in so close I could feel the rasp of his mildew breath against my neck. "So, you see, there's no need to provoke. No need to try and goad me into killing you. Bide a while, get yourself ready for the hereafter; prepare yourself for hell."

"I've been to hell. Didn't much like it."

He laughed. "No. Me neither. Nice ring you have there." I didn't think to draw my hand away as I was busy choking on the gristle of his speech. He grabbed my wrist and tugged Malin's ruby ring from my finger. "You don't mind if I take this, do you? I mean, it would be a shame to bury such a pretty trinket."

Although it felt like my ribs were made of broken glass I had to laugh. Doc slapped my cheek, all friendly like, as though we had an accord, which we did, only it wasn't the one he understood it to be. He was in part right. I had wanted to die after losing Malin, and I was getting old. I was sixty or thereabouts, ancient for a human, unheard of for a thoasa. I should thank him, for with the theft of the ring, the bastard had given me a reason to live. I was going to make him permanently dead; give him the gift of death *he* fucking craved. As he walked away, he glanced over his shoulder, smiled, and put the ring on.

***

When the door to the carriage closed, something with wings swooped down from the far corner of the cage to my right and begged with a spidery black hand for water. The child crept forward and handed over the ladle. Like Edie, this young, shaven-pated human showed no fear as a beaked face poked from behind a pair of leathery wings and slurped the water.

"Thank you, Sonam." The bird creature squawked and passed the ladle back through the bars before stretching its wings as far as the cage would allow. It had a humanish torso, arms, and legs, but its feet were clawed, and it had the head of a vulture. It wiped its beak with the back of its hand. The child, Sonam inclined his head.

Using the bars for support I stood up as far as the chain would allow. "Oi, kid— come here." The vulture shuffled back into the shadows of its cage and wrapped its wings around its whip-scarred body. The child didn't hesitate to approach me and offer me the dipper. "Thanks. Sonam, is it?" The boy nodded. The water was brackish. I sluiced it around my mouth before spitting it out. The boy stepped back, reluctant to get blood on the hem of his ochre robes. "You work for the Black Pennies, eh?" He shook his head. "Not much of a conversationalist, are you?" He shook his head again. An unmistakable growl came from the next carriage along. I knew without a doubt that it was a dragon because I had been one on and off for the past forty years. This was a young one by the sound of it; young and afraid. The child dropped the bucket and ran to the door.

"It's sick," said a voice on my left. I turned, but despite knowing it had an occupant because I could hear it, the cage appeared empty. All I could see were bars and the re-enforced floor of the carriage. Something caught my attention. I had a closer look whereupon a section of floor and cage rolled itself up like a rug and stood on its end. A rudimentary face pushed out of the flesh at the top of the 'body', which molded itself into segments. A tiny pair of hands pushed out of each segment. "I'm a chameleon, if you're curious."

Sonam opened the door to the next carriage. Inside was another, much larger cage. Imprisoned within was a very young, purple dragon. I say purple, but its color had faded almost to grey. The poor creature's head was resting sullenly on a pair of massive paws. Its crest was flaccid and had flopped to one side. The child ran over to the cage and reached between the bars. The last thing I saw before the door slammed shut was the dragon opening its great, amber eyes.

"It won't eat." The chameleon wiggled closer to the bars separating us. "Not even the dragon's boy, Sonam can make it eat." Tiny silver shackles gleamed on its lowermost pair of hands. "Ah, yes. I was ensorcelled by a maiden in *gay Lutetia*. I would like to say she was worth it, but that would be a lie."

"Who are these culls, and what the fuck do they want?"

The chameleon's mouth rounded into a shocked 'o'. "You really shouldn't swear so much, it's terribly vulgar and uncouth."

"They're going to kill me. That's a good enough reason to curse in my book." Anything was a good reason to curse in my book, but he didn't need to know that.

"Your book is somewhat low-brow." He added sniffily. "And I believe they intend to kill everyone in this carriage, but you don't hear me swearing." The winged fellow on the other side of my cage squawked miserably before wrapping his wings around his body.

"Very sorry, old fellow. Don't take on now," said the chameleon to the bird man. It then leaned in closer to me. "He's very sensitive. A lifelong slave, he was bought from a sultan's menagerie when his satrapy became a protectorate of the Empire, sort of a going-out-of-business sale". It chuckled at what it evidently considered to be a hilarious joke.

"I don't have a fucking clue what a satrapy is, but I swear I will look it up as soon as I get out of here."

"There's no getting out of here, old love. Oh my, no. We're going to be used as bait dogs to help hone the deadly skills of Madame's star performers. She runs one of the best arenas in Britannia, if not the whole of Europia." It slouched against the cage. In the time it had been upright its skin tone had taken on subtle shades of grey and black that blended perfectly with the walls and metal bars, so much so that I had to squint to focus on its outline. It smelled loamy, like rich dark soil, although it talked like a toff of the highest order.

"I'm no bait dog. And how come you can shapeshift while you're wearing warded chains?"

It chuckled. "Oh, my, darling. Bless your ignorance. No offense." It folded five pairs of hands over its mottled abdomens. "The ability to blend into my surroundings is innate and entirely natural, like breathing. The ability to *shapeshift* into any creature I choose is where I employ my learned, arcane skills." It chuckled. "I was guised as a Bulgarian Count when that big-breasted doxy ensnared me with her gorgeous, kohl-rimmed come-hithers."

"Speaking of peepers, what if anything do you know what these penny-eyed dead culls?"

"You've never heard of the infamous, Black Pennies? Where have you come from, sweetie? You must live under a rock not to have heard of them." It canted its head. "You don't know much about the Veiled World, do you?"

"I know nothing of this world, veiled or otherwise. I'm not from here."

"Ah. That would explain it. They're thugs and miscreants who Madame Darzka has saved from certain death, but oh, the price they pay." It shuddered. "They are strong, ruthless, devoted to their mistress, and greatly feared." It leaned in again. "Not even I would want to tangle with them openly, and I'm a bit of a whiz when it comes to fisticuffs."

I coughed, which hurt my ribs, but it was more polite than laughing in his face. If it could be called a face.

"I say old chum, you're hurt." It tutted. "That doesn't bode well for your chances in the arena, I'm afraid. Which, I suppose might not be a bad thing, eh?

Get it over with quickly rather than lingering, and dying by inches, after days or even weeks of torment."

"You seem pretty sanguine to say that it's the same fate which awaits you."

It leaned in again. "I'm an insignificant cove *in this form*. I'm easy to ignore or indeed, forget about, an ability which has kept me alive for nigh on... Well, let's say for a very long time. I'm hoping my luck holds a while longer." Its almost spherical mouth narrowed to a gentle smile. It had half a dozen dried currant eyes all of which were shining bright with mischief.

"Have you a name?"

"Yes."

Silence grew. "Ah. I see. I am Loftur." It inclined what I guessed was its head segment. It might very well have been its ass because I'd known a fair few coves who talked out of theirs with a surprising level of erudition. "And you are?"

"Breed."

"I'm sure our meeting would have been a pure delight had it occurred elsewhere."

Our conversation was cut short when the door to the dragon's carriage pen burst open, and another penny-eyed cove came in dragging Edie. I was pleased and impressed that she remained full of fight, as attested to by the dust spilling from the bite marks on the Penny's hand. The undead almost threw the dark-haired little cave bear into the next carriage before following her through. The door slammed on her youthful screams.

I sat down heavily. "D' they use kids as bait dogs here?"

"They use anything they can get their hands on, petal, even old coves like you and I. But that was the Goblin Queen; the Mistress of the Wild. Darzka isn't going to waste her precious claret in the arena. She's to be sacrificed."

"So I've heard. Do you have any idea why?"

"I'm not one to gossip, but I heard some of the Pennies talking. They say that Madame intends to destroy the Wild and therefore every creature born of it, which is a pity really, particularly for the girl."

"Yeah."

Chapter Four

The train stopped twice on route to our destination, jolting me awake both times while whatever mechanical or physical needs were taken care of. I was stiff and sore and had a cramp in my knees. *I'm going to inhume that dead-eyed bastard, am I? I can't even stay awake.*

The door to the dragon's carriage opened again and Sonam emerged this time carrying a mop and bucket. He began sluicing the floor and urging the accumulated slops out through the gap between the wagons. Rain impatiently drilled on the bowing canvas slung between the carriage roofs, which had probably been put there to hide us from any curious 'mundies' as my fellows called the locals. The boy poked at the sagging cloth with the butt of his mop, tipping the water off the makeshift roof. The door to the dragon's wagon remained open, perhaps to reassure the sickly beast, or perhaps to reassure the child. Either way, they shared many a pensive glance, growl, and whispered word as the boy went about his task.

"You're hurt," he said to me when he'd finished washing down the floor of my pen.

"Does it show?"

Guileless, and therefore oblivious to sarcasm, the child nodded. "It isn't good."

"No, it isn't." I smiled. "What's your dragon called?"

"He isn't my dragon."

"What's the dragon called?"

The boy looked towards the beast who was watching the boy with the fierce intensity only a dragon can muster. "Druk."

"He's sick?"

The dragon yowled in response. The boy made a placatory gesture towards it and cast a nervous glance to the other door to the carriage. "He needs his mother."

"How come she can't track him down and eat these bastards." I leaned in close and lowered my voice so as not to distress the beast. "Is she dead?"

"No, the Dark Queen is hiding us with her magic. If they aren't reunited soon, I fear he will perish." The boy leaned on the mop. He looked exhausted, doleful.

It was passing strange to me that something bigger than an adult uxatzi could still be hankering for its mother's tit. The boy finished his chores in mawkish silence before returning to his beast. My companions and I were left in the darkness without even the roar of the engine or clatter of the wheels to drown out the cries of the other members of our miserable crew. The sound of young and old bemoaning their plight rang around the carriages as all manner of creature called out for their gods or their mothers, oft times both. Those who still had some fight left in them cursed and swore vengeance upon their eyeless captors. Those without speaking pipes just moaned and gibbered like dispossessed spirits.

Light slowly faded from the rivet-hole in the wall behind my cage that had become my window onto the outside world. The rain abated. I tried unsuccessfully to pick the lock on my shackles. My neighbors whiled away the tedious hours of waiting in markedly different ways. The winged fellow withdrew further into his misery and started fearfully at every unexpected sound as though the Carnival of Death was capering towards him, carrying a bloody invitation for him to join their crew. In contrast, Loftur slept soundly and hour by hour, seemingly without any effort on his behalf, blended in more closely with the floor until he was virtually indistinguishable from it. His natural camouflage was so good that I kept forgetting he was there and only remembered whenever he rolled over or farted, which was quite often, and possibly of some detriment to his efforts to go unnoticed. For all that his gas might give him away, the blending was still a neat trick, and one which I greatly envied right now.

Despite not knowing what fate awaited me, I was glad of the chance to get some rest. I needed a few hours of quiet, *wakeful* contemplation to gather what wits remained after the beating Doc had given me. I needed to come up with a plan that would get me out of this embarrassing pot of arsepickle. At worst, I needed a plan to get me out and back to the angle gate. At best, a way to get me and Edie out.

Even though I wasn't her mythical guardian, I'd taken a liking to the kinchin cove and would like to help her if I could. Of course, that might prove easier said than done. I couldn't use sorcery thanks to the warded manacles, I didn't have a weapon, and even if I did, I wasn't as quick with the steels as I used to be. The only thing left to me were my wits, yes things were that bad. Why, the very thought that I'd have to rely upon my aged brain soup, conjured an image of Mother slouched on the Rat Bone Throne telling me that if I had an ounce of sense I'd be dangerous, and that was years ago. I shoved it aside. Not for the first time, I was going to have to prove the old monster wrong.

***

"Ladies and gentlefreaks!" Doc's abrupt pronouncement snapped me to startled wakefulness. "It's time for you to take a bow, to put your best foot forward and shine like the stars you are." The cove strolled from carriage to carriage rattling the bars of every cage with a tin mug.

It seemed that the miscreant crew had been waiting until darkness to unload us, their wretched cargo. The engine huffed as though tired from its labors and cocooned itself within a shroud of steam. It had pulled into a shed some hundred yards distant, which was open at both ends and covered by a concave, glass-paneled roof.

It was a warm, clear night; the air was fresh, redolent with the smell of sweet grass and wildflower meadow. Alas, we were not granted long to bask in the cool clean air, as we were quickly hustled from one mobile prison into another. Half a dozen horse-drawn wagons waited for us on the road outside of the shed. I was shoved into the first along with the feathered fellow who I noticed had a pronounced limp. I didn't see Loftur in the coffle and made no mention of his absence. More than a little jealous, I wished the bastard luck.

Too many were shoved into the wagon, and the journey was cramped and hot but thankfully short. When the wagons drew to a halt everyone breathed a sigh of relief. A heavy door was unbolted and opened and then, much to the consternation of some of my fellows, the horses were urged on. The clatter of hooves and wagon wheels rattled over cobbles. The change in smell and temperature, the subtle shift in air pressure and the gradient of the wagon indicated we were heading underground. The deeper we went, the hotter it became. When the wagon stopped, and we were left to sweat for over an hour while others were unloaded, and the horses were unhitched and taken back to the surface.

At last, when some poor coves were near to fainting, the wagon doors were unlocked and thrown open. Blinding light poured in. A dozen or so Black Pennies were waiting to receive us, guns aimed and at the ready. Half blind and stiff from standing in one place for hours, we staggered down the ramp. The strong, handy looking types were sent to the right and marched off into a brightly lit tunnel. My winged friend was ordered to the left. Two more culls were sent to the right. Then it was my turn.

"Left," the woman said accompanied by a wave of her handcannon. It wasn't unexpected, but at the same time I was disappointed to be amongst the broken, the sick, and the old.

Bait dogs. Loftur's words came back to mock me.

"Wait." It was Doc. "Not that one. You come with me." He gestured for me to follow like he was summoning a pet to his side, and like a whipped cur, I obeyed.

"What is this place?" I said as I trailed after him.

"The Druinen. Not that it's any of your business."

"If I'm going to die down here, it's my business."

He laughed and urged me on with a shove. "You don't have any business anymore. You're meat. You're gonna' die down here like hundreds before you, maybe thousands if you count those from the old times, before Madame claimed this burgh." He gestured expansively. "But as you're a stranger to our world I'll give you a little history. See now, these caves were dug out of the earth thousands of years ago by creatures that could barely call themselves human— things like you maybe— and yet they dug this labyrinth with nothing more than antler picks. The stones they raised above echo the dance of the stars. They say that in ancient times the markers were made of dragon bones."

"Bollocks."

"Aye, probably, but it's a good tale, is it not?" He tilted his head to the ceiling, now blackened by soot, it was still easy to make out the thousands of tiny antler pick scores that had gnawed away at the soft stone over gods only knew how many decades. Somewhere close by, a muffled cheer went up, followed by a collective gasp. "Sounds like a good crowd tonight. Now come on, old timer. We don't want to keep Madame waiting."

He led us through a tunnel that sloped up at a right angle to the one that the wagons had been driven down. Ancient mold and candle smut dappled the walls and ceiling. Chains and broken cages— the trappings of slavery— lay discarded here and there. After a few minutes of silent marching, we came to an ironbound door where an aged wench was slumped in a chair, head resting on a gnarled staff. She looked up as we approached.

The old relic wore her hair in a long, grizzled braid. Her lips and chin were tattooed blue, and the coins in her sockets shone gold in the waxen lamplight giving them a disturbing semblance of life. "Evening, Doc. What you got there?"

"It came through the gate."

The crone nodded, pursed her tattooed lips. "Madame was right then." As she got up her old bones cracked and popped. Her withered fingers unhooked an ornate key from her belt, and she unlocked the door before hobbling aside to let us pass.

"Thank ye, Dagda," Doc touched the rim of his hat. The woman leaned on her staff that up close I could see was carved with writhing serpents.

She inclined her head. "You are most welcome, brother."

***

We emerged from the dimly lit labyrinth into a polished marble hall. Light blazed from sconces, lamps, and candelabras and rebounded from the white tiled floor and fabulously intricate gilt mirrors hanging on every wall. To the right of the cellar door, a grand, floating staircase swept up to a galleried landing.

Across the hall from the entrance to the undercroft, two humans in blue velvet livery and powdered wigs flanked a porticoed entrance. They attempted to maintain an air of stoic vigilance, but their eyes widened when they saw me stumble out of the darkness. To the left of the bewigged varlets, a pair of doors stood ajar. The sound of voices and smell of pipe smoke drifted from the room beyond and into the hall, accompanied by the ruffle of papers and the clink of glasses. Doc grabbed my arm and marched me towards the noise. Malin's ruby shone fiercely on his finger, reminding me of the promise I'd made to myself.

"Word to the wise," Doc whispered. "If you antagonize *her,* she will hurt you a great deal before she kills you. So, keep a civil tongue in your head and she might do you quick and easy, let you die with some dignity."

"Thanks for the advice."

He balled his fist and kissed the ruby. "Don't mention it."

A woman I took to be Madame Darzka reclined on a silk couch, robed in a long, silver-grey nightdress and matching dressing gown. A pair of fluffy woolen slippers completed the ensemble. She was smoking a pipe and had a pile of ledgers on her lap. She gave me a cursory once-over. What she thought of me and indeed, what she looked like was a mystery as her face was covered in a mask of white cream. A rotund fellow with a waxed mustache and a neatly coiffured garland of hair was curling her dark tresses with a pair of hot irons. He was garbed after the style of an Imperial Senator, which was somewhat at odds with his trade. A mousy looking girl in a plain tunic was kneeling beside the couch, filing her mistress's fingernails. The tunic reminded me of the Valenese style of dress; simple, pale cotton, belted and folded in drapes and pinned at both shoulders.

The fine salon was done out in yellow, silk wallcovering and was hung with more gilt-framed mirrors. A harpsichord stood in a bay window. Painted in exquisite detail on the inside of the instrument's lid was a battle scene between demons and Mage Lords. It was a strange thing to recognize participants on both sides. I could also taste the distinct blood and steel tang of magic hanging in the air. It would have been a grand room had it not been for the stacks of ledgers and official looking documents that were piled on every available surface. A fusty looking scribe in a sober grey suit and black-rimmed spectacles was pacing by the windows, pencil and notebook in hand.

Doc encouraged me to kneel with a foot in the back of my knee. Madame frowned. "That will be all, Doc, thank you." I heard the Penny's dead muscles creak as he tensed and bit down on his undoubted objection. Like the girl doing Madame's nails, the hairdresser pretended he wasn't all ears. When Doc's heavy step receded and the door closed, Madame shooed the girl away and sat up. The fellow doing her hair looked most perturbed but was too fearful or perhaps too wise to say so.

Madame didn't say anything for a minute or two. She just looked at me and puffed thoughtfully on her pipe. Whatever she was smoking smelled like pel, only not as strong. "You don't look like an Annurashi," she said at last, the pipe still clamped in the corner of her mouth.

"I'm not."

She nodded. "If you aren't an Annurashi, are you their creature? You look like some kind of warspawn."

"I am indeed, some kind of warspawn. But I'm not the Annurashi's creature, I assure you. I escaped from them." She had to be another renegade like Ozbert. Which meant there was no love lost between her and the Annurashi, a fact that I might be able to work to my advantage.

She took the pipe from her mouth and sniffed. "Show me your hands."

I held out my hands, palms down.

"The other way."

I turned them palm up. "It's complicated. Really, really complicated."

She laughed, cracking the cream mask. "I'll bet it is."

Before I could spin her a tale, there was a knock at the door and another grey suited cove rushed in. He looked worried yet determined as he approached. The woman with the pen and notebook gave him a reprimanding look, which he ignored.

"Madame, the Han Du office want to know if you'll raise your bid to eight hundred."

"For both?"

"Yes."

She tapped the bowl of her pipe and took another deep draw, waking the eye of fire slumbering within the pungent herbs. "Tell Mr. Trinh I'm a witting fool. Seven-fifty, not a ding more. He'll push to seven eighty. You go to seven seventy-five and that will be that."

"Yes, Madame. Seven-fifty, seven seventy-five. Thank you, Madame." The flunky tipped a nod and hurried out the way he'd come.

Darzka turned to the other cove in grey. "Trinh is a reliable fellow, so I'll give him the benefit of the doubt after those twins. If the next pair arrive in the same state however, I want an example making."

The scribe wrote something in her notebook. "His sons are at school in Guang Province. We have people there."

"Splendid." With a gesture, the fellow with the curling irons put down his instrument of hair torture and retired to the far end of the salon, where he began to fuss over a midnight blue gown decorated with stars that was hanging on a mannequin.

Madame clamped her pipe into the corner of her mouth, got off the couch and came over to me.

"I like this world," She offered me a hand up, which I was more than happy to accept because my knees were killing me. "I like this corner of this world in particular. I'm sorry I haven't introduced myself. I am Darzka."

"Breed."

"You're a sorcerer?"

There didn't seem much point in lying. She'd seen the star steel flowing in my hand as I had smelled the reek of sorcery upon her. "I am."

"And you have come here to kill me?" Bespeaking her confidence— or stupidity, she turned her back on me and went over to the harpsichord.

"I… what? No. I didn't even know you were here. I don't even know where *here* is and no offense, until very recently I'd never heard of you."

"I would like to believe you, but your arrival is uncannily bad timing. For you that is."

Here it comes. "It doesn't have to be. You could just let me go back through the gate."

"No. I couldn't."

"I'm sure you could if you wanted."

"If I let you go back you might tell the Annurashi where I am."

"I won't, I swear. I loathe the meddlesome fuckers."

"Language, please." She gestured to the girl. Nadia scuttled over with a towel and dropped a curtsey as she handed it to Madame. Darzka wiped the cream from her face revealing a middling pretty mug. "I can't take that risk, Breed, I'm sorry." Either she was a superb actor, or she was genuinely contrite. "Please, take a seat. You look quite done in." She gestured to the velvet stool beside the harpsichord. I accepted her offer. "The thing is I've built a life here; a business.

People rely on me. I can't risk their livelihoods on the promise of a stranger."

"Don't think of me as a stranger. Think of me as a friend you have only just met." Cringeworthy I know, but I was of a mind to try anything to get me out of these manacles.

She gave me an arched look. "I prefer to think of you as an asset." She opened an ivory box that was on the harpsichord and took out a pinch of dusty red weed, which she stuffed into the pipe and lit with a click of her fingers as she took a pull.

"Might I ask what business could so captivate a Mage Lord?"

She grimaced and held her breath before exhaling, bluing the air with a thick billow of smoke. "Businesses. I deal in all the good things in life; flesh, drugs, games of every stripe." She took another pull on the pipe. "I give the mundies so much more than they've ever had before. That's why they come to me. My drugs are alchemical wonders, the flesh I find for my customers is exotic and rare, and as for the games.
. ." She stretched and smiled. Her eyes glistened, and her erect nipples stood out through the thin fabric of her gown. I didn't flatter myself that her arousal was down to me. Whatever she was smoking had most likely provoked her ardor. The only thing that I might arouse in her was pity, but I'd take what I could get right now. "My games are renowned throughout the

world. No one puts on a better show, and do you know why?"

"I do not."

"Because I bring the monsters. I bring the legends and the myths to life. It is the greatest show on Earth."

"I've no doubt of that. You're a Mage Lord. I would expect no less. Look, I have no desire to do anything except go home and live out my last few years somewhere nice and quiet. I'm no threat to you and, if I'm being brutally honest, no use either. You'll waste more money cleaning up my remains than I'll earn you."

She sighed. "Look, don't make this difficult. I'm not a bad person, I just...if you hadn't so readily mentioned the Annurashi, if you'd feigned ignorance of them, it would have gone better for you. Too late now, because I know that you know them, and if you know them, they know you."

"I...go on." I assumed she had a point.

"I'll be brutally honest with you, as it seems only fair. Compulsion isn't my forte, as they say here. Oh, I can control simple folk, but the Annurashi? They are masters of that, most dark of arts. For all I know they might have set a geas upon you without your knowledge."

"I assure you, I'd know. My contact with them has been slight and very unpleasant it was too. They're monsters without a doubt."

"You have no idea. I can't go back. I won't, and very soon they won't be able to make me. Ah. I wish I could let you live. It's been so long since I spoke to someone from home. So much must have changed."

The image of Shallunsard popped into my head. "Indeed."

"But I just can't take the risk."

"You could."

"No. I'm severing all ties to Edolis. Everything."

Fucker. "I'm no threat to you, Darzka. I could be an ally."

"You were found trying to protect the Goblin Queen and her warlock."

"It was just a coincidence. I was in the wrong place at the wrong time." I tried to look harmless and pathetic, which wasn't difficult given my current state.

"You killed one of my Redeemed."

"An accident. I thought they were trying to kill me."

"That's not what I heard and as we've discussed, I'm hardly going to take the word of a stranger, and a dangerous one at that."

This is getting me nowhere. "Speaking of dangerous coves. Why are you planning on slotting a child?"

What little color she had drained from her cheeks. "Who have you been speaking to?" The demand was accompanied by a weak attempt at a compulsion spell. Even wearing warded manacles, I was able to ignore it.

"You're right; you don't have much skill with compulsion magic. I'd stop smoking the pipe if I were you. It ruins concentration."

The servants stopped fussing over the gown. The sober-suited cove gasped and snapped the nib of her pencil on the notepad.

Darzka hurled the pipe across the room. It clattered on the polished marble. "You think you can judge me? You're nothing but an abomination. You're no warspawn, and certainly no true sorcerer. How could such a...*mismatch* possibly understand my motives, or why I do what must be done? I have sworn to protect this world from the real monsters that lurk upon the shores of the Void, your fucking masters." She stormed around the harpsichord, hands in fists. "One child will die by my hand. *One.* Every day in this or any other world, thousands upon thousands of innocent lives are snuffed out by hunger, war, and greed, never mind the vagaries of nature. I will slay one to save this world from true evil."

"Oh, well, that's all right then. Listen, I know the game went tits up for your lot after you almost-but-not-quite slotted Shallunsard, but to go from hero to child killer? That's quite a fall." I aimed my gaze at the battle scene lovingly detailed on the lid of the harpsichord.

A slew of emotions chased across her face. Anguish foremost amongst them, which offered me the tiniest flicker of hope. As was often the case, I was to be disappointed. Sorrow and regret followed but were swiftly replaced by fury. She swiped at the prop holding up the lid. It slammed down, unleashing an inharmonious cacophony.

Her fingers turned black, her nails silver. She lunged for me, forgetting in her rage that she was a sorcerer. I was, for the most part, a warspawn and something of my old instincts remained. I caught her by the throat. Tears coursed down her cheeks. I had a second to break her neck before she remembered she could use magic. I'd killed another sorcerer this way—snapped her neck without a thought.

I let her go.

She gave me a puzzled look. "Why didn't you kill me?" Before I could answer, she cast a bolt of something dark and horribly painful. It didn't throw me across the room or blow me to pieces. It dropped me to my knees and burrowed through my flesh with fingers of ice that clawed at my heart. The room furred at the edges.

"I am not a monster…unlike you." Iron knives of pain stabbing through my chest left me gasping for breath.

"You call me a monster?" She laughed without humor. "The Annurashi destroyed everything to protect that bastard Shallunsard. They tried to kill us to save that demon. I won't let them do to this world what they did to mine, do you hear me?" I couldn't help but hear her because she was shouting in my face, but I couldn't tell her because I was having my heart and lungs squeezed by tendrils of dark, sorcerous energy. She grabbed me again. The pain in my chest lessened but her touch was colder than death. "A child will die, the Wild will bleed, and the gates to this world will close forever. But I will be safe, and this world will be safe. One child, *one.* The Annurashi, the mundies of this world have killed thousands." She kissed me then. It was not an entirely pleasurable experience truth be told for when our lips locked she drew my star steel from me, rendering me powerless with or without warded chains.

Chapter Five

Something poked me. The smell of shit and mold told me I was no longer in Madame Darzka's elegant drawing room. I opened my eyes. I was in a cell. One side faced onto a tunnel, the other a sand-floored arena lit by tallow candles. The air smelled of rancid fat and offal.

Sonam was standing on the tunnel side of the cage. Ice crystals coated my eyelashes; my clothes were stiff with frost and I was no longer bound by magically warded chains. I sat up, my chest hurt like hell, and I was frozen to the marrow.

"You cried out in your sleep," the boy informed me.

"I did, did I?"

"You were very loud. Everyone heard you."

"How rude of me. Do pass on my apologies to everyone. I don't know what I was thinking." I drew my knees to my chest and tried to hug some warmth into my frozen body. I looked at my palm. Rowan's mark was still there, pale as an old scar, and Shallunsard's sigil was as black as the day he'd marked me, but the star steel was gone and with it my sorcerous abilities. I felt the loss as keenly as I would have felt the loss of a limb. I say *gone*. It had been stolen. I rubbed my eyes, felt ice crystals dissolve. Sweet salvation, but I was tired.

"Do you know how long it's been since I had a proper, *physical* fight?"

The boy squatted on the other side of a cage door. He shook his head.

"No, me either. But it's been a long time. What have they done with Edie?" He shrugged. "Doesn't matter. There's nothing I can do to help her now."

"How do you know?" The boy toe-poked a sliver of bloody bone against the bars.

"Because I know what I'm capable of." *Which isn't fucking much*. I was taken by another fit of shivering.

"But you haven't tried to do anything yet."

"I've played punch bag for Doc and his cronies. Not the most fun I've ever had it must be said, not the worst experience either, but still. Hey, did you know, I used to live in a palace?" *Fuck's sake. I sound like one of those old codgers who sit in the park waylaying strangers with their inane conversation.*

"No, I didn't. You should try to avoid their blows."

"Splendid advice. So, that's Madame's arena, eh?" The cage was set in the wall of the arena which was in a cavern. The enclosure was about ten meters at its widest with the cages housed beneath thirteen-foot-high walls. There was a gate at the narrow ends of the oval.

"No, this is just where they practice killing."

"Ah. Yes, of course." I had to laugh. "I'm not here to fight." Now that I'd been stripped of my power, Darzka was going to get her money's worth and use me as a bait dog. As Loftur said, the job of a bait dog was to whet the appetite and hone the skills of more dangerous coves. I felt insulted to my core. I dug my claws into the soft limestone ceiling, as dozens had done before me. The walls were marked by names, dates, prayers, and curses; a scratched memorial to the poor souls who'd spent their last, miserable hours in these pens. Somewhere in the tunnels, dogs began howling. Chains rattled, and then there was snarling, and snapping followed by the sound of flesh being torn and bones being cracked. It was feeding time and judging by the smell nothing went to waste down here.

With warmth, came feeling and the ache in my chest lessened.

"Sonam! Get your ass over here now, boy," Doc's voice echoed through the tunnel. The boy glanced fearfully down the corridor, spared me a last, pensive smile before racing off.

I could just about stand in the cramped cage, though I had to stoop. A few minutes passed, then metal grated on metal and the gate on the left side of the oval slowly opened. Sonam was standing beside Doc, who was gripping the boy's shoulder in his meaty paw. He carried a whip in his other hand. The boy's eyes were locked wide, his face was frozen with fear. The Black Penny pushed the boy into the arena as two lumpen golems emerged from the darkness behind them, hauling on chains as thick as my wrist. I didn't need to see what was on the end of those chains to know what they were dragging. I could smell him. As soon as the dragon reluctantly emerged, the boy squirmed from Doc's grip and ran towards Druk, only to be swatted away by one of the Golems. The boy sprawled in the sand. The dragon howled.

"Sonam, get over here," I hissed. The child didn't hear me, but Doc did.

His blind gaze turned to me. "Hush now, freak. You'll get your chance to play." He turned to the other door. "Bring it in, Torsten."

I could hear crying as the gate was thrown open. A Penny dragged a hairy, ogrenish fellow into the arena. He was about five feet tall and clung to his tormentor as he begged for his life. The creature's fangs were brown with age and its fur was almost entirely grey.

The Penny ignored its pleas and threw it down between the golems, in front of the dragon. The hairy cull reached out to Sonam and tried to make a dash towards the boy but the Penny, a shady looking cull with long red braids, kicked the cull in the face sending it sprawling with a bloody mouth. He grabbed Sonam and marched him over to Doc before taking up position before the right-hand gate.

The thing rolled over and screamed. "Nulwal! Nuwal, meshuch-ba!"

The young dragon shied away but was stopped from retreating into the gate by the golems, who dug their heels in and held on to the taut chains.

"All right, my lovely." Doc addressed the dragon, mindful to stay out of biting range. "Eat the…whatever the fuck it is. But mess around with it first. Snap at him, claw him a bit, toy with him. Do. You. Understand?" Doc spoke slowly and loudly, turning from time to time to address Sonam as well as the dragon. "Tell him boy. Tell him to play with his food."

The boy's lips hardened into a defiant line. Doc held the boy at arm's length and raised the whip. "Tell him."

The dragon growled. Doc grinned. "Oh. You understand me, eh? That's good. Now come on, be a nice doggy and give him a lick."

The ogren cowered, clasped his paws before him. "Meshuch-ba. Meshuch-ba, tulun…"

The dragon shook its head from side to side. The golem's muscles flexed as they fought to keep control of the dragon.

Doc sighed, theatrically. "Very well. You leave me no choice." He flicked the whip and caught Sonam a stinging blow across the back of the legs. The child yelped and tried to bend away from the blow as the first strike was followed by a second. The other Penny sniggered. The dragon roared its distress, pawed at the ground.

"Yes, you big silly bastard." Doc grinned. "That's it! Bare your fangs, flex them lovely, nasty claws. Show the good people what they're getting for their gold. You'll have to imagine the good people for now." The dragon snarled, revealing juvenile teeth that could snap a man's arm and unsheathed foreclaws, each as thick as my wrist.

Sonam shook his head, tears stained his scarlet cheeks. "Mena, Druk, mena." The child sobbed.

Whatever he said had an effect on the beast. The dragon gave a protracted yowl and settled on his haunches. The old ogre tried to scuttle away from the huge creature, but one of the golems menaced it into staying put. Time was I'd have made a wager on whether the dragon would eat the ogren before Doc whipped the boy to death. But not now.

The penny-eyed bastard whipped the boy across his shoulders. He was so skinny that almost immediately a bloody welt bled through his yellow robe. He reminded me of Malin when I'd first met him; thin, stubborn, and stupid. The dragon reared, the golems strained against the sudden tension in the chains.

"Hey. You made me do that," Doc bellowed at the dragon, while maintaining his grip on the boy's robe. "I don't want to do this. You're making me hurt your friend. Now just kill the fucking monkey man… but slap him around a bit first. Fucking amateurs." He looked at the Black Penny standing by the gate. "This is what happens when you go for exotics. They don't want to work for their keep."

More yowling. I couldn't stand it any longer and turned away, tried to block out the sobbing and the wailing, tried to ignore the dragon's whimper. It wasn't easy.

"Listen to me you big fucking idiot," Doc continued. "If you don't kill and eat that nithing, I will skin this little bastard. Do you hear me?" Doc's threat echoed around the cave.

"It's a bairn, you thick fuck." The words leaped from my mouth before good sense could keep them in.

Doc cast the boy aside and marched over to my cage. "What did you say?" His voice was a study in pre-fight provocation.

A little of the old fire woke within me. I recalled a time when I liked thumbing my nose at arseholes and be damned to the consequences. It was a vague recollection due to the many, *many* beatings that ornery attitude had earned me, but fuck it, I had to die sometime. "It's a baby, it can't eat the fucking monkey man. It doesn't understand what you want because it is a juvenile." While Doc and the other Penny were busy glaring at me, the ogreish cull crawled away from the dragon. Not being entirely devoid of intelligence, Doc chewed over what I'd said. Sonam tried to sneak away too but the undead slaver's hand shot out and grabbed the boy's collar. "Will it drink cow milk?" Sonam nodded. "Get it out and get some fucking milk. Milk! It's a fucking dragon…"

The boy ran to his dragon and whispered something in its massive ear. It nuzzled the boy and shuffled back, towing the golems behind it. Doc tipped the nod to his comrade, who dragged the sobbing old ogren out of the arena. I relaxed and considered that had gone surprisingly well until Doc came over, took a key from his waistcoat and unlocked the door. "Come on then, smart ass. Get out here."

"I'd rather not."

His smile was as disconcerting as you would imagine. "Get out, or I'll lock the door and set fire to the fucking cell."

"Well, as you ask so nicely." I left the cell. We stood facing each other in the poorly lit arena. It was disconcerting not being able to read his eyes or discern his intent by the smell of his sweat.

"There's just no helping some people, is there?" he said.

"No. there isn't."

He canted his head as though he was trying to read me, which was a laugh. "You've brought this on yourself, you know?"

"Like the boy made you whip him, eh?"

"You're old enough to know better, and it was the stupid fucking dragon that caused me to punish the kid."

"Ah. My mistake."

"If only you hadn't killed Vasquez, if you'd stayed out of our business, you could have been on your way."

"It's been said that I have a nose for trouble."

"A pity. I bet you've seen a few things. In another time and place we could have shared a pint you and I, swapped tall tales."

"No. We couldn't, because even in another time and place, even if you were alive and not a sadistic piece of rat-fucked coffin stuffing, you'd still be a cunt, and I don't drink with cunts."

The air became charged. I waited for him to strike. I had a few ideas as to what I might do when he made his move. How I'd disarm him and shove his fucking whip where the suns don't shine. But he didn't attack. He leered and shook his head in mock sorrow. "Like I say, you just can't help some people. But you can teach them. Torsten!" He called towards the gate where the other penny had taken the ogren. He returned. His hands were bloody to the wrists. "Teach this old fool a lesson."

"Madame said to save it for the show on Sunday."

"I'm master here, and I say you fight now."

Torsten shrugged. "Whatever." He strode into the center of the arena, rolled his neck and cracked his knuckles. "Come on then, old timer, let's see what you've got."

I sighed and tried to shrug the knots out of my neck. Doc grinned. "That's the spirit, freak." He took off his hat before executing a deep bow. "My lords, ladies, and gentlemen. We have saved the best for last!" He nodded and smiled as though accepting the cheers of an imaginary crowd. Torsten grinned and also waved to the empty stands. Their performance drew the attention of my fellow prisoners, who pressed their faces against the bars as well as a couple of passing Pennies, drawn perhaps by the sound of laughter instead of the more common screams. "In the center of the arena is Torsten Scaldsson, reaver, raider, ravisher of nuns... and priests." Doc winked.

Torsten cupped his nethers. "What can I say? A pretty face is a pretty face."

Some of the prisoners cheered nervously.

"His opponent tonight is from the lost land of Lemuria, the last survivor of a forgotten, reptilian race known to feed upon the flesh of virgins. My lords and ladies, I give you Breed!" He tipped me the nod.

"I'm not bowing to a pretend audience."

"Bow to your fellows then, give the condemned their respect, 'morituri te salutant' and all that bullshit. Come on, Breed, don't be churlish, play the game."

"Fuck's sake." I waved to my fellow, idiot prisoners and was rewarded by hoots, howls, risible laughter, and the odd, unexpected supportive cheer. Doc left the arena, leaving me and the ravisher alone. I not only feared for my life but my virtue, such as it was.

"Don't worry, Breed, I won't fuck you. I don't like scaly buttocks," said Torsten as he began to circle.

"No? Well I'm planning on killing you and fucking your corpse while it's still fresh-ish because I do quite like a bit of hairy-assed barbarian. Ah. I forgot, I can't kill you— you're already dead."

His smile faded. My comrades in chains raised a hearty cheer, and I saluted them with enthusiasm. Something crunched in my neck.

"You know, if everyone on the other side is as stupid as you, I'm surprised Madame doesn't go back and take over." Doc taunted from the gallery.

"I bet you are, Doc."

He laughed. "In all seriousness, it boggles the mind how even in the face of death you can't shut your trap. Did I not warn you? 'Don't antagonize her' I said, and what did you do?"

"What can I say? It's a gift." I circled in the opposite direction to Torsten. He was shorter than me but stockier.

"When I heard you screaming like a bairn I thought she'd done for you. But no, you vexed her so mightily she left you alive, lying in a puddle of your own piss. At least, I assume it was yours." A crowd began to gather in the gallery, silver-eyed Pennies ringed the arena. While his captain flapped his lips, Torsten slowly narrowed the distance between us. "Oh, I almost forgot. Torsten, catch." Doc tossed a machete to the redhead, who caught it with practiced ease.

"Really?" I sighed. "Why not just fucking hamstring me, you blank-eyed shitmonger?"

"Hey, Torsten," Doc called. "Cut the cunt's tongue out, would you? I want it as a memento."

"Right you are, boss. Stand still, *odjur,* and I'll make it quick." Torsten slapped his chest with the flat of the stubby blade and let loose with a battle cry as he charged.

I'd like to say his attack was clumsy and slow, only it wasn't. He was fast and the blow he leveled at my head missed by inches. Still, it missed. It missed because a part of my brain that had lain dormant for forty years or so was starting to wake up.

Quite detached from the process, I found myself leaning away from the blade's path while sending a kick towards his knee. The next surprise was that it connected, not enough to break or dislocate but enough to throw him off balance. He staggered. I righted myself and took a long stride back. I enjoyed the muttered displeasure of my captors while my fellow prisoners raised another nervous cheer, as much out of surprise as appreciation of my skill. My limbs tingled. I was starting to remember how to do this.

Torsten stumbled. Alas, the blow didn't hurt him or slow him because the dead feel no pain, and I hadn't done enough to break the limb. Head down, he set himself and barreled towards me, swinging the blade. I dodged the first two wild slashes, got the measure of his timing and stepped inside just before the third blow which was aimed at my head, could land. I caught his wrists, drove him back and smashed my forehead into his nose with all the force I could muster. He staggered, tore his hands from my grasp. I danced back as he swung again. This time he caught me and sliced the front of my thigh. Blood flowed. I stumbled but managed to catch his arm as he swung past me. We stood a moment; eye to coin, before he tried to pull away. I grabbed his elbow, turned his arm in towards his body and guided it into his gut. There's a funny thing that happens to people when you outmaneuver them in a fight, even the dead ones. They don't let go of their weapons. Whatever it is, be it knife, sword, halberd or broken bottle, they hold onto it and allow you to use it against them while their brain attempts to catch up. If you move quickly and surely, you can vent someone *with their help*, although for every rule there are exceptions. Torsten wasn't one of them.

There wasn't a hot gush of blood as usually happens when inners become outers. The air wasn't filled with the iron tang of fresh, living claret, or piss and viscera as the contents of bladder and gut sack mingled in flight. What fell from the rent was a dried-out knot of intestine and a pile of dust.

"And you called me a monster?" I enquired and then drove the blade deeper.

Sandy residue trailed from his desiccated guts. Silence fell on the arena.

"Finish it," Doc commanded. I wasn't sure which of us he was talking to as I wasn't going to take my eyes off Torsten, who seemed to be staring at the rent in his stomach. It isn't often that you catch a glimpse of a being's true nature— of their thoughts as they unfold. It is even less frequent that you will recognize these fleeting moments of clarity. But I saw him then. I saw the artifice stripped away as this sorrowful creature standing in the dry and dusty remains of its once vital umbles, realized it was no longer a man but a thing.

He shook himself and came on, the blade gripped in both hands. I suspected the overhead cleaving posture was a feint, and with good reason it turns out. At the last second, he flipped the blade and turned the downward chop into a sideways swipe. I decided that I would sidestep, spin on my heel, grab him from behind and wrestle him to the ground.

That was the plan.

I love making plans. I love the way they turn to shit the second I try to enact them. Unbeknownst to me, buried beneath a light dusting of sand and sawdust of the arena were the sticky remains of some poor bastard's excreta in which I planted my heel as I charged towards Torsten. By a stroke of luck this slip was actually beneficial. Had I continued my run unimpeded I would have caught Torsten's blade in my teeth, as it was I skidded under the swinging steel while simultaneously taking the bastard's feet out from under him.

My attacker flailed and fell on top of me. Not one to waste a gift, I gouged at the coins in his eye sockets much as I would if they'd been proper, fleshy peepers. There was an unpleasant sucking noise as the metal tore free of the dead flesh, releasing greasy tendrils of necromantic energy. He gagged, spewed a torrent of shadows, and then the empty shell that had been Torsten collapsed with a sigh.

I pocketed the tarnished pennies, which depicted a bird on one side and an equally beaky man on the other. Now that the fight was done, pain rushed in like a tide reminding me that I was not the ferocious Guild Blade I had once been. I pushed the corpse aside and stood up. "So then, who's next?" I declared fearlessly. "Because I'm in a killing mood." If I was going to die, I would die as I lived: lying out of my backside.

Doc clapped. "Not bad, old stick, not bad. I like the bravado. It plays well in the arena." He paced, out of reach. "Maybe I can use you after all? Put you in a warm-up bout. What say you, freak? D'you want to live another day? Another two?"

I spat onto the ashen gut stuffing of the recently spent Torsten, whose passing appeared to be mourned by none.

"Well, what's it to be? Glory in the arena or taking a dirt nap now with poor old Torsten? No need to overthink it; time is money and I assure you, the choice is that simple." He tipped his hat back on his head. Malin's ring, *my* ring winked blood bright on his finger. I dropped the blade.

Doc nodded. "Perhaps you're not that stupid after all."

Chapter Six

As well as a promotion, my accidental victory earned me a change of lodgings.

"This burial crypt was excavated by the Romani thousands of years ago." My guide and jailor informed me as we emerged into another fucking cave. "This weren't for no commoners. This was where they buried their equites."

"Their whats?"

"Horse soldiers— knights or some such. They done this place up nicer than the local Chieftain's manor, 'an just for their dead." She shook her head and chuckled, causing her dead dumplings to bubble up and almost out of her grimy blouse. I was conflicted. The coin-eyed cull had lived well in life, as attested to by the ample chesticles and the broadness of her plumptious beam. She was so well endowed top and bottom, that she was forced to traverse the last few yards in a crabbish, sideways shuffle.

While I waited for my 'guard' to squeeze from the narrow passage I took in my new surroundings, under the watchful coins of a gun-wielding Black Penny lazily patrolling the cave. Fake, fluted columns lined the long walls of the mausoleum in a pretense of supporting the barrel-vaulted ceiling. Between the columns, tombs for the wealthy and the not-so-wealthy had been dug into the limestone. The more modest tombs were at this end. Some were little more than shelves, barely deep enough to stash a body. The next tier up in the funereal pecking order were small chambers of decorative stonework, with room enough for two to six shelves. At the far end, grand porticoes marked the entrance to palatial tombs.

The fine tombs were no longer the final resting places of the equites; now they were home to the just-about-living. Bones had been swept aside to make room for bedrolls; mournful statues of angels had been draped with laundry.

In the most salubrious funereal residences, the bronze doors had been torn from their hinges, no doubt at Darzka's behest and set aside to be replaced by flimsy curtains. Halfway along the vault, a pair of bored looking Pennies guarded an arched, barred gateway, which bespoke a certain measure of confidence, for this cave appeared to be the exclusive domain of monsters— some of whom I would not want to tangle with on a good day.

"Ah, Kate, at last. I almost started without you." A skinny cove scolded my escort. Unlike most of the inhabitants of the cave, he was a living human, complete with peepers, although he was a poor example of the species.

Kate fixed him with her dead, copper coin stare. "Don't give me no sass, Ennis. You ain't one of us yet."

Ennis turned his attention to the group of prisoners standing before him in an attempt to hide his embarrassment at being put in his place. I recognized some of the captives who had been deemed able-bodied when we, the useless, had been winnowed from their ranks upon arrival. They were all cleaner than when they'd arrived and had been dusted in what I guessed was louse powder, giving them a ghostly appearance, enhanced by the uniform, grey overalls those with regular body parts were wearing.

"Go join the line, Breed," said Kate. "And do what you're bloody well told, or someone'll put a bullet in you," she said loud enough for those close enough to hear before leaning in and whispering. "I'm gonna put a few shillings on you lasting out your first games, so don't let me down, eh?" She tipped her head in what might have been the eyeless equivalent of a wink.

"I'll do my best, milady," I replied, which made her titter.

"You, over here now!" Ennis barked, transferring his ire at Kate's rebuke to me, as she ambled to the far end of the hall. I took my time, making my way to the end of the line as indicated by Ennis who, in the meantime, began coughing. He pulled a grubby kerchief from his waistcoat and used it to absorb what sounded like a lungful of phlegm, before tucking the bloody rag back in his pocket. I'd seen this malady before and didn't need to smell the canker on his breath to know his days were numbered.

Unlike the rest of the culls at this end of the room who were all garbed in uniform grey, Ennis, like me, had been granted the privilege of keeping his own clothes. He was wearing a faded black overcoat, a black jacket, green waistcoat, and a blue shirt as well as patched black trousers and a worn pair of boots, one of which was held together with twine. He must have been weed thin under the tatty garb, certainly, he was as pale as a dead fish and had bags under his eyes as heavy as a rich man's sins. He took a battered flask from his overcoat pocket and had a generous nip before addressing his audience.

"Ladies and gentlemen. A delight to meet you and welcome you to the esteemed ranks and proud traditions of the Ephemerals."

I looked down the line. Everyone who had a face I could read appeared as underwhelmed and confused as I was.

"Ephemerals— *you* will play a vital role in the bloody revels." He scratched his greying stubble with brown-stained fingers as he picked his way across the sawdust-strewn floor like a long-legged wading bird tentatively striding through viper infested waters. A couple of Black Pennies armed with firelances ensured nobody wandered away while Ennis recited his obviously well-rehearsed speech. He cut a pathetic figure, as did all those who straddled the gap between prisoner and jailor.

"You lovely bastards will open the finest arena show in the whole of Europia," he continued. "Your sacrifice, your brief antics, will stir the blood of our guests." He grabbed a crab-faced cully by the faceplate and peered into her tiny eyes. "You sweet, dear freaks will sanctify the sand and anoint the air with the heady stink of viscera. Your blood will invigorate Madame's honored guests." He released the poor cull and strutted along the line. "It's like magic: where blood flows, gold follows. They won't bet a penny on you lot, but your ludicrous deaths will set the stage for the majesty that is to come." He gestured to the far end of the cave where a group of handy-looking beastkin were training. A two-headed fellow made a gesture that left no one in any doubt as to what he thought of Ennis's florid screed. Another of them, this one with the upper body of a human and the lower quarters and antlers of a stag, snorted dismissively. I caught his eye and held his gaze long enough to appear neither cowardly nor bullish and was rewarded in return with a curt nod.

"Oi, Snake eyes," Ennis snapped at me.

I knew he meant me, but I feigned ignorance and looked along the line before pointing to myself. "Do you mean me, cockling?"

He came over and jabbed me in the chest. My first instinct was to snap his bony finger and shove it where the sun didn't shine, but the guards' were watching, which caused me to reconsider.

"Yes, I mean you." His breath smelled of sickness and pickled eggs. "Harken unto my words and you might learn something useful." He spoke slowly and loudly, enunciating every word as though he was talking to someone who was either hard of hearing or hard of thinking.

I slow blinked my disdain at the skinny louse farmer but held my tongue. He fumed but moved on. Had he been your average thug he would have probably punched me for my insolence, but I could tell that Ennis didn't have it in him.

"You lot are the entrée. While the great and the good enjoy Madame's hospitality and get nicely liquored up. You will tear each other to pieces. But do not despair, for you will burn brightly, if briefly and die with the cheers of the crowd ringing in your ears. For the glory of the games!" He flung his arms wide. Some of the fighters at the other end of the tunnel cheered. Some beat their chests, some tried to beat their comrades' chests and had to be separated by the

Pennies. The cove with the antlers merely stood by and watched.

"The games will take place in two days' time. Until then, relax, entertain yourselves, and make peace with whatever gods you pray to, if any at all. Dinner is served at seven sharp each evening, informal dress." He chuckled alone. "My advice to you is let *them* eat first." He chinned in the direction of the fighters before wandering over to his little piece of necropolitan heaven which was an alcove tomb on the right-hand wall that had a mattress *and* a table and chair crammed into the tiny space. Upon entering, he flicked up his coattails before taking a seat like he was the nib of the manor, surveying his domain. Dismissed though we may have been, we were also in a fucking tunnel, so my fellow ephemerals and I milled awkwardly until Ennis slapped the table. "Don't just stand there, for goodness sake. Grab a bunk. Where do they find these idiots?" He addressed his comment to the nearest of the Pennies who ignored him.

There followed a pathetic stampede as my fellow prisoners fought over the vacant tombs in this half of the room, which was divided midway by locked double gates. I didn't fight for a place to put my head down. If I needed somewhere to kip, I'd just evict one of them later.

"You're a cool one, eh?" The woman who spoke hobbled over, propped up by a crutch. She was young, with bright eyes, choppy brown hair and an open, friendly smile. Beneath the underlying stink of shit and piss that stained the air in the tunnel crypt, when she got up close I noted that she smelled of booze and predator. Like everyone else here, except for the Pennies, a warded shackle was locked around her ankle. "My name's Antoinette, but please, call me Nettie." She offered me her hand.

I shook it. Her wicked sharp claws tickled my wrist. "Breed. Pleased to meet you. So, what are you in for? I know you're not supposed to ask such things in the clink, only you and those coves over yonder don't look like the rest of us humble ephemerals."

She laughed. "We're not ephemerals according to the fucked-up rules of this place. As to how I came to be imprisoned, I can only be honest and say that cognac was my undoing. I got drunk in a bar in Kathmandu after the successful completion of a job and woke up on a train wearing this pretty bracelet." She glanced at her ankle cuff. A dirty bandage was wrapped around her right thigh from knee to groin. She saw the drift of my gaze. "I know what you're thinking, but I'll have you know I won my last bout. Alas, I got a little sloppy when I was playing to the crowd." She shrugged. "But enough about me. How about you? What's your story? Nuanu says you're not from here."

I smiled. "No."

"I mean not from this world, at least that's what I think he means. Bucky is a good sort, but he talks in riddles. I understand him better when I'm drunk, but as you see, I am currently, mostly sober."

She didn't seem in the slightest bit sober, but the glint of fangs suggested it was best not to dispute the point. "So how did you end up here, Breed?"

"I had a disagreement with…er, thingy. You know? What's her name? The thin wench, bit shorter than me, dark hair, no sense of humor." I couldn't for the life of me remember what the cunt was called.

"Darzka?" Nettie offered.

"Aye! That's her."

She cocked her head. "And yet you live? Maybe Bucky's right. Come, let me introduce you." She clapped her hand on my shoulder. "I have a bottle of brandy an admirer sent me. We'll have a party. Oh, don't call him Bucky, eh? Like Madame, he has no sense of humor and will most likely kill you if he feels you have insulted him." She gestured with her crutch to the end of the room. As I had nothing to do other than fight over piss-soaked straw pallets with my fellow forgettables, I decided to take her up on the offer.

Ennis had other ideas. "I say, where do you think you're going?" He marched over, keeping his focus on me while politely trying to ignore Nettie. "Ephemerals don't mix with the talent."

Nettie's smile vanished, and she fixed him with a cold, grey stare. "Fuck off, Ennis, or the talent might decide to eat you."

"You wouldn't dare, and anyway, you couldn't. The ward won't let you kill me."

"I could maul you a little before the pain got too bad."

His nervous gaze darted from Nettie to the nearest Black Penny who gave no indication that he was about to support Ennis up. He backed away muttering all manner of dark imprecations.

"Can you shapeshift in the shackles?" I asked Nettie as we headed up, past the gate into the plush end of the crypt.

"How did you know…?" she enquired blearily.

"Your smell."

"Ah, of course, and no, I can't, but I could still give that little collaborator a kicking."

"So how does it work in this here arena?"

"The magic in this thing stops working when we're in there, allowing us to use our abilities within the arena. Of course, the moment one leaves, the magic returns. It's a neat trap, but then, Madame Darzka is a most cunning witch."

"She's just a no-mark Mage Lord. But yes, she has a modicum of cunning and it seems some small skill with wards."

She chuckled. "Small skill, eh? What are your skills?" She guided me to one of several, larger chambers that had been delved from the cavern.

"That is a very good question. I used to be good with a blade. I also used to be a fair old sorcerer, but in truth my ability ran more to the destructive end of things. Now?" I spread my hands. "Finding trouble appears to be my *forte* as they apparently say here."

In Nettie's tomb, the walls had been painted with scenes from a typically bucolic, human afterlife. The coffins and contents had been cleared out long ago and replaced by a couple of mildewed chairs, a tattered rug, and a pallet of reasonably fresh straw that had been bound into a bed with a blanket thrown over it. Candle stubs of varying lengths filled votive niches. None of them were lit because a creature like Nettie with her luminous green eyes could undoubtedly see well in the dark.

"Be it ever so humble, there's no crypt like home." Nettie entreated me to enter with a flourish of her crutch. "I inherited this domicile when poor old Patrick 'Knuckles' McNally was sucked dry by my dear friend Aaiko." She sighed a breath of melancholy into the spore-laden air. "Mon Dieu, but that nukekubi was a formidable wench. Sadly, now also departed." She tossed the crutch aside and rummaged in the straw until she came up brandishing a bottle like it was a gilded trophy before drawing the cork with her teeth. "It's cognac and Gaulish so, *naturellement* it's excellent."

"After you," I said. I was beginning to remember how to play these games. I had to be careful now that I wasn't a dragon or a sorcerer which annoyed me. I enjoyed life much more when I could just eat anyone who annoyed me.

She acknowledged my caution with a wry smile as she savored the smell of the drink. Evidently satisfied that it met her clearly, very high standards, she took a long, grimace-inducing pull. "I was going to save this, but what's the point, eh?" She offered me the bottle. The honey-colored liquid smelled of oak and spiced fruit. I took a swig. It had a mellow burn on the way down my gullet, which blossomed into a pleasant fire.

"Ah, here he is." Nettie chinned to the entrance. The part man, part stag fellow walked softly for someone who must have been seven feet at the withers and composed entirely of rippling muscle. He stopped at the entrance to the cave, precluded from entry by his magnificent crown of antlers.

"Greetings, stranger and well met— that is, I hope 'tis well met." He tapped the ground with a forehoof.

"Well, Antoinette?" His voice was resonant, his breath smelled of berries and green shoots. He regarded the shapechanger with an unwavering gaze, his fierce golden eyes bright to the point of iridescent, like twin pools of sunslight burning through a leafy bower. He was naked and his torso, like his flanks, was crisscrossed by scars, some of which had faded to silver while others were freshly scabbed.

Antoinette shrugged. "I don't know. Breed, this is Nuanu, the Master of the Hunt or some such tree fairy nonsense. Nuanu, this is Breed."

He didn't look like he appreciated the description and snorted before turning to me. "I am the emissary of the Lord of the Wild. I came here to negotiate with the outland mage, whereupon she broke the ancient laws and incarcerated me."

"Some people, eh?"

"Quite. I sense a similar, otherworldly aura about your person. Is it true?"

Nettie sniggered.

"I did come through the portal as you call it, although I refer to them as 'gates', but I'm not like her, honest." *I'm much, much worse, all told.*

"Gate, portal." He waved his hand dismissively. "Why are you here?"

I took another sip of the cognac. *Well, funny you should ask. My best friend died because he was a stubborn, fucking idiot. In the throes of a righteous sulk, I nicked his body and legged it through the gate without the faintest idea of where I was going, and then I got summoned by mistake by a cove who got vented shortly thereafter.* "I came here to stop Darzka for she is a most dangerous cove and an affront to all that is decent and good in this world or any other." *Much better.*

The Master of the Hunt nodded, seemingly pleased by what he heard. "Then it is as I hoped."

In desperate need of allies, I decided to run with it. "Indeed, I feel a keen sympathy for your plight, not to mention the kinchin cove she's fixing to slot."

"Kinchin cove? Slot?" He looked at the shapeshifter.

"Child. Sacrifice," Nettie clarified and gestured for the return of the bottle. "I wouldn't ask but it's all I have left until Sunday— maybe longer if I'm not fit to fight by then." She flopped onto her pallet. "Damn Monroe. The scorpion tailed bastard caught me a good one. Gods rest his soul." She eased herself onto the straw.

"You should not have played to the crowd. It is demeaning," said Nuanu. "But back to the matter. If the outlander has her way, the Wild will die and we will die, and the solstice is mere days away."

"The what now?"

"The estival solstice. The end of spring and beginning of summer. If the Goblin Queen is slain on the day of rebirth on the most hallowed ground, the Wild will be cut off from the breath of the universe, and we will wither and die." He sounded impatient, like I should have known what he was talking about when I was still struggling to get my head around what the fuck an estival solstice was.

"I don't want to wither," Nettie added drunkenly. "I mean who would want that, eh?" She shuddered. "Although, and I mean no offense my friend." She waved the bottle in Nuanu's direction. "But I find it hard to believe that one teeny tiny sorcerer can destroy a world of Wild magic."

"That is because you're a child." Nuanu smiled. "I am old, but the Lord of the Wild was born when the first fires of the sun quickened. He knows what will happen if Darzka closes the portals to this world."

"If you say so, grandfather." The shapeshifter teased. Nuanu stamped his hoof, drawing the attention of a couple of the Black Pennies who were patrolling nearby.

"What's going on in there?" one of them shouted, his hand drifting to the trigger of his firelance as he approached.

Nuanu swung around to face the guard who had to back up sharpish to avoid being impaled by the massive antlers. "Begone, gaunt. Your corrupt stench offends me."

"Nuanu's a decent sort, but he's the least diplomatic emissary I've ever met," Nettie side-mouthed to me.

"Oh, I offend you do I, Your 'ighness?" The Penny laughed. "You're fucking lucky Madame don't like venison, or your arse would be on a plate and your head on the wall where it belongs. In fact, I've bet half a crown that your number's up this Sunday. So, don't let me down, will ya?"

Nuanu reared, but before his hooves could land a shattering blow upon the head of the Penny, the sigils on the stag's shackle glowed, and he crashed to the ground in agony.

"You lot never fucking learn." The eyeless guard spat on the emissary, who writhed in pain. "Come on, why don't you try again? I love seeing you squirm." The Penny kicked him. Enraged, Nuanu lowered his head, ready to impale the fellow before the warded shackle once again reduced him to a quivering mess.

"All right, that's enough." The buxom Penny who'd brought me here shoved her way through the crowd that had begun to gather. "Go on now, get about your business, the lot of you."

Nettie nudged me. "Help him up, eh?"

"How, exactly? He's all hooves and pointy bits."

"I do not need...help." Nuanu's voice was ragged, frayed by the sudden fire of the wards that I knew from personal experience had lit through his bones like a lightning strike.

Whether through arrogance, lack of imagination due to being dead, or painfully accurate estimation of skills, the Pennies paid little attention to the injured shapeshifter and none at all to me. The threat as far as they were concerned was Nuanu, and he'd been humbled by Madame-What's-Her-Face's wards. Having grown an ego as befitted a dragon, it stung to be so overlooked, to be invisible but then that blade could cut both ways.

I crouched beside the stag, careful to avoid the dagger points of his thorny crown. "Lean on me, and for fuck's sake be careful with those antlers." He was heavy, and I hadn't fully recovered from my own injuries, but between us we got him back on his feet. He mumbled something that might have been 'thank you' before hobbling over to the wall for support.

"The way I see it we're in a massive pot of arsepickle," I said, making sure that no one but Nettie and Nuanu were within earshot. "Now, I'm not bound with warded shackles, because I can't do fuck all. We need to get you useful coves free."

"Everyone here must be set free," Nuanu corrected.

"Well, yes, obviously, but we need to get the shackles off you lot first."

Nettie growled and took an angry slurp of rapidly vanishing booze. "Don't you think we've tried? These things are impervious. Trust me, I have the scars to prove it. The poor bastards who persisted in trying to break them have been shot or worse. They burned poor old Southey at the stake."

Nuanu lowered his head. "The warlock will be missed."

An air of misery settled over the pair. I loitered awkwardly. Unable and unwilling to share in their grief, I was about to excuse myself until they were in a more receptive mood when the gate halfway down the hall was unlocked.

"Grub's up!" a phlegmy voice shouted, and a pair of trollish coves dragged a cart into the crypt. Riding on the back of the cart like the captain of her ship was a human woman with a ruddy face, and a mouth big enough to swallow a boulder. A massive cauldron, of what smelled like rendered down dog rat bubbled and steamed behind her on the cart. A crowd of hungry ephemerals and warriors began to gather impatient for whatever swill was in the pot. "Don't shove, you miserable fuckers. You wait your turn like proper bleedin' ladies and gentlemen." She tapped her pipe out on the side of the pot. "I won't hold wiv no bad bleedin' manners." The brazen cull's voice carried the length of the cavern.

Like magic, bowls and mugs were produced from a variety of hidey holes as the prisoners jostled for position in the line. Well used to the routine, Nettie unearthed a bowl from her pallet. "We get fed once a day and not much at that. On Sundays we don't eat until after the games." She grabbed her crutch and hobbled to the back of the growing queue.

Hidden behind the stew pot was Sonam. I hadn't noticed him until he began handing out hunks of bread as the woman ladled out gruel. The moment I laid eyes on him it hit me. "Of course."

When the last scoop of slop had been poured into the cupped hands of one of my less fortunate ephemerals, she gave Sonam leave to clean the inside of the cauldron with a crust of his own. I waited until he'd scooped up some juice and jumped off the wagon to eat his meager portion before joining him. The serving wench directed the trolls to turn the wagon around. As I approached, I felt the kiss of fresh air blowing down the tunnel. Alas, despite my new-found powers of being inconsequential, I didn't think I'd make it past the Pennies guarding the tunnel.

"Hello, Sonam. Do you mind if I join you?"

The boy shook his head. "You don't have any food," he said as I settled myself beside him.

"Not hungry but I do have a juicy proposition for you."

He locked his hands together in a complicated knot of fingers and adopted a sage expression far beyond that which suited a cove of his tender years. "It is taught that we should move beyond desire."

"How about reuniting Druk with his mother and seeing your homeland again?"

His expression changed immediately. "I...I would like that very much."

"Then this is your lucky day, old pal."

Chapter Seven

I stood alone in the amphitheater. Save for one, the stepped seats were empty, the sand unsullied. Torches guttered, and a chill breeze hissed across the arena whirling glittering dust devils into the air.

"Still alive then?" Tobias was sitting in the seat of honor, front and center beneath a gold and purple canopy amid a scatter of velvet cushions.

"I thought I told you to fuck off."

He tried to look hurt. But I saw the smile before he could hide it. "Since when have I done what you told me to do? You look tired."

"And you look dead, what's your point? What do you want?"

He rubbed his head with his stump. "To rest in peace. When are you going to finish this, Breed? When are you going to stop running?"

"When I run out of worlds."

"Forget worlds, you're running out of time, thoasa."

He was right. I could feel the sand of my life draining away. "Half thoasa, and you speak like this is my fault, which it isn't."

"No, you're right. It isn't." He stood up, turned to leave.

"Wait. Is that it?"

"Is what it?"

"That. I expected something more, a bit of advice or something."

He tucked his hand and his stump into his sleeves. Fixed me with his smugly pious stare. "Stop being a cunt, how about that?"

"Well, that's a bit keen for a priest."

"It's the company I keep. That you dare even ask for advice—"

"Ah, now, I didn't ask as such, I just wondered if you might have some insight, some clue as to how I might extricate myself from this predicament."

"What? Something like, 'you have the power, Breed. It was within you all the time."

"It was?"

"No. She drained it out of you, idiot. You're nothing more than a Guild Blade of small renown."

"Oh." *Shit*.

He drew a breath. "Just get up, Breed."

"What?"

"Up!"

"No, sorry, I'm still not getting it. Is it a metaphor or—"

"GET UP!"

The words thundered through my mind, shattering the dream. I jumped up and hit my head on the low roof of the coffin ledge where I'd been sleeping.

"Are you deaf?" Ennis was standing over me. Spit flecked his lips. "Move it, you lazy, old bastard. The day of reckoning has arrived."

"What?" I didn't know where I was. Just for a few seconds, amid the noise and confusion I was completely at a loss as to what the fuck was going on. Then the last two days came rushing back. I was in the catacombs. We'd made plans, well, *I'd* made plans, the others just had to follow them. Prisoners and guards were rushing around, the frantic activity fueled by an air of panic and excitement. The gate was open, the 'talent' were preparing for the games, and the Black Pennies were driving my fellow ephemerals towards the gate like cattle to the slaughter.

"I said, move." Ennis grabbed me, started shoving me towards the gate.

"It is Sunday, isn't it?"

"That's right, freak. Today is the day. I must say, I thought you'd be trouble, but there hasn't been a peep out of you. You're like a little dog…"

I glanced down to the far end of the tunnel. Nettie had just picked a glittering cloak out of a pile of costumes. When she saw me, she tipped me a nod and glanced at Nuanu. He snorted, released a burst of musk that no corpse would notice. He was ready. We were still on. I was shaking. Was I ready? "Yes of course I'm fucking ready."

Ennis prodded me in the chest. "Glad to hear it, freak. Now get a f—"

I grabbed his finger, bent it back stopping just short of snapping it. He dropped to his knees in a bid to save himself from the pain. "Don't poke me, Ennis, not when I'm trying to think."

"Oi, you, Breed." A red-haired Penny with matching copper peepers shouted over. "Put him down and get over here or I will shoot you where you stand." I released Ennis, who climbed unsteadily to his feet clutching his hand.

"I hope you go down hard, freak," he said through gritted teeth. "I hope you die screaming."

"Why, Ennis? Is that what gets you hard?" I gave him a suggestive wink.

The Penny laughed. "All right, that's enough. Come on. You too, Ennis."

The blood drained from Ennis's face. "What?"

"Tonight's the night, old son." She stopped smiling. "You do still want it, don't you, Ennis?" As one, the Black Pennies in the catacomb stopped what they were doing and turned their inhuman gaze upon him.

He shrank under the weight of their scrutiny. "Yes." He coughed. "Of course."

***

While the stars of the show were given time to primp and prepare themselves for the battle to come, we ephemerals were given no such consideration. The Pennies herded us at a run through the labyrinth of tunnels until, breathless and disorientated, we burst from a vault in a graveyard. I drank the sweet, evening air like it was nectar. Despite gloom and almost certain death being the sky under which I lived, the cold stars were a balm for my tired, old eyes. I'd spent a lot of time underground about forty years ago but honestly, I hadn't missed it.

I looked to the horizon beyond rustic, thatched roofs and a twisted steeple to where the sun's dying fire burnished the tree-toothed horizon. It was beautiful, and as much of a day as I'd seen since being dragged into this shithole world. A lively breeze slapped my cheek and carried with it the scent of meat and ale, of wood smoke and incense, strong wine, beast sweat, sorcery, and most importantly, dragon. A hard shove in the back sent me sprawling.

"Get up and get moving," the red-haired Penny took a swipe at me as I scrambled to my feet. Knees creaking, I stumbled out of the graveyard behind the worried herd of ephemerals. Dogs held in check by dull-eyed locals barked at us as we passed. Their masters drank cider from stone jugs and jeered at our monsters' parade from behind a hedge of brambles entwined with barbed wire and wish ribbons.

The path we were taken down led to a gate that was set between the first of a pair of earthen banks. Each bank must have been twenty feet high and wide enough for two Black Pennies to patrol side-by-side. The gateway was between two monoliths of schist stone, each one eight feet across and eighteen feet high or thereabouts. As we were driven through the gate, I saw that there were dozens more stones stretching in an arc which, if it was a circle, would be half a mile across. Between the banks were animal pens and wagons piled with all manner of props required for the bloody performance that was about to be enacted. What sounded like the drone of a million-bee swarm drew my attention to the indigo sky, where five lozenge shaped balloons were rising, propelled by what looked like massive windmill paddles attached to what I guessed was the stern of the flying boats. "What the fuck are they?"

"Airships," said Juanita, the cully who looked like a crab. She was moving as slowly as me on account of her only having three and a half legs out of six.

"Magic?"

"Gas."

"Come the fuck on," the red Penny hissed. I guessed that her sudden discretion meant that we were in earshot of Madame's guests. Beyond the banks and between yet more giant, irregular monoliths the path was boxed-in by high wooden palisades. To the left, the clink of glasses and soft flutter of laughter danced upon the bright trill of strings. Warm torchlight swayed from a web of wires strung from poles which followed the curve of the earth banks. Billows of intoxicating pipe smoke drifted ghostly and sweet between the waxed paper globes, and I was sure I could hear the silvery chime of a fountain. Truly, Madame had spared no expense to entertain her guests before the bloodletting began.

The amphitheater dominated the center of the circle. It had some age about it; moss and fungus mottled the once white stone, but the gods and nymphs carved into the façade were still recognizable. I had little time to study the finer points of its architecture as we were hurried within. A vaulted passage was blocked off on the left but rolled around to the right. Like the practice pit, cells opened onto the arena.

"Those two, in here," Red gestured to one of the cells with the barrel of her firelance, and another of her crew shoved me and a blue-skinned old lamprey creature inside. The cage door slammed behind us, and I had the first opportunity since being roused from my kip to catch my breath.

My cellmate didn't have a face as such, it was more a head with a giant mouth in place of eyes and nose. In his youth I would not have liked to get a kiss from the three rings of angled, saw-edged gnashers, but like me he was past his best and half his teeth were missing. Still, he looked like a handy...whatever he was. Upon seeing me staring, he scratched something that might have been words in the sand and pointed to himself.

"Sorry mate, I don't understand your script, but for what it's worth, I'm Breed."

The lamprey rested his knuckles on the ground, no mean feat to say he was standing up and roughly as tall as me. His hide bore barnacle scars and old slashes and bites. Five thick tentacles sprouted out of the back of his head. I noticed that each tentacle ended in an eye, two of which were fixed on me, one looked towards the tunnel, and two gazed out onto the as yet empty arena. The sound of cell doors being slammed ran along the right-hand side of the arena, quickly followed by pensive faces appearing at the bars to stare out onto the pristine killing ground.

"If you're lucky they might drop some weapons in," said Red as she made her way back along the passage, checking that the tunnel side cage doors were locked. "If they do, my advice is to grab 'em quick and work as a team… until the end that is." She grinned; her copper eyes twinkled in the dying light.

"Why the advice?" I asked. My companion slobbered something incomprehensible.

"I brought you to the arena so that makes you and Minnonuk mine in the sweepstakes. If you last longest I get the pot this month. Ave."

"Fuck you too," I said, more bravely than I was feeling. Minnonuk made a wet fart noise with an accompanying hand gesture indicating he felt the same. The Penny walked away laughing.

Keeping my toothsome new friend in view in case he decided to improve his odds of survival by doing me early, I had a closer look at the arena. It was uncanny how like my dream it was save that the four tiers were now packed. *No not uncanny. I had a dream is all, and how different can one amphitheater look to another? Forget ghosts and all that bullshit, stick to the plan*.

"Stick to the plan?" I laughed at myself. "Yes, rely on luck and trust in strangers, when has that not worked out well?" Minnonuk canted his head and turned a couple of eye tentacles in my direction. I think I smelled the musk of pity but chose to ignore it.

Braziers set around the arena above the highest tier of seats burst into flames, casting dramatic slashes of light and shadow over the sea of conspicuously wealthy spectators. All that glistened was most certainly gold, and all that shone were diamonds, emeralds, sapphires, and my favorite, rubies. Dozens of servants tended this most splendid jewel garden and didn't let a glass run dry or a velvet cushion go unplumped.

Minnonuk joined me to gaze at the glittering gathering. He puckered his vast mouth and whistled through his gill holes.

"My thoughts exactly. The Penny was right, by the way. If we fight together we have a good chance of getting out of this."

His shoulders shook, and he clapped his tentacles, which could either have meant 'You've got to be kidding, elderling', or 'that sounds like a marvelous idea.' As I was feeling apprehensive but optimistic, I decided he'd gone for the former and offered him my hand. He shook it. We were golden.

At an angle of about forty-five degrees from our cage, on the first tier of seating, was the canopied box where Tobias had sat in my dream. In his place was Madame Darzka. She wore a black, velvet gown and two strings of diamonds that fell to her waist like stars. Her glorious, well coiffured mane hung loose about her slender shoulders. Her cheeks were wine-flushed, and firelight danced in her eyes. In contrast to the slight Mage Lord, the cove sitting beside her was comfortably rounded. I initially took him to be a Penny but when he turned his whiskered face I saw that he was just wearing spectacles. A gold watch chain dangled from his brocade waistcoat. An equally curvaceous female sat next to him, garbed in white silk with emeralds glittering at her throat and feathers in her hair. Doc stood at Darzka's shoulder, as impassive as a corpse. I couldn't see it from here, but I knew he was wearing Malin's ring. My nerves vanished instantly upon seeing him, replaced by a strong desire to rip the bastard's head from his shoulders.

More troubling even than the sight of the thieving, undead cocklouse was the sight of the cage at Darzka's feet. In all my plotting and scheming of the last two days, I hadn't once considered that Edie might be here. Her presence made things awkward and added an unwanted piece to an already unfair game. The Goblin Queen sat with her knees drawn up to her chin and was unusually quiet, but her dark eyes still shone fiercely through the tangle of black curls.

"Do you see her, Minnonuk?"

He nodded.

"Do you know who she is?"

He nodded again.

Before our riveting conversation could continue, someone blew a single note on a horn and a hush of sorts fell over the crowd. Darzka stood up and bestowed a dazzling smile upon her guests.

"My friends, new and old, welcome to our revels. Tonight, the most magnificent, terrifying, and wondrous creatures ever to walk the earth will fight to the death for your entertainment, but first you will witness a rite that is rare and dear to us. You shall witness the birth of one of the Redeemed." Even though the arena's design gave the stadium excellent acoustics, her voice carried with unnatural clarity around the vast space. I fancied that I could taste star steel in the air and by the gods and all the demons, I craved it like the lowest sot drooling over a pail of week old beer slops.

Clearly already in her cups, the woman sitting with Darzka leaned across to the Goblin Queen's cage and slopped a half glass of wine over the child. "Have a little drinkie, eh?"

Edie lunged through the bars and tried to claw the woman. Darzka kicked the cage, which served only to rile the feral child more. The fellow with them roared with laughter. Darzka again smiled politely at the couple before whispering something to Doc. He nodded and vanished down a flight of stairs behind the royal box.

A few minutes passed. Tension mounted, and the crowd began to grow restless in anticipation of the games. Just before restless became surly, one of the gates on the left side of the arena burst open, and a flustered and nervous looking Ennis was marched onto the sand by Red and Doc. He appeared almost luminously pale in the fading light, paler even than the dead coves standing either side of him. He was in his shirt sleeves and breeches and his boots that were held together with string. His gaze darted furtively around the arena but settled on no one in particular even though all eyes were upon him. A solemn hush fell upon the crowd.

"Ennis Thomas Cranston stand forward," Darzka intoned. He did as he was bid. "You are a murderer of innocents, a panderer, a trafficker of flesh. Are you ready to cast off your sinful past and serve me, now and forever?"

He swallowed so hard I could hear it. "Yes?"

Darzka gave the nod to Doc and the other Penny. The initiate held out his trembling hands. The woman dropped two coins into one and Doc slapped a small bladed knife into the other. Both of them took a step back, just behind him. My guess was they were there to grab him should he try to scarper.

Darzka smiled benevolently. "Give me your eyes, Ennis Cranston, and be redeemed."

Trembling, Ennis raised the knife until the tip of the blade was level with his peepers. His hand was shaking. I sniggered. Minnonuk gave me a stern 'look' involving head mouth and tentacles in an expressive combination.

"Oh, come on, he's a proper cunt."

My companion considered my comment a moment before shrugging, and we got back to watching Ennis fail to cut his eyes out. The hot wind blew towards our cage and again brought with it the smell of dragon. Again, I was reminded of the precarious stack of incidents that had to balance if my plan was going to work.

While I went over the details in my mind, details that me and my conspirators had painstakingly worked out in slyly whispered conversations, Ennis continued to stand there like a eunuch in a brothel. Lustful for blood and violence, the crowd began to murmur. Attentive hostess that she was, Darzka was quick to notice. The gracious smile faltered. A fleeting look of consternation crossed her face.

"Even a mediocre Mage Lord can cast a spell of compulsion," I informed my companion whether he wanted to know or not. "She should be able to make him cut out his eyes. But maybe…" I clapped him on the shoulder. "Maybe she can't cast into her own arena."

Before I'd even finished patting myself on the back, magic rippled through the air as Darzka cast the spell of compulsion on Ennis. The expression of fear on his face became one of frozen dread as the Mage Lord bent her will upon him. Screaming, he plunged the knife into his right eye and twisted the blade. He did not do it quickly. A spurt of eye water sprayed the ground before him while claret flowed down his cheek. He ran the blade around the socket deliberately, agonizingly slowly. Darzka must have thought his pitiful screams unseemly. Another ripple of magic burned the air and Ennis fell silent.

"Bollocks." Wishful thinking had caused me to hope that Madame couldn't cast into the arena, that by some fortunate oversight on her behalf, she had failed to allow herself that capability. I should have known better; as my dear old Mother used to say, "*Hope is for fools*".

Minnonuk screwed up his mouthface, and he turned his tentacle eyes away from the grim spectacle. I suppose having five peepers made him squeamish when it came to watching the overseer destroy his own. When both eyes were in the dirt, Darzka allowed Ennis to drop the knife and fall to his knees. The puppet's head rolled forward onto his chest as though in deference to his mistress. It was a nice touch. The Mage Lord maintained the façade and raised her glass in salute before forcing him to jam the coins into his bloody sockets. A cloud of dark, necromantic energy engulfed him, eliciting gasps and the odd, strangled cry from the crowd. A gust of wind screamed across the killing ground, whipping up dust and perhaps carrying Ennis's soul off to whatever hell kept tally of the Black Pennies. As Darzka released him, Doc and Red hooked him under the arms and dragged him out.

Far from quenching the spectator's thirst for blood, Ennis's sadistic demise and rebirth inflamed it. There followed a round of polite applause, and as flies feasted on the mangled eyeballs, the guests feasted on suckling pigs, and roast birds with extravagant, iridescent tail feathers. All dishes were presented on silver platters the size of shields. My guts rumbled embarrassingly loud. I told myself that I was warspawn, bred for battle, able to go days without food, run twenty miles, and fight at the end of it.

I didn't convince me.

I was sixty years old and so hungry I could have eaten the ruined eyeballs. Not only that, but I was tired and sore and dreading the next few hours as much as I'd dreaded anything in my life. "I'm warspawn, you know," I said to Minnonuk, as though by saying it aloud I might start to believe it. "Well, half warspawn. Although, I used to be a dragon." His mouth tightened like a giant anus. I think he was trying to tell me something.

The gracious hostess drained her glass as her companions messily fed each other butter-drenched crustaceans. When Darzka put her glass down, a phalanx of trumpeters stationed on the highest tier sounded a single, imperious note. Silence fell. In the pens behind and beneath the amphitheater's walls, beasts roared. Darzka stood up and spread her arms as though embracing the crowd. "Highnesses, my lords, ladies, and gentlemen." She smiled with all the warmth of a glacier. "Let the games begin!" When the echo of her words died away, our cage doors were flung open.

Chapter Eight

Minnonuk shrugged his shoulders and stretched his powerful legs. For such a big cove he moved quietly and with grace. In his prime he must have been a formidable hunter, swimming silently through whatever swamp or sea he called home, catching fish, but I could tell that the poor fucker wasn't a fighter. It isn't muscle that makes a cove a killer; it's desire.

Of course, if a fellow has both, so much the better. By the looks of things, the other four ephemerals that were being goaded from their cages had some of one and none of the other. The leery crowd began to jeer.

"After you," I said to Minnonuk. He curled the upper part of his lip in such a way that it looked like he was frowning. "Fine then." I headed out onto the sand. As there wasn't much point in hugging the wall, I strode to the center of the arena, got a good look at the leering crowd. My blood ran cold, my limbs began to tingle which was a good sign. I just hoped that my body remembered how to do that which it used to be so good at.

Killing.

I was built for killing— born with the tools and yes, *the desire* to use them. I was lithe, strong, equipped with claws and fangs and speed. No human could stand against me. I was warspawn, bred for battle.

Was, thickwit, and not to mention, those I was about to fight might not be born warriors, but they weren't soft humans either.

The crabbish cully didn't make it half a yard out of her cage before the fellow she was paired up with, a cove that looked like a small spew maggot from my homeworld of Edolis, leaped upon her back and began furiously chewing through the soft neck parts that the plates of her crabbish head did not protect. She fell on her face, pincers flailing ineffectually as the maggot man crunched through flesh and spine in less than a minute.

Unlike a professional pit fighter, the maggot had taken her down close to the wall, denying a portion of the audience a good view of a kill they'd paid to see. They loudly declared their displeasure and pelted the cove with whatever was to hand, which included a couple of velvet cushions. Rightly confused, the maggot looked up, just in time to see one of our fellow ephemerals' elephantine feet descending towards him. The maggot's head exploded like a ripe, grey peach.

The segmented body spasmed and twitched as Big Feet made sure and stomped the maggot's brain box flat before turning to face me and Minnonuk.

"Get your dancing shoes on, Min, we're up."

Big Feet was a ridiculously out of proportion fellow, being as he was a giant below the waist and regular-sized human above it. In truth, I would rather be killed by his partner, who looked like a mulchy pile of desiccated, brown leaves that had been loosely swept together prior to burning. A flashing blink of copper betrayed where the creature's eyes, and presumably its head, were located in the center of its body. The razor-edged leaves of its limbs were furled protectively around its gut face. While I got their measure, the rowdy spectators continued to throw things as much for sport now as to show their displeasure. The steady rain of fruit and empty wine bottles drove the pair of them into the open and closer to me and Minnonuk who had followed my lead.

We stood awhile, beyond the range of the barrage of improvised missiles; a quartet of fools, bound by Fate to dance this absurd, bloody jig. I had no idea what misfortunes had caused Big Feet, Mulchy, and my old mate Minnonuk to end up here. I hoped like me, they'd earned their place in hell. But given that they all looked scared, they might very well have been as innocent as the day they were born.

"Which would be a shame."

"Nie rozumiem," said Big Feet.

"Quite." I began to laugh. It felt good so I continued. "As one who knows first-hand, I must warn you," I said between giggles, "dying is shit. The idea of dying *here* for the amusement of these, minge-faced cum-jugglers I find particularly irksome, so I'm going to try and avoid that, sorry." Laughter being contagious, it wasn't long before the three of them were also chuckling. At least, Big Feet was laughing, the other two trembled and bobbed about, but I took their spasms to be the equivalent of a good, old belly laugh.

For the most part the half-drunk audience looked bemused, clearly unused to the entertainment being entertained. I glanced at Darzka and savored the expression of discomfort on her face. After what she'd done to Ennis I knew I shouldn't provoke her ire, but fuck it, I was probably going to die soon, no matter what I did, so I might as well have a bit of fun.

It was Mulchy who broke up the party when it spread its spidery limbs and leaped at me. The fine, saw-toothed edges of its 'leaves' flashed in the torchlight as the creature caught the breeze and floated through the air. If this cull had ever killed, it must have done so by stealth, using its natural camouflage to close on its prey. I had almost too much time to decide what to do as it kited across the space between us. Its face nestled in the middle of the slender stem of its body was the only part of it not covered in razor-sharp thorns. Big Feet stumbled back to give his partner room to maneuver.

I legged it. The crowd erupted in laughter and gave those with a mind to throw bottles a new target. Mulch was light enough to ride the air, but it wasn't flying, and I quickly outdistanced it as it lost the wind and drifted to the ground. With a reasonable space between us, I stopped running and feigned confusion. Sensing victory, the leaf creature drew its limbs close to its body and leaped again. I yelped theatrically and pegged it. With laughter ringing in my ears I got within four feet of the arena wall and jumped. I wasn't trying to clear it, just gain purchase about six feet off the ground with my feet, which I did. My claws bit into the mortar and I pushed off and back. I could do this.

As I flipped over the leaf creature, some of my hair spines drifted too close to its uppermost limbs and were trimmed like silk. Ignoring the pain, I landed directly behind the prickly cove. Because its leafy limbs were for the most part forward facing, it would have to turn to attack me. Before it had a chance to do anything, I smashed my fist through its back and out through its face. I felt some resistance that I hoped were its vitals. It convulsed, its tiny teeth bit down and broke against the scales on the back of my hand before the thing folded on itself like a dead flower.

I pulled my hand free. The crowd cheered wildly. My fist burned, my bleeding hair spines dripped down my back. Before I had chance to catch my breath, the ground began to shake. Big Feet roared and charged Minnonuk, who set himself, tentacles flat against his elongated skull, eyes peeping from behind his back. Lacking much of a repertoire, Big Feet launched a two-footed kick. Minnonuk's lamprey mouth grew wider than I had hitherto thought possible. He sidestepped the kick and latched onto his attacker's shoulder, almost engulfing the poor cull's entire torso. Minnonuk's teeth began to tear into him. Blood flowed. Big Feet kicked Minnonuk. Bone snapped. My comrade buckled on his left side but kept biting. I should have jumped Minnonuk while he was locked onto the other fellow, but I didn't. Not because I was feeling particularly loyal, but because I'd noticed a commotion in the pens under Darzka's throne. I backed away just before the cage door burst open and a two-headed, trollish cove strode purposefully into the arena, brandishing a spiked club as thick as my leg. Dozens of spectators jumped to their feet and cheered enthusiastically. He accepted their praise with a raised fist salute.

"Fucking cliché," I said as I circled around to put Minnonuk and Big Feet between me and the newcomer. My heart was pounding, the wound on my leg where Torsten stabbed me was bleeding again, but damn it, I was alive. *I can do this.*

Another cage door opened behind me. I dived aside, landed, and rolled into a crouch. A fellow with the head of a bull set atop a mountainous body burst onto the sand near where I'd been standing. He was wielding a double-headed ax and spinning the blade in a looping arc which was all very showy. "You've outstayed your welcome, maggot," he bellowed and charged.

I'm not sure I can do this. The crowd gave a collective groan as though in sympathy, but more likely due to some horror happening behind me. I didn't dare turn around to see what it was. I kept my eyes on the bull as he swung the ax in a disemboweling sideways sweep. I hollowed around the blade, grabbed his flaring horns and pulled. I had no chance at overpowering him, he was far stronger than me, but that wasn't my intent. I was trying to provoke a reflex. I might not have been fast or strong, but my experience told me he'd do one of two things. He'd either charge forward, crush me and then hack the rest of me into dog food or do what I wanted. Happily for me it was the latter. With an angry bellow, he threw his head back. I went with him. I tucked, flipped, extended, landed, and dropped flat.

Something twinged in my back as I rolled over, scissored my feet, and hooked his ankle. Balance is a wonderful thing but not particularly faithful. Sometimes you have it, sometimes you don't. Certainly, this fine fellow was used to compensating for his massive noggin, but the blade he was swinging was also moving as he turned, whereas I was stable, laid flat and gripping the ground. I braced and forced one foot against the inside of his calf and the other against the outside. My thighs screamed. The ligaments holding my knees in alignment creaked like old rope. I yelled unashamedly as muscles tore, but I took the bastard down. Driven by adrenaline and an overriding desire not to die this day, I threw myself on top of the winded bull, drew my legs beneath me and anchored my clawed toes in the one part of him that, as with many coves, wasn't protected by thick hide or muscle. And then I kicked back.

Even I winced as I turned the bull into a steer. Deafened by his screams, I rolled off the stricken beast. In the center of the arena, the two-headed cull stood triumphantly over Minnonuk and the remains of Big Feet. The Lamprey's back was broken. His eye tentacles gazed weakly at the blood-flecked face of his killer. With a roar, the troll brought the gore-streaked club down on my cellmate's head. Teeth, blood, and flesh splattered across the arena and clotted the sand. The hot iron scent of death chummed the air and drove the crowd into a lustful frenzy. I was faced with a choice; I could either go for the ax or finish Bull Head. I went for the ax.

Being a consummate performer, and not in the least concerned about the puny, half-human half-warspawn ephemeral limping across the arena, the troll grabbed the bloody rag that had been Minnonuk by the tentacles and held him aloft for the crowd to admire. I glanced at Darzka. She was smiling with her mouth while giving me a dagger stare. Ominous rumblings echoed from the cells beneath her throne.

I grabbed the ax. Unsurprisingly it was bloody heavy, too heavy for me to wield with any proficiency. *What I'd give for a nice pair of sharps.* Making it look heavier than it was, I picked it up and held it at waist height in a wide two-handed grip. The crowd were most entertained by my pathetic effort and cheered. I roared a battle cry and charged the troll. Frontal attacks weren't my style; I preferred to stab people up all nice and quiet preferably from a distance, and if possible from behind, but this was a show after all. The troll threw Minnonuk's skin bag aside, raised his brain-greased weapon above his head and unleashed an ear-splitting battle cry as he came on.

"Time to take your final bow," he said as he swung the club.

"After you, bumfiddle." I threw the ax between his legs and let his own momentum do the rest. Confusion spread across his ugly mug as his legs knotted beneath him. I took a sideways step, and, as he sailed past, clawed his face with a vicious swipe. I lost a claw as he tore past me, but the gout of blood and fluids told me that I'd destroyed his peepers.

The troll cried out and rolled in the viscera of his fallen comrade, clutching his ruined face. The arena was by now a bloody mess. I knew it would be, because Nettie had told me that Darzka didn't allow for clean-up teams to come in and 'spoil the flow'. I was relying on the bodies being left where they fell, while hoping that mine wasn't one of them, and yes, I know what Mother said about hope, but she didn't know everything.

"Get up!" Doc bellowed from behind Darzka. I followed the track of his blind stare to the bull man. He was rolling around, clutching his nether region and bleeding profusely. If he heard the Black Penny, he ignored him and got on with the important business of dying while being pelted with bread rolls.

"Cunts," I said under my breath, but the bread rolls bouncing off his horns gave me an idea. "A knife, kind gentles, I pray you." Nothing. "A knife and I will carve my benefactor's initials in the bull's worthless hide." Solid silver eating irons peppered the sand around me. A smile spread across Darzka's ice-cast face. I hoped it was because she thought I was playing the game, and not because she was about to force me to cut my own throat for spoiling her games.

I picked up a couple of knives. They smelled of butter and liver pate. I ran at the troll who was blindly stumbling around and took him to the ground. Before his muscle-bound arms could enfold me, I stabbed him in the neck. I wasn't familiar with any of these spawn, but I'd performed enough exsanguinations to know that some serious pipework was required to keep even a tiny brain working. Tendons squeaked as I drove the knives in. Muscles contracted around the blades like lips on a love pole and a gush of hot blood washed over my hands. I withdrew the cutlery. The poor fucker didn't know whether to grab his bleeding face or his neck and clutched ineffectively at both. I climbed off, flicked the blood from the blades and went over to the bull. As I walked away, I heard the gates beneath Darzka open again and smelled a familiar scent. *Finally.*

The bull lifted his head as I approached. His great, dark eyes were mad with pain, his snorting breaths labored. The crowd bayed like the blood-hungry shitmongers that they were. I raised my arms, spun the silverware between my fingers, teased out the moment as I paced towards the bull.

"Clean or dirty, your choice," I said to him.

He held out his hand and gestured for me to give him a blade. Standing would have been an uncommon form of self-torture given that I'd ripped his fruits to ribbons, so I guessed that his intention wasn't to fight me. I handed him one of the shivs, hilt first. Some of the more stupid spectators cheered, thinking perhaps that we were about to perform a blade dance for their delectation. I was pleased that he disappointed them and rammed it into his throat. Cheated, the crowd booed.

"What?" I shouted. The word graveled the air, heavy with an anger I hadn't realized I felt. "Did you really think I'd carve him up to entertain you cake-faced poxmongers?" I turned slowly as I spoke so that they could all see what contempt looked like.

The whole parcel of them drew an indignant breath. I watched Nuanu's shadow lengthen as he came up behind me. Not that any of this had been what you'd call 'fun,' but turning around so that he could gore me in the stomach was the least amusing part of my plan. I turned, and he gored me and my word, did it hurt.

As we'd planned, I gripped the offending tine he'd skewered me with and supported my weight on my hands as he lifted me off the ground. The crowd I'd just insulted favored my attacker with their cheers. I gasped as the antler point fish-hooked me in the gut. He dug his forefeet into the sand, lowered his head as though he was trying to drive his antlers deeper. He actually went in and out at an angle which caused a lot of pain, but little damage. The stamping and snorting gave me the chance to adjust my grip before he raised his head and charged across the arena wearing me like a headdress. I clung on, while making it look like I wasn't supporting my weight on my hands. Blood ran down his antlers.

"Ready?" he said.

I braced.

"Now," he pulled up suddenly. My back tingled in anticipation of what was to come. I let go and flew backward, mindful to spread the impact across my back as I hit the wall. Nuanu made a show of mauling me when I hit the ground, while hiding me from view with his bulk. I screamed, yelled, and flailed as befitted someone being gored to death. Finally, after I'd begun to entertain the thought that he might actually be trying to kill me, he turned and reared to accept the adulation of the crowd. I slumped against the wall and feigned death, which wasn't difficult. After all this there was still one more move that had to be executed if my plan was to have any chance of success.

As though in answer to my anxious thoughts, the dragon's roar thundered from the bowels of the earth and shook the air.

"Behold." Darzka's voice rode the echo. "Ladies and Gentlemen, our champions will face the mighty dragon!"

With all the enthusiasm of youth, the 'mighty dragon' bounded into the arena with Sonam beside him, guiding him into the open. The crowd were naturally stunned to see the magnificent beast. Some cheered. Many screamed. I stole a sly peek and saw some run for the exit. *As well they might.*

Nuanu stamped and shook his bloody crown. In response, Druk crouched on his haunches and hissed a stream of steaming breath. Even on the other side of the arena I could feel the heat wash and hear the gurgling, flammable gut juice began to rise in the dragon's gorge. I was so jealous I could taste it. To my right, another cage door was thrown open. Nettie strode out, clad only in a sparkling, black cloak. She waved to the crowd, blew kisses to a favored few before standing beside Nuanu who acknowledged her with a nod. Another cage opened, and another spawn slithered into the hellish spotlight on her powerful tail. It was Padma the naga. Her hood was up; her scaled face and torso were dusted with turmeric powder and she wore a garland of roses and jasmine, so out of place in this slaughterhouse.

The three champions fanned out. The baby dragon swung his head from one to the other, unsure. Sonam stayed out of the way behind Druk's knee. I got a cramp in my arse because I was lying in an awkward position where I'd been 'killed'. *Hurry the fuck up.* Nettie threw off her cloak. The simpleminded whistled appreciatively, threw roses and jewels. She accepted their salacious adoration with feigned modesty. After blowing a kiss to a cull who looked like an egg wearing a monocle, she dropped to all fours and her skin split in a dozen places. Blood flowed as bones broke. Muscles twisted and distended as she became something altogether more savage than that which she had been. This wasn't a sorcerous transformation, this was what she was. When it was complete, she stood on her hind legs. Her dark fur shone in the torchlight, her grin was made of knives and death.

The naga coiled her sinuous body beneath her, Nuanu snorted and lowered his head as though about to charge. This was the fight the wealthy patrons had paid through the nose to see. Once again, it was not a pity then that they were to be disappointed. *Oh, please, let them be disappointed.*

I couldn't see who tipped the wink to whom from where I was lying; all I knew was that the heat from Druk's breath almost baked me into the sand. I closed my eyes against the brightness, smelled the metal of his shackle burn and heard Darzka's panicked shout rise above the confused tumult as the spectators realized something unexpected was happening. I looked up and saw Druk tear the cuff from Nuanu's foreleg with a swipe. He spun gracefully to face Padma, who bowed and extended her arm. The dragon bobbed his shaggy, purple head and snipped the band from her wrist like it was made of soap. Glittering beads of gold dripped from his lips and turned the sand to glass.

I stood up. The world was slightly off-kilter but not enough to stop me running to Druk, scooping Sonam up, and climbing on the dragon's back. I made sure the lad was safely sat between his massive shoulders before heeling the beast in the flanks. By now, Nuanu and Padma were racing towards the tunnels beneath Darzka's box. Nettie was the last champion to be freed. When Druk shattered the band on her ankle, she threw back her shaggy head and howled before leaping the twenty feet up to the stands and sinking her teeth into her egg-faced admirer's neck.

"Welcome to the Wild, ladies and gentlemen." I could only imagine the damage the three of them would wreak, let alone what would happen when they freed more of their brethren. For my part, I was trying to steer Druk towards the Goblin Queen's cage. It was a frustrating task. Being a child, Druk wasn't receptive to the crude commands relayed by heel, voice, and seat. Sonam was no help as he was understandably scared witless. Somehow, I managed to turn the dragon and make a grab for Edie's cage. Doc saw what I was trying to do and kicked the cage out of reach. Meanwhile Darzka was weaving wards about herself. I knew that as soon as she was done protecting herself, she would turn her power on us.

I tried one more time to guide Druk towards the cage, and once again, Doc leaped to intercept. I didn't plan it, but when I was close, I jumped from Druk's back and grappled the bastard. While Druk set fire to the seats, me and the Penny tumbled into the arena, wrapped in each other's bruising embrace. Doc's fist grazed my cheek. I ignored the lights dancing before my eyes, grabbed his wrist, and squeezed. Even though he was dead, tendons still controlled his movement and his hand sprang open. I saw the golden shank of Malin's ring and bit his fingers.

I have a big mouth in every sense of the word and encompassed three digits. Now, I'm not fond of sinking my fangs into undead flesh, but in Doc's case I was happy to make an exception. I bit down and severed the thieving bastard's digits and then I punched him. He reeled back, and I spat his fingers into my hand. Druk wheeled above the arena, pulled a sharp bank, and dropped down behind me. I dived aside as he opened his mouth and breathed at Doc. The Black Penny saw the attack coming and threw himself into the dark maw of the tunnel and vanished behind a wall of fire.

"Breed, quickly— we must go," Sonam shouted. I didn't like leaving unfinished business, but the boy was right. We were out of time.

Bone weary, I climbed up behind Sonam, and he urged the excited dragon into a vertical climb. The wind stole my breath, threatened to tear me from the Druk's muscular, if still downy, back. I held onto the boy with one hand. My other hand was wrapped around the severed fingers, one of which still wore Malin's ring. The fucking things were still twitching, tickling my palm like fat maggots.

Wards blazed around the arena as the freed warriors began to liberate their fellow prisoners. I hoped they caught Madame, but I doubted it. She was a Mage Lord and would make sure she was safe before addressing the revolt. As we soared into the nightling sky, none of my many aches could compare to the despair I felt when I recalled the look on Edie's face as the cage rolled out of my reach.

"Hang on, Edie, I'm coming." I made my promise to the wind in the hope that it would carry it to the Goblin Queen.

Chapter Nine

To ensure the direction of our escape remained unknown, we flew high enough for frost to crisp the edge of Druk's silken wings before heading for the rendezvous. When the youngster began to labor, I urged him to level out and head for a particular corner of the silvered mosaic of fields, villages, and woodland. If I'd read the map Nuanu had scratched into the floor of the crypt correctly, this inconspicuous parcel of land folded in a glacial crease was in the heart of the Wild. Apparently, we would be safe here, hidden from Darzka and her accursed Black Pennies by old magic. Apparently.

The Mage Lord proof sanctuary did not inspire faith. We landed beside a copse of strangle-branched trees in a small meadow. A Rubbled cottage stared dead-eyed and impassive as we came to land between the wood and a river. It was…unremarkable, but it would have to do. I slid off Druk's back and fell gratefully into the long grass.

The dragon's massive head blotted out the sky above me. Sonam peered over his shoulder. "Are you hurt?" the boy asked.

"Aye, and his breath isn't helping."

Sonam urged Druk to lower his shoulder, and the boy clambered down his foreleg. "Where are you hurt? Is it your stomach?"

"Ish. Mostly it's the full weight of sixty that's done the damage."

"I don't understand."

"Sixty years of age just fell on me, and it hurts boy, it really fucking hurts."

Druk made a throaty, snorting noise. Laughter. It was the first such sound I'd heard him make, I liked it. The sound reminded me of happier times. Sonam, being a sober cove and more serious than his age should have permitted, planted his hands on his hips and gave me a reprimanding look.

"In truth, my gut is wicked painful where that great, horned fool gored me." Sonam didn't look convinced. "It's true, but aside of that, everything hurts, everything aches, and to use the common argot, I'm knackered, also, my mouth tastes like dead man's fingers—which is as nasty as you would imagine."

A river burbled below the meadow in which my misery and I currently resided. I couldn't be bothered to move, but Druk, who must have had a raging thirst after all that fire-breathing, prowled cautiously towards it. This dragon was nothing like my dragon. He was a real dragon for a start, but his body was sinuous, and he moved with an undulant grace that belied his power and strength. When, *if,* he grew to maturity, he would be a magnificent cove and no mistake. I sat up.

"Sweet salvation." I lay back down and tried not to cry. "I felt less dreadful when I was dead."

Sonam regarded me with a familiar, calmly judgmental stare, which reminded me of my other priestly friend. "You complain a lot."

"It helps with the pain."

"You should get up and have a drink. It will make you feel better."

"I doubt it very much. How's your back?"

He shrugged.

"Ah, well, never mind."

"You should try to move."

"Fuck's sake. If it will stop you pestering me." I got up. Halfway down the slope I regretted the decision. Druk was crouched at the water's edge, biting at his reflection like a giant, toothsome puppy.

"You did good, Druk," I said as I eased myself down beside him and peeled off my shirt, an act as necessary as it was unpleasant.

Druk made a noise somewhere between a yowl and a purr and rubbed himself against me, almost knocking me off my feet. I changed my mind about bathing in the river just in case I didn't have the strength to get out and drowned, which would have been embarrassing. I settled for rinsing my shirt in the water.

"I suppose you boys will be off home now, eh?"

The dragon turned his head to the sky and yowled.

"Don't take on, you're free now. Safe… ish." We had flown northeast about twenty miles, which didn't seem far enough given that we'd just pissed off a Mage Lord. But I had to take the local expert at his word because it wasn't my world, let alone my manor. Sonam lay his head against his dragon's cheek and gently rubbed the soft skin beneath his eye. Malin's daughter Althea used to do the same to me. *When she was sad, when the hurts of the world could only be soothed by the strength and the love of a dragon.*

"The what now?" The voice in my head, if indeed it was in my head, didn't sound like mine. Startled by the intrusion, I jumped up and stumbled into the water. I gasped as I scrambled out, all maudlin thoughts murdered by the shock of ice cold water.

"Anyway—fly by night, lay low during the day, and don't trust anyone. If you can make it back to your home in one run, so much the better; these are dangerous lands. Druk, stop biting your tail and listen." The dragon stopped chewing his tail and cocked his head. "Fly low or fly high, above the clouds." I put on my wet shirt, which was bracing to say the least.

Sonam nodded. "What will you do?"

I gave him my best heroic, devil-may-care grin. "I'm going to save…What's-Her-Face-"

"— Edie?" Sonam reminded.

"Yes, her. I'm going to save the Goblin Queen and keep the gates between worlds open."

"Why?"

That stumped me. "Because… Well, I'd like to leave this world, and Edie seems a nice enough kid. I also owe Darzka a basting." He didn't look like he believed me. "It's what I do, all right? I get in amongst things. If I try to avoid trouble, live a quiet life, trouble finds me. Or…" *Senescence, death, loss.* "It gives me purpose. I'm warspawn, it's what I was born to do."

"You must learn to accept life as it is or else you will never grow."

"Did you read that in a book?"

He blushed. "In a book and at the knee of my master."

I leaned in. "Don't believe everything you read, son, or everything you're told. If you must abide by something, my advice is, go with your gut."

"You are alone; you are old and weak. You cannot win against Darzka and her minions."

"No don't couch, Sonam, say what you mean."

The boy canted his head. "We will stay and help you."

"It's tempting." It really wouldn't hurt to have a dragon on my side, and I was about to say yes when Druk must have caught sight of his tail out of the corner of his eye and pounced upon the offending appendage, tumbling himself onto his back. Sonam giggled. *Kids. They're just kids.* "But no. You must go home to your kin."

"But—"

"No. Now go on, shove off."

The wind shifted, and I smelled Nuanu before his shadow detached itself from the darkness and the emissary limped into the timid moonlight. "Harken to Breed, child. Take your charge and leave this land."

"Ah. You made it," I said, noting the many wounds on the stag's flanks and the broken points of his antlers.

"Aye."

"You almost gutted me by the way."

Nuanu snorted. "You said, 'make it look good'."

"I don't recall saying 'make it hurt' though, which it does, a lot, thanks for asking. Did Nettie get out? Any of the others? What's her name, Padma?"

"Nettie cut a bloody swathe through the ranks of Black Pennies and escaped. Padma fell, but it was a good death; the naga sacrificed herself for others."

I didn't care overmuch about the others, and neither did he by the sounds of it. The difference between us was that if I'd been the emissary of the local nib, I would have at least feigned concern.

Sonam bowed. "Thank you, Breed. I did not think to tell Druk to burn his shackles when we were taken to the arena." Druk growled his agreement. "I should have known that he was capable of destroying the magical bindings."

"No, you shouldn't. I only knew because I've been a dragon; not much made by mortal or god can withstand elemental fire. Now get going, while you still have the night on your side."

Druk extended his leg to Sonam, who climbed up and nestled between his shoulders. "We will not forget you." The boy waved.

I barely noticed. I was lost in a distant, painful memory of a life that had ended the day Malin died. The dragon unfurled his wings. The wind filled them, and they billowed like rippling, violet silk. Druk coiled his tail beneath him and whipped into the air like an arrow trailing a ribbon. The backdraft of his ascent caused waves to skip on the river and spun the long-necked grasses into rustling whorls. Yearning to fly with him, I watched until he vanished amongst the clouds.

"Did I hear you say that you were going to save the Goblin Queen?" Though he looked like he'd had seven bags of shit beaten out of him, Nuanu still had the strength to mock.

"No, please don't mention that I planned our escape, you're entirely welcome, and yes, you did hear me say that."

The Emissary of the Wild pawed the ground. A wolf howled in the distance. "As the boy said, you are old, and—"

"— not deaf. I heard him, and as far as advice from children goes, his was excellent, thank you for the reminder." I wrung the water from the hem of my shirt.

"I will indulge you, Breed. As you say, you provided the catalyst for our escape. You *were* the catalyst; the rogue element."

"I've been called worse."

"But the Wild takes care of its own. My lord Volund will free the Queen."

"That's great. But I want in. I've got scores to settle, debts to pay."

He nodded. The smile faded. "As do we all. I shall take you to see my master."

I clapped him on the withers. "Wonderful. There's a couple of things I need. Maybe your nib can fix me up."

"What do you need?"

"A sword...preferably two."

***

"That is not a horse," I said as we looked down upon the massive thing that had been inexpertly carved on a hillside at the head of the valley we were crossing.

"It is the sacred totem of Epona," Nuanu huffed as he led us down the hillside, across the skinny rib of the thing he called a horse, and into a wooded valley.

"It's got a beak. Where I come from horses don't have beaks."

Nuanu tossed his mane evidently irritated by my disparagement of local folk art. "It's... stylized."

"It's shit."

The stag gave me his profile. "Have a care, outlander."

I left the 'or what?' go unsaid. We'd both fought enough for one night. Despite his haughty, nib-of-the-manor demeanor, the poor cull looked like he'd had a shit in an outhouse made of knives. He was limping, his rear right leg was open to the bone, and his tail flicked constantly to keep away the plague of flies that were trying to feast on his raw behind.

We plodded on for another half mile or so, to where the trees thinned, and a track shone like a dull, steel knife as it cut through a wheat field. The tall stems sang like the sea, and the wind rolled the feather-tipped sheaves into waves. Nuanu paused, tilted his head to catch a taste of the wind before venturing into the open.

That he'd shown caution made me wonder how safe the 'heart of the Wild' really was. Some two-hundred yards away, on the far side of the grassy surge, was an ancient woodland. The smell of wood smoke and star steel caught in my nostrils. I quickened my pace. The track through the wood was flanked by trees bearing an abundance of white flowers, quickened to shimmering silver in the moonlight. As we made our way towards the hold of Nuanu's master, creatures gathered and stalked us from the shadows. They didn't speak or growl but hung their feral scent in bower and reed, knotting the heavy air with the smell of soil, blood, worms, and bones.

"Are they on our side?" I side-mouthed to Nuanu.

"What?"

"Those things that are dogging our steps; those who dwell in the shadows."

"The Wildkin? They are not our enemies."

"Oh."

The trees opened onto a clearing. The sound of metal hammering on metal, and the hot dull thump of lump iron smashing hot steel patterned the air. Sparks flew, light blazed, died back, and blazed again. The sound of roaring bellows lent a semblance of breathing life to the woods and sounded so much like a dragon that I was disappointed to see a humble, turf-roofed forge hemmed by giant stones.

"Hail, Volund." Nuanu called. The scalding quench of metal, and the sound of tools being racked followed the greeting. Nuanu folded his forelimbs and sank onto his haunches, exhausted. The shadows lengthened, the fiery blaze diminished to a roseate glow, and Volund, Lord of the Wild, emerged from his smithy. He wasn't what I expected. He was a few fingers short of six feet, soft in the middle and broad in the back. He was bald, had pig-pale eyes, and a small mouth that was comfortably set in a sly smile.

"Well met, my son," he said to Nuanu. He wiped his hands on his leather apron and turned his scrutinizing gaze to me. "Bene darkmans, Breed."

"That's as maybe."

He laughed, and his breath fogged the air with blood and smoke. His hands were big, his knuckles stood out like rivets on a ship's hull. He wore his shirt sleeves rolled up, revealing spirals turning beneath his skin in a dance woven of blood and woad.

"Care for a drop?" He gestured to a stone jar set beside one of the stones which flanked the entrance to his forge. "I've a raging thirst upon me."

I might have said yes but for the sudden tension that creased Nuanu's brow. I recalled some scrap of lore cautioning against accepting food and drink from fey creatures.

"Thank you kindly for the offer, but I'm well enough. I could do with a blade though, if you've got one lying around."

He laughed again. Beneath the jovial rumble I could hear the rattle of bones. "Here's a bold one. You will not sup with old Volund, but you'll take my steel?"

"Aye, if it pleases you."

"And what if it doesn't?"

"Then I shall bid *thee* a bene darkmans and be on my way, the good service I've done you and your kin left unpaid." The words fell out of my mouth before my brain had time to counsel my tongue. Nuanu groaned, but his misgivings were unfounded. Volund rasped the iron grey stubble on his chin with thumb and forefinger. Humor lit in his eyes. He stepped from his forge, his shadow with him. As you would expect, it matched his human bone bag in every detail, save that in place of his human noggin, a stag's hollow-eyed skull crowned his corpse, betraying his more than mortal lineage.

"If I sell you a sword, what will you do with it, stranger?"

Scratch my behind, what do you think?

"Go over some of the finer points of a disagreement I'm having with a cove of my acquaintance."

"Come again?"

"Stab Madame Darzka, repeatedly."

"Is that all?" He smiled paternally at Nuanu and brushed a blood-matted lock of hair from the injured stagkin's face.

"Isn't that enough?"

The Lord of the Wild shrugged.

"I also intend to stop her sacrificing the Goblin Queen."

"You say 'sacrifice' like it's a bad thing. It used to be currency around here."

"How lovely for you, but if she dies in the right place at the right time, the portals to this world will close and, I'm informed that, aside of a child being slotted, that will be a bad thing for you lot."

"Hmm. Good point." He rubbed his chin again. "Let me see what I've got lying around." He headed back to the forge, muttering and trailing his uncanny shadow behind him like a pet. "I usually work on commission you know, the price of steel being what it is. And don't get me started about unicorn horn…"

The hobkin lurking in the trees crept a little closer and gathered on the ragged, blossom fringe like bad dreams. Here and there I saw a flash of claw, a gleaming fang, the luminous yellow blink of a hunter's eye. In the distance, hidden behind the hills, I could hear the thunder of a train tearing through the night on its steel tracks. This might be the heart of the Wild, but only for as long as the land was of no use to the ever-rapacious humans.

"Here we are." Volund emerged carrying a sword. He held it up, turned it to catch the light, all the better to admire the blemishless steel. It was a heavy looking thing with a straight blade and two, deep fullers. The stubby hilt terminated in a hawk's head pommel. Decoration aside, what caught my eye was that it was laced with star steel.

"Why is it wet?"

He wiped the blade on his sleeve. "It, er, got dropped in a lake." He flicked the blade with his calloused thumb. The steel sang. "Hear that? I made it for a sorcerer who gave it to a mortal, which was a bit of a waste as it turns out. Anyway, it's all I've got in stock."

"May I?"

Volund plucked a strand of pond weed from the hilt. "There is the small matter of payment."

I looked at Nuanu, he shrugged.

"I just rescued your emissary."

Volund sighed much like any salesman about to sell you his patter. "If it were up to me, I'd give it to you, but there are rules."

I folded my arms. "Do the rules involve coin?"

"Do you have coin?"

"No."

"Hmm. I suppose we could bargain for services…"

"Oh, no. I've played that game before."

"Then I can't give you the blade, which is a pity, for it was made to be used."

"Fuck's sake, I don't have anything." I thrust my hands into my pockets and was about to pull them inside out to illustrate the truth of my words when I felt the coins I'd taken from Torsten and Malin's ring. I handed him the coins.

"Are these worth anything?"

A sly smile crept across his face. "Raven pennies? It's been a while since I've seen any of these." He bit the corner of one of the bloody relics I'd torn from Torsten's eyeholes. "They'll go some way to paying the price the Wild demands, but they have no value to *you*, do they? What else do you have in your pockets?"

He knows. The cunning shaver knew what I had in my pocket and the value I placed on it. *Value to another 'you', fool, to the dragon sorcerer who, like the owner of the ring, no longer exists. The you who has to save Edie needs that fucking blade*. I was torn. Volund began to whistle tunelessly. I gave him the ring.

His smile broadened. "How does the saying go? 'He fishes well who uses a golden hook.' Nice fire stone too." His meaty dabble closed around the ring, hiding its fire. So much for my old life. Volund flipped the sword and offered me the hilt. I took it and turned it in the light to admire the star steel glittering in the blade. Now that I got a better look at it, I noticed that it was longer and more slender than I'd first thought, and the pommel wasn't the head of an eagle but that of a dragon. It was perfectly balanced. "This is a nice blade."

"It's some of my best work. So how about we have a wee drink, to seal the deal?"

"Perhaps just a small one." Well, what could one drink hurt?

Chapter Ten

Ididn't recall falling asleep, so woke with a start having mislaid a sizeable fistful of time. I was lying on the grassy roof of Volund's forge. A goat was standing over me chewing a mouthful of grass loud enough to rouse the dead. I felt my noggin just to make sure no one had actually driven rusty nails into my brain, despite what it felt like.

"I've been poisoned." I told the goat. "Either that or I've got the worst hangover anyone has ever had. Sweet salvation, even thinking hurts." It bleated, breathed rancid grass and fart breath in my face, which didn't help my delicate condition. *Warspawn indeed.* I flailed at the goat, which fixed me with an insolent stare before wandering away.

It was evening. Wisps of cloud unspooled across a purple-tinted sky where faint stars were waking. To the west, the sun was slowly sinking through the trees, laying off shreds of gold that enlivened the murky, viridian undergrowth. I would have closed my eyes and sought sanctuary from the pain in sleep, but then a panicked recollection seized me. I flailed, groped through the grass as vague memories troubled the surface of my consciousness without having the decency to make themselves plain. The fear that I might have lost the weapon was quickly banished when I found the sword lying beside me, cold in the grass and pearled with evening dew.

I picked it up. The ball of lead in my skull rolled from one side to the other, but the substantial ache faded to a mere background irritant as it was supplanted by the realization that I was naked. I sat up. Nuanu's head poked above the curve of the roof. He smiled, a rare and somewhat suspect expression for him.

"Good eve, Breed. I shall not ask if you slept well for all who sup our mead and eat from the Lord of the Wild's table enjoy the sweetest of dreams."

"Shit."

"Not quite the response I expected."

"You don't know me, then." I jumped up, lithe and agile and lacking a great many of the cuts and bruises I'd carried the day before. "How long have I been out?" *You ask this question far too many times.* Vague memories of folk tales cautioning against accepting fey gifts bullied their way to the functioning portion of my mind.

"Twenty years," Nuanu intoned.

"Oh, shit. No. That can't be..." I'd failed the Goblin Queen and worse, I was eighty, which was beyond ancient.

Nuanu laughed and slapped the mound. "I jest. You've slept for twelve... fifteen hours at most."

"Bastard."

The emissary continued to laugh. A chittering, nut-brown impling clambered onto the mound, followed by a sprite with straw slender limbs and long, gossamer wings. A pair of ravens flapped like wet linen onto the two great entrance stones to what I saw now, in the waning light of day, wasn't a forge at all but a tomb. "I'm really confused now. What the fuck happened? Why does it feel like someone's filled my braincase with rocks and then shit in my mouth? No one has...?"

"No, of course not." He gave a sly grin. "You struck a bargain with the Lord of the Wild for a sword, and then we celebrated our freedom. You were a most enthusiastic participant in our hunt." Unlike the previous day, Nuanu appeared to be in rude health, the scars across his flanks miraculously healed where they had been open wounds the day before. My own hurts looked months rather than days old.

"I hunted...?"

"You hunted, caroused, and wassailed."

I tried to squeeze a recollection from the shit-soup of my booze-battered brain. Again, vague, half-formed thoughts bubbled up; dancing fauns, giggling maidens, and the deep-throated fuck bellows of rutting cattle were swept together into a wild canter across moon-crested hills and shadowed vales. From menhir to dolmen, from ugly, duck-faced horses carved into hillsides to blackwater meres. "Did I…did I dance?"

"Let's say you moved vigorously and with enthusiasm."

"Sweet salvation." I brushed my hair spines from my face. They too had healed, although they were sticky and smelled of vomit— thankfully my own. It was interesting how much like my old self I looked after Darzka had stolen my power.

I stood up and the world swayed. "I need a piss and a moment to think. By which I mean throw up." The implings giggled as I half jumped, half fell off the mound. Something stirred in the long grass just beyond the tree line. Without a moment's thought the blade quickened in my grasp, alive and eager to be used. A fellow with a goatish lower and a hairy, mannish upper staggered into view.

In a blink he went from sleepy to startled when he saw the bright end of my blade.

"Good evening, friend Breed. If it's about the breeches…"

"Breeches?" I looked to Nuanu.

"It's a long story. This is Theil, you're firm friends."

"I knew that," I lied.

Theil trotted forward, his beard was plaited with flowers, and his red eyes were bright with merriment. "I'm truly sorry about thine breeks, the fire had a mind of its own, eh?"

"Aye, it did." I laughed, although I had no idea what the fuck he was on about.

Theil offered Nuanu a polite bow and winked at me before heading off along a woodland path as other sleepers began to stumble from the undergrowth. The more timid culls scarpered without so much as a word or a wave, some sought friends amongst the disheveled before staggering off into the gloaming. Most showed due deference to Nuanu before departing.

After I purged myself of whatever honey based skullfuckery the Wildlings had fed me my head felt clearer. I also felt stronger than I had since I'd arrived in this world. Whether brought on by my newly acquired clarity or just the natural tumble of thoughts that take their own sweet time to gain prominence, it suddenly occurred to me that I had a knack for finding renegade Mage Lords. I didn't know if I was being guided by the Eldest of the Annurashi or if Fate was steering my course. Whichever it was, it was passing strange that in all the worlds there must be in the star-scattered Void, I'd found another Mage up to no good. But first things first. "Does anyone know where my clothes are?"

"Hold a moment, if it please you," said a woman I couldn't see, her matronly lilt accompanied by the *clackety-clack* of cartwheels and the steady plod of horses hooves. "And cover thyself, hob. 'Tis the Lord's day and I've no wish to see thy bare behind *again*." I knew the voice but couldn't recall the owner until the cart trundled around the tomb. Seeing the ruddy-cheeked couple driving the manure-loaded wagon provoked a flash of memory. I remembered something about an orchard with small apples as tight as fists birthing on the bough, and a gaggle of humans singing, and sharing jugs of cider.

Nuanu must have seen my confusion and came over and whispered in my shell. "These are cunning folk, the keepers of lore. Their roots go deep in this land."

"That's lovely. Do they have my clothes?"

The emissary snorted before trotting over to the rickety break as the cunning man drew the cart to a halt beneath the black bead gaze of the ravens. "John, Gert, be welcome."

The woman tipped a courteous nod to Nuanu. The fellow tugged the brim of his hat, eyes deferentially lowered. The woman pulled a bundle of clothes from under her seat.

"Here, take 'em," she said to me. "The breeches are John's and should fit thee well enough, if a bit short in the leg. The shirt is thi'own and mended as best as I could. I would ask ye to kindly refrain from doffing off in the orchard next time. You gave old Tam a proper turn."

I took the clothing and dropped my most winning smile upon the wench. "Thank you kindly, ma'am. A cloak? How thoughtful. You have my word, I shall never doff off in thine orchard again as long as I live."

"A hollow offer. The Blood Moon rises tonight," said Nuanu quite souring the mood.

"I take it you know where she intends to perform the rite?"

"Aye. 'Tis commonly known as the Giant's Dance. The approach will be guarded by magic as well as mundie means, but the Hunt will ride the paths no mortal or witch-bound soul can fathom."

"You say 'no mortal'. How then am I to get there, being as how I am most certainly mortal?"

He looked at the cart. Steam rose from the dung and straw.

"Really?"

He nodded.

"Fuck's sake."

***

Full night came cold and brought with it a heavy fog. I
lay in the back of the cart, under a blanket, under the
steaming manure, which was apparently bound for a
local mundie nib's rose garden. As the cart trundled
along the rutted track, the couple discussed the
weather, and I wondered why I always ended up in, or
as in this case, under the shit. I suppose I was just
lucky.

Some few miles further, a coldly hollow voice
called out. "How do?"

The cart continued, although the horse danced in its
traces. Like me, the beast had caught the unmistakable
whiff of corpse emanating from the Black Penny
watching the road.

"Olright?" said Gert, her tone questioning and
cautious.

"Where are you good folks headed this eve?"

"What business is it of yours where we're headed?"
John jumped in.

I gripped the hilt of my new sword. The reassuring
tingle of star steel woke a hot itch in the sigils branded
in my palm.

"Now, John. That ain't no way to greet a Christian
soul." She lowered her voice theatrically. "An' look,
the poor fellow is wearing blind-folk spectacles. We're

bound for Amesbury, Mr. Our youngest has had a babber. Lil' boy, God love him. Here, buy yourself a mug of cider to wet the baby's head." Fingers dabbled in a coin purse.

"Steady on woman. I won't be able to buy my own bloody cider if you give every blind beggar we pass a penny," John huffed.

"Thank you kindly, missus." He played the part of a blind beggar as well as they were playing the parts of doting grandparents. "I'll raise a mug to yer babber."

"Bless you, dearie," Gert's voice dripped pity.

"Listen here, mother. You know I don't hold with telling the world my business. Blind or sighted, a stranger's a stranger."

"And I don't hold with bad manners…"

"I was just sayin'."

"Well don't."

The conversation bounced between the couple until the beggar cleared his throat, as bored as was intended by the exchange.

"I'd turn down the road near Hopgood Farm, go on past the Hog's Head," the Penny said. "The road by the Dance is flooded some."

"Is it, by God?"

"John, language."

"Aye, sir," said the Penny. "A cart got stuck there all day yesterday."

"We shall avoid it then," John declared. "Thank you, and good eve."

"Good eve, Mister. Missus." The reins cracked. We rolled a little quicker as we passed Darzka's checkpoint and until the odor of corpse was swallowed by the foggish mizzle. Pensive silence reigned for another half mile before the cart left the road and pulled over.

Someone slapped the side of the wagon. "We're 'ere," said John.

I extricated myself from the bedding, and while John unhitched the horse, I got my first look at the Giant's Dance. We'd pulled over behind a dense hedgerow which the track cut through before continuing across the gentle camber of sheep-sheared downs like a pale scar. Drifting in and out of the fog, the Giant's Dance stood aloof, some three hundred feet from the hedge. Silent as old bones, the dance looked like an angle gate, which didn't surprise me overmuch given Darzka's plans. However what did throw was that it looked deserted.

"I'd expected the place to be crawling with Darzka's crew by now," I said.

The couple exchanged a knowing look.

"This is the right place?" It wasn't that I didn't trust them; Nuanu had vouched for them, but this was passing strange.

Gert drew her chin into her neck and pursed her lips. "Now let me see; there are so many sacred temples to the old gods around here, I might have got it wrong…"

"Really?"

She laughed, slapped her thigh. "No. Of course not, you scaly dolt. I thought 'ee was supposed to be cunning?"

I was taken aback by her rudeness, (an irony that isn't lost on me). But before I could take the wench to task, John whipped a sickle from his overcoat. The crescent blade was cold grey. Clouds raced across the rind of the blade; a neat trick given the sky was lost in the fog. I backed up, suspecting betrayal, but he moved away from me and took a tight hold of the horse's bridle. The animal paid little heed, being as it was intent on eating the hedge. He whispered something in its ear, which had no discernible effect as the animal continued to chew.

John raised the blade and in a swift strike, slashed the chestnut mare's throat. Hot blood gushed, and showered the butcher who held fast to the bridle as the horse staggered against him.

"This is Epona's hold. No outsider magic can stand against the old ways." Gert's voice was thick with the blood and iron that suffused the air. The horse did not fight its death. Its legs folded beneath it as its lifeblood pumped onto the track and ran, counter to all logic and law, uphill. The ragged flow crawled along the track until it came to the ditch that ringed the giant angle gate. The unnatural flow split and followed the course of the circle, bloody fingers parting the grass where it passed.

Like a tatty-jacketed psychopomp, John guided the animal's head to the dirt as blood continued to pump. He knelt beside it. His dun-colored breeches dyed the color of sunset as the hot blood soaked into the fabric. "Go on, Willow, go to Epona, and reveal that which is hidden. Go on, old girl, hurry on home now." The old fellow clicked his tongue, his gaze tracked across the plains as though he was watching something run.

That was enough blood magic fuckery for me for one day. Gert dropped to her knees by the cart, raised her gaze to the blanketed sky, and began to mumble words that snaked through the air, sibilant and dangerous. My hackles raised, my palm itched fiercely, and the sword warmed in my grip as the unmistakable stink of sorcery filled my nostrils. It smelled like power, and I was immediately and intensely jealous.

"Come, Breed, be anointed with the blood of the goddess." John came towards me, bloody hand outstretched. I waited patiently, content that I could drop him if he tried to get slashy with me. He didn't; he just daubed my face with warm horse claret.

"Thank you that's very…" I was about to scarper when I happened to glance towards the stones and saw that the air around them had begun to shimmer. I peered into the gloom and saw a fractured lattice of blood crawling up and over an unseen barrier that surrounded the Giant's Dance. The bloody web pulsed and then vanished, taking with it the illusion.

"Well, I'll be." Light blazed from the ring, sending spindle shadows racing across the plain. "That's a fine glamour. I couldn't even smell anything was amiss."

"Aye, she's wicked talented…for an outsider. None but the Wild and you will see anything amiss even now," John admitted grudgingly.

"The stones. I've never seen anything like it, and I've seen a fair few gates."

"It was made by the goddess Epona from the bones of the first dragons."

I didn't have the heart to gainsay him, to explain that this 'Epona' cove was probably the Eldest of the Annurashi and that the stones were nothing like dragon bones.

The gate consisted of concentric rings of different heights. The outer ring of uprights was almost as grey as the fog and somewhere close to twenty feet tall.

They were locked together by equally massive lintels. Six feet within this outer ring was another circle, this time of waist-high, blue stone monoliths. Within this ring stood an imposing horseshoe arrangement of five grey triliths that were as tall as the outer stones. Dozens of severed heads sat atop these giants. Their dead eyes shone gold, reflecting torchlight as they gazed towards an inner semi-circle of more waist-high stones.

Darzka stood at the midpoint of this configuration, a bloody knife in her hand. Before her was a horizontal slab of stone about eight feet long and four feet thick. It gleamed dark and slick with the claret of those poor culls who she'd already sacrificed to empower the gruesome rite. A couple of Black Pennies were carrying a headless corpse from the inner circle to the ditch where they tossed it. The fellow's arms windmilled in grim farewell as his body flew through the air.

"Gerroff me, dungpuzzle," It was Edie. Doc had her by the arm and was dragging her to the inner ring where the cage awaited. She kicked and bit and scratched him to no avail. He thrust her inside and locked the door. I didn't have much time. On the eastern horizon, the world was lipped with the faint promise of red. My guess— *my hope,* was that Darzka would wait until the Blood Moon was overhead before she killed the Queen.

"Good girl." John's voice startled me. I turned to see him release the dying horse and ruffle its forelock. He wiped the crescent blade on his jacket and approached the kneeling woman. Her eyes rolled back in her head, her lips worked over the knots of a whispered prayer.

"Er...What are you doing, John?"

"I'm going to open the blood path for the Hunt."

"By slotting your missus?"

"A willing sacrifice so that they might cross over. The time is nigh."

"I'm no expert in the Wild but couldn't they just skip across the fields?"

He looked at me blankly. There was a time when I'd have let him get on with it, after all, I couldn't take on Darzka and her Pennies on my lonesome. John turned his gaze to the sky, began chanting. I didn't know these culls and as John pointed out, her sacrifice was willing.

And yet...

No matter which way I sliced it, it didn't sit right. I gave it a moment, tried to recapture the callous indifference of my youth. *Might as well try to weave the wind.* There was no going back to the good old days. Somewhere along the way I'd grown a conscience.

I crossed the space between us and caught his hand as he swung the blade. The fellow was shaking, and sweating, trapped as he was between priestly duty and simple affection. He turned his fear-riddled face towards me. "I can't open the way for the Wild Hunt if we don't give the gods their due."

"I hear your words, but they lack conviction. I used to be an advisor to a king, for more years than I care to or indeed, can even remember. I therefore pride myself on knowing when to step in. Now is one of those times, John."

"But the Hunt…?"

"They can fucking walk like us mere mortals. It'll do 'em good."

"You cannot beat Darzka alone."

"Perhaps not, but I can slow her down long enough for the Hunt to slot her sentries and get themselves here the old-fashioned way." I plucked the sickle from his clammy hand. Relieved of the onerous responsibility of murdering his mate, he sagged. I licked the blade. The mix of horse blood and silver tasted sweet, but as I'd suspected, it was the hot iron tang of star steel that lit a fire in my veins. "Would you mind if I borrowed this?"

Chapter Eleven

Gert and John, or Relieved and Sheepish as I liked to think of them, left without further argument now that the whole, sacrificing your wife issue had been dealt with. I watched them trot off down the muddy track until their huddled forms vanished in the drifting banks of fog. And then I put my back to the cart and breathed my anxiety into the night.

The enormity of the task I'd set myself wasn't lost on me, neither was the fact that I'd made it more difficult by stopping John slotting Gert. If I couldn't pull it off, if I couldn't stop Darzka, or at least slow her down long enough for the Hunt to ride to the rescue, that child's death, and the death of the Wild would be on my head.

"I just won't fail, then. It's that simple. I'll keep her busy until the Hunt arrives." On a distant hill, lightning flared, and the report of a dozen guns thundered. My resolve wavered. "I've fucked up. I should have let him kill her." I smashed the blade against the cart. It cut clean, bit deep, got stuck. "Oh, for fuck's sake." I took a two-handed grip on the blade and pulled it free. There wasn't a mark on the edge. "That's something at least. Now come on, you were a Guild Blade long before you were a sorcerer or a dragon." A little of my old confidence returned. I was a damn good thief, and an efficient killer, unburdened by a conscience. I was fast, I was strong, and I was good with the sharps.

Was.

Once again, my confidence vanished like smoke. I felt better than I had but I wasn't fast, I certainly wasn't strong, and I was also thirty years older than any thoasa who'd ever lived. A crow swooped from the fog and alighted on one of the blossom burdened trees, showering me in petal snow. It cawed as if to say, 'get on with it fool' and bestowed upon me a sharp-eyed stare.

"I don't want to 'get on with it'," I said, as though the conversation was anywhere other than in my head. "I want to sit down, drink a glass or three of good wine, and curl up beside a warm hearth." It cawed again, mocking this time. I turned my back on the harbinger and saw that the Blood Moon was rising through the haze. Gunfire boomed in the distance. If I was going to do something, it had to be now. I rotated my wrist, spun the blade and tried to work a few knots from my neck. For a professional, killing is an art and a skill. For some, it is also a pleasure. Although I have never particularly reveled in slaughter, when the need has arisen to inhume someone, I've given it my all. I could do this.

I smeared myself and my blades in dirt and plotted my route to the stones. I took note of the stationary sentries and timed the patrols as they passed the point where I'd decided to make my assault on the gate. My plan was to find Edie while avoiding Darzka; a trick worthy of any sorcerer—and if the Mage Lord or Doc, wherever he was lurking, were kind enough to present their backs, I wouldn't hesitate to slot them.

When I was sure of my route, I headed out, moving with the drifting fog while angling ever closer to the stones. Even from half a field away, I could feel the subtle vibrations of power emanating from the gate, although from this distance I couldn't tell which was the keystone. Given the size and complexity of the gate, there might have been more than one for all I knew. I'd worry about it later. Right now I had to focus on killing the sentry that was in my way.

After scouting the circle, I chose this particular cove because out of all the fearsome Black Pennies on guard, this one looked like the weak link. That the sentry happened to be Ennis was merely a happy coincidence. I stalked across the open ground, low and quiet—and downwind, just in case he still retained a sense of smell, magical or mundane. The newly minted Black Penny adjusted his grip on the rifle he was inexpertly wielding. His cough had improved, but it was still a poor deal in my opinion. He shifted his weight from foot to foot, which could only have been out of boredom rather than fatigue. I slipped behind him as he cast his desultory gaze across the plain.

I crept closer, the sword was hanging from my belt, and the sickle was tucked into my shirt, cold against my skin. Ennis cradled the rifle in the crook of his arm. This was a sickle job. I slipped the weapon from my shirt, crept the final couple of feet and had a quick check for any wanderers before clamping my hand against his mouth and pulling him close.

Ennis might have been undead, but he was still a barley backed coward.

"Hello Ennis," I whispered in his ear. "Did you miss me?"

He fumbled the rifle, which hit the ground with a soft thud as I opened his throat. A dribble of stale blood ran across my hand. Had I intended to bleed him, I would have been disappointed. But all I wanted to do was stop him yelling while I kicked him to the ground, put him in a headlock, and tore out his pennies. Wisps of oily shadow spirited from his still raw sockets and into the fog. I tucked the sickle into my shirt and retrieved his weapon. It looked much like a firelance, but there wasn't a zanth crystal or calthracite powder pan. There was instead a hammer mechanism and most importantly, a trigger. I was sure I'd work it out if the need to use it arose.

Thunder rumbled, and the clouds above the stones scudded away from the face of a gibbous, red moon. I rolled Ennis into a shallow scrape and kicked dirt over his pale mug. The grave wouldn't conceal him from anything but the most cursory glance, but it was the best I could do in the circumstances.

A child screamed from within the stones. I held my breath, prayed to no one in particular that I wasn't too late. She yelled again. Shadows danced through the paths of light cut between the stones. I crouched, waited for a patrol to pass, pocketed Ennis's eye coins and headed in.

This was going surprisingly well, I thought, until a claw of lightning split the sky above the altar stone. I hit the ground and crawled into the shadow of one of the triliths before making a run for the stones themselves. My hair spines tingled, the air tasted of ash and iron. I could feel power flowing through the stones. Another bolt of lightning arced into the sky. It was as though the weight of the universe was pressing down on the gate, trying to break through. It occurred to me then that Darzka might not have a fucking clue what she was doing.

"Let me go!" The Goblin Queen yelled gamely as the last grumble of thunder died upon a distant hill.

My palms were not only itching but sweating. That was a new one on me, I didn't even think they could sweat. Another bolt of sorcery-wrought lightning tore the night gloom asunder. The young queen yelped.

"The bowl, Doc," said Darzka. I inched around the stone. Doc headed out of the ring. I raised the gun. *Choices.* I could kill Doc and nick the bowl. Killing the prick would grant me a modicum of satisfaction but I doubted not having the right blood catcher would impede the Mage Lord overmuch. I could try to kill Darzka, which was highly bloody unlikely as she was a sorcerer and most likely warded to the hilt. There was one thing I could do that would at least stop her destroying the Wild. She would kill me, but for what I was contemplating, I'd deserve it. As she said herself, thousands of kids die every day.

I put my head against the stone and let bitter regrets run like rain. I shouldn't have told my ghosts to leave. I shouldn't have stopped old farmer scrote from killing his wife and bringing the Wild to this place. I banged my head against the stone. Perhaps if I hit it hard enough, I might shake loose a brilliant plan to save the kid and the world. *Nothing.* I moved around the stone until I could see the inner horseshoe.

Darzka was garbed in black robes, no doubt to hide the bloodstains. A silver crescent knife, the twin of the one in my possession, gleamed in her hand. Edie was bound to one of the stones behind the altar.

"Doc?" Darzka turned her back to me. "Doc!" I aimed at Edie. I was so close I couldn't miss. *Do it. Do it, now.*

I've always had a bit of a problem. Often when I've been faced with a choice between doing something I should do and something I've wanted to do, I've done the thing I wanted to do, no matter the consequences.

Today was...no exception.

I changed my aim to Darzka. The timing couldn't have been worse as right at that second, Doc returned, clutching a silver bowl. He saw me instantly and yelled a warning to his mistress. I pulled the trigger as she turned, dark hair veiling her face, but she saw me. The echo of the gunshot caromed around the stones. Light flared around the Mage Lord. A brief, blue flash lit inches from her face and told me I'd failed.

"Bollocks."

The next instant, the gun was wrenched from my hands and thrown against one of the outer uprights, but this was the least of my concerns.

Darzka's face twisted into a mask of rage. An invisible force gripped me and pinned my arms to my sides.

"I'll give you this—you're tenacious," she said, as she lifted me off the ground. I would have come back with something devastatingly witty if I'd been able to breathe but at that moment all I could do was gasp and listen to my ribs crack. It was agony but lucky me, it didn't last long. Pressed for time now that the Blood Moon was up, Darzka hurled me from the stones. Light exploded before my eyes as I hit the ground, skidded, rolled, bounced, and rolled some more, before finally coming to a halt. A few seconds passed in the blissful, numbness of shock before various pains woke.

I opened my eyes and saw Doc's long shadow stalking towards me, followed by the man himself. I tried to stand but the world moved, and I fell back. I tried again, but it was a trick that I couldn't quite master as one of my legs refused to do what I wanted. I wiped the blood from my eyes and saw that my kneecap wasn't where it should be, a situation easily, if painfully, remedied. I grabbed it with both hands, pulled and twisted. My whole leg tensed and spasmed as the knee popped back into the correct alignment. Doc started running. I stood up, drew the sword that by some miracle hadn't stabbed me when Darzka hurled me from her sacrificial circle.

"Kill it!" Darzka bellowed. Arcane fire lit the sky across the valley. Guns spoke.

Doc pulled a small handgun from his waistband. I tugged the sickle from my shirt. He shot and missed. I hurled the curved blade. Hit.

Doc looked down at the hilt of the blade sticking from his chest. He laughed and tugged it loose.

"Let me go!" Edie screamed.

Someone, Darzka perhaps, yelled in pain.

"You do know I'm dead, don't you?" Doc tossed the sickle into the grass.

"Yes. You do know that's a sacrificial blade?"

He looked down. His smile faded as his chest began to collapse as if made of paper. "What have you done?"

"Don't blame me, blame goddess er, what's her face." He staggered forward, reached for me with his mutilated hand and watched his remaining fingers flake to ash as his, suddenly brittle legs crumbled beneath him. "It begins with an 'E'." He gave a strangled cry as his throat began to crack and disintegrate. "No, don't tell me—Elona?" I looked to Doc, but he was busy watching himself fall apart. And then, it came to me. "*Epona*! That's the cove. She sends her love." Doc fell forward and exploded in a cloud of dust. I coughed, tasted blood.

"Breed!" It was Edie. The fierce kinchin cove had managed to get away from Darzka and was running towards me as fast as her twisted little pins would carry her. A handful of Black Pennies came running through the fog behind her.

"Run, Edie!" I shouted and began limping towards her.

"Oh, no you don't." Darzka's voice echoed across the plain. Shadowy tendrils snaked through the stones, bashing aside the Black Pennies that were chasing Edie as the Mage Lord took matters into her own hands. My knee screamed as I put on a turn of speed. The tendril coiled around Edie's leg and pulled her to the ground.

"Breed help me!"

"Fuck's sake. What do you think I'm trying to do? Just hold on." Edie took me literally and grabbed at the grass. I caught up and slashed at the darkness with Volund's sword. The tendril flew apart like raven feathers. I picked the girl up and set her on her feet. She looked no worse for wear. "Now run, Edie. Don't look back and don't stop." The child scrambled to her feet and legged it. By this time the five Black Pennies had also got to their feet.

"Five. Right." I gulped a lungful of sweet, sweet air and leaned on the sword. *I can do this*. A shot rang out, whipped past me. Muzzle flash lit the culprit. I charged her. It was my old mate, Kate. She raised the gun to protect her head. I brought the sword down, cut through the barrel and split her skull in twain. This was a damn good blade. The coins that were her eyes popped from their ruined sockets. I sidestepped as she stumbled forwards a couple of feet before crashing to the ground, trailing darkness in her wake.

That left four.

Two split right, one left, and the other held the center. The sky for miles around came alive with storms that raced across the heavens like giants running through the clouds, lighting the earth with every pounding step. Thunder and gunshots boomed. I had to get in amongst them or…

Another shot rang out. Despite the obfuscating fog and distraction of sheet lightning, this one didn't miss. It passed through my thigh, missed the bone, but tore a messy chunk from the muscle. The impact staggered me. I windmilled my arms. It wasn't graceful, but it kept me on my feet. A bank of fog drifted between me and the Pennies, I moved with it as best I could and circled around to the left.

My senses were nowhere near as good as they used to be, but they were still better than those of a human, particularly a dead human. I tasted the air, peered through the veiling fog, and put my shells to the task of listening for footsteps. I could hear water trickling through the grass. Sheep shit and chalk milled the air with a pastoral bloom and mingled with the sharp tang of lightning and of course, gallons of claret. I picked away at this crusted agglomeration of smells and sounds until I found the anomalous gems I sought. The Black Penny smelled of mold and dust, wet wool, leather, whale oil from the lamps, and cheap rosewater.

I closed in, mindful that his comrades were also skulking in the fog. I bit down on curses as every step made my growing collection of pains sing.

The Penny's tightly curled black hair sparkled with dew. I took a two-handed grip on my blade and removed his head from his shoulders. He gasped. His body trembled but remained standing. I chased the head down and dug the coins from his face. The body fell as the dark essence of Darzka's sorcery escaped. Three to go.

Click, click, click. I knew the sound of a gun being cocked, and this one was behind me. *Fuck.* I tried to spin and drop but was hampered by my injuries. The mouth of a gun barrel was ten feet away and leveled at my face. It seemed I wasn't the only cove good at sneaking although, in my defense they hadn't already been shot and hurled across a field. The Penny, a robust fellow with braided hair, stood a moment, obviously savoring the dead shot. And then he stood a moment longer, and then his coin eyes popped out of his face and a pair of fingers wiggled in the smoking black sockets.

This better not be a demon.

"Boo," said a most un-demonic voice. The cove standing behind the spent Penny withdrew their fist from the ruined skull and let the body fold like a linen sheet, revealing themselves to be someone with whom I was intimately familiar.

"Did you miss me?" She—or he, it was hard to tell which, stood about six feet tall, had bright yellow eyes, and an insolent grin. Long hair spines hung over their broad shoulders and down to their narrow waist. The back of their clawed hands were covered in scarlet scales. They were wearing a dark suit and white shirt. "It's me, Loftur."

"You've changed."

Loftur grinned. "Oh, this?" he giggled. "Do you like it?"

"I have a level of affection for that bone bag, eye."

Loftur chuckled. "You wouldn't believe what you've been up to in the last few days. Nothing terrible I hasten to add but best keep your head down, eh?"

"You got the feet wrong, chameleon. And my hair spines aren't that red anymore."

Loftur looked down. Instead of seven clawed toes, he had hooves. "Ah, silly me. What is it they say? The devil is in the detail?" He flicked his hair spines. "As for the color, consider it artistic license."

"Why are you helping me?"

"I'm not so much helping you as having a bit of fun; adding a little more chaos into the mix before she spoils things." He put his hands on his hips. "In truth, I was a bit bored just scaring drunks and servant girls in the city."

"While looking like me?"

He waved off my concern. "I told you, it was just a bit of fun. *You* are a lot of fun, Breed, you wonderful, chaotic sprite." He began to retreat into the gloom. "You remind me of me."

"Wait, don't go— there's plenty more mischief to be made."

"Never change, Breed."

Gone.

One more down, another two to go. I continued to circle to the left when I saw the remaining pair heading towards the angle gate, carrying a struggling Edie. While I'd been busy, they'd nabbed the girl. "Bollocks."

I was feeling a little lightheaded by this point, due in no small way to the amount of blood I'd lost and the inability to draw a good, deep lungful of air without scraping my bellows against the ragged edges of broken ribs. I plodded over to the stones. When I got there the two remaining Pennies had taken up position behind Darzka between the inner horseshoe of stones and the triliths. The Mage Lord stood at the head end of the altar on which Edie was bound. They'd thought on and gagged the young queen, but her eyes shone with rage and fear.

I'll give her this, Darzka didn't look like she was enjoying her role as a child killer. Her jaw was clamped tight, and her gore-slicked hands were shaking as she raised the knife above her head, ready to exsanguinate Edie. There might have even been a tear.

I stepped between the giant outer stones and into the light. The eyes of the dead gazed down from the lintel stones upon my folly. "Darzka! Don't." I could feel the vibrations from the stones. The buzzing, gnat wing whisper of power bored into me, made it hard to hear anything else. The air smelled of blood and incense.

She looked up. One of the Pennies, a fellow with a shock of grey hair, raised his gun. The other was Red, who drew two knives from her belt and ran towards me.

Darzka lowered the knife. "I don't fucking believe this. Siobhan, Niall. Wait."

The moon was at its zenith now, full, heavy, and as red as sin. "Darzka. Give it up." I used my best city watch voice. "Whatever you're trying to do it won't work. If you slay the child, the Wild will come after you."

She threw her head back and laughed. "Let them. I've slain demons made of eyeballs that spoke with my dead mother's voice and vomited poisonous spiders. Do you think I'm scared of a few fucking fairies?"

I sighed. "Very well, I concede, you're made of sterner stuff. But you can't fight the whole world."

"When this is done the Wild will come to terms or they will all perish." While she talked I saw Red out of the corner of my eye, edging around the stones. I kept track of her and the gun at Darzka's shoulder.

"It doesn't work like that, Darzka. They're not like the Annurashi. They won't make a deal whether it's expedient or not. They've got principles."

"Speaking of whom, the Annurashi would destroy a thousand worlds to have their way. All I want is to live freely. Is it so much to ask?"

"What about the kid?"

"I've told you; thousands die—"

"Every day. Every day. Yes, you said."

A look of anguish crossed Darzka's face. Tears fell as she looked down at Edie, who was begging with her eyes not to die.

"I'm sorry, child." Darzka raised the knife.

Time's a funny thing. An hour can feel like a day, and a minute like an hour. Like now.

In the briefest explosion of a second, I charged towards Darzka, and Niall shot me in the stomach. Red leapt onto one of the horseshoe stones and propelled herself towards me, knives flashing. Edie squirmed aside. Darzka slashed down and struck sparks from the altar while casting a tendril of darkness at me, which as luck would have it, slapped me out of Red's deadly path. I twisted and threw my sword at the blade-wielding Penny. Even wounded I would have struggled to miss at this distance and it took her in the chest. Her blades flew in opposite directions like shards of light as she somersaulted backward over the stones. I crashed into the ground. Niall brought his gun to bear once more, before vanishing under a couple of tons of angry baby dragon. Druk shredded the undead henchman like he was a straw doll. Upon seeing her minion reduced to rags, Darzka levitated out of his way and began to weave lightning.

This all happened in less than a minute. After which, time rushed back upon me at its normal pace. The air crackled, sparks lit in the quartz embedded in the outer ring of stone. Clouds gathered over the gate, gravid and threatening they masked the moon.

Druk looked up, the stringy remains of Niall trailing from his mouth. He seemed unconcerned, or innocently unaware that Darzka was building up a storm to destroy him. I lacked the strength to do more than watch this latest tragedy unfold.

A horn sounded, and then I understood why he wasn't afraid.

Druk bore a close resemblance to his mother, save that he was less than a third her size. Her lion-dog face appeared above Darzka, the creature's enormous, sinuous body wrapped around the outer ring of the gate. Stone groaned, storm winds filled her billowing wings, her iridescent scales reflected fire, and lightning danced in her eyes.

A five-toed paw lashed out of the darkness and struck the Mage Lord, hurling her into one of the outer uprights with unparalleled force. The stone cracked, and the lintel fell, bringing down another of the giants. Darzka's wards flared, saving her from certain death but not from a wicked basting. She hit the ground like a sack of turnips and that was all I saw.

***

"And I say we burn her."

"Rend limb from limb, then burn."

"Can I eat her?"

A cove I took to be Mother Dragon roared so loudly my teeth rattled. I opened my eyes to find that I was lying within the gate on the altar stone. "This is still sticky."

Sonam was standing beside me. Mother and child were high above, frolicking in the lightning-laced clouds. "It's covered in blood."

"Yes, I know what it is. I just think someone could have washed it down before putting me on it or just not laid me on a sacrificial altar at all, now that I think about it." Sonam helped me to sit up. Edie was on Nuanu's back; Nettie beside them in her human form, as naked as the day she was born. The Wild Hunt were crowded within the stones. Darzka was gagged and bound with what appeared to be strands of ivy to one of the trilith uprights. Her face was bloody and furious.

As I got off, a nut brown imp hopped onto the altar. "Cut off her head like wot she done." He put his hands on his hips. Some agreed. Others grumbled their dissent. Amongst the Wild I recognized some faces from the arena and was pleased to see that some of my fellow bait dogs had survived their ordeal.

I have to take her back. I wasn't sure how or when I'd come to that conclusion, but there it was, leaving the burning question of *how* hanging in the air. I was quite badly hurt and very outnumbered. Someone had seen fit to slip Volund's sword into my belt, but if things got nasty, it would avail me little against this crew. That's if things got nasty. "And why would they?"

Sonam cocked his head. "Why would who do what?"

"What? Never mind. Thanks for coming back. I take it mama came looking for her nipper?"

The boy nodded. "We did not get far before she found us."

"I'm happy for you," I ruffled his shaved pate. "And for Edie. Or should I refer to her as, 'Her Majesty' now?"

He shrugged. "I don't know. Their ways are strange."

"So, are we burning her or not?" a trollish cove enquired, as he and a friend shoved the fallen upright back into its hole. "Only we're due rain in about an hour."

Nuanu stamped his hoof. Edie hung on to his neck and whispered in his ear. "The Goblin Queen would hold a trial for Darzka," the emissary intoned. I could see the stuffy cull was loving every minute of this.

The Hunt fell to bickering, which was perfect for me. "Look, Sonam, it's been a pleasure and all, but I have to get back to my own world."

"And you wish to take Darzka with you."

"Er...yes. How did you know?"

"Just a guess. Goodbye, Breed. I hope you don't bleed to death."

"Er, thanks Sonam. If you could do something distracting while I cut her loose, I'd be obliged."

He looked up at the dragons feeding on the storm and nodded. Slowly and painfully I made my way around the circle until I found the keystone. It was one of the small blue stones just inside the outer ring. None of the hobgoblins were paying the slightest heed to me. They were too busy arguing the finer points of fairy law. I had to smile. No matter how wonderful, how rare, and magical, they were just as petty and argumentative as a village hall full of humans.

I didn't turn the stone yet, instead I made my way to the back of the trilith to which Darzka was bound. *Bring her back.* The imperative was painfully strong. "Back where?" I didn't understand me sometimes. The ivy rope was looped around her wrists then around the stone, so it would be a simple matter to cut the rope from behind and drag her to the keystone. A simple task, perhaps, if I hadn't been limping and leaking.

I'd give it a go. If I got caught they might go easy on me for all I'd done to save Edie. *Edie.* It would have been nice to say goodbye, to wish the kinchin cove well as Queen of whatever the fuck she was the queen of. But it was not to be. She was alive, and she was well, and would no doubt think ill of me forever for thwarting her royal decree, but there you go, bigger fish and all that. I took a moment then, put my back to a stone as I caught a glimpse of the winding path of my life. It was more complicated than I would have liked, than anyone would have liked. I didn't know if I felt proud to have survived this long, or bitter that there had been so much shit I'd had to survive. Was this all there was for me? Or perhaps my woes were no greater than those of anyone else. I drew my blade quietly. Who knew I'd be grateful for a cloak?

Keeping the blade out of sight, I waited until I was in position before I tipped Sonam the nod. He steepled his fingers and closed his eyes. Lightning cracked the sky as mother and son swooped from the cloud layer. The Wild cowered, momentarily unsure. I cut Darzka's bonds and dragged her behind the trilith.

"Don't do anything, or I'll gut you where you stand," I said.

She stamped on my foot and reached for her gag. I butted her in the face. There was a soft crack as her nose broke, and she fell against me, instantly transforming from prisoner to unwanted burden. I dragged her to the keystone as Druk and his mother swooped, dived, and wove between the stones like ribbons. The keystone turned easily enough, and a slice opened in the world above the altar. I groaned as I heaved the semi-conscious Mage Lord onto my shoulder and barged through the crowd. Before anyone could stop me, I was diving for the sliver of nothingness.

Chapter Twelve

As we tumbled through the gate I gave Darzka a kiss. It was only fair to take back that which she had stolen from me. The rush was extraordinary, star steel flooded my body, as the aching cold of the Void bored into my bones. Darzka opened her eyes and they filled with stars. It was a beautiful moment…for me.

I'd never fixed a destination when I'd entered an angle gate that spanned worlds, but this time I felt pulled in a specific direction, as though we were caught in an unseen current. I could have fought it, I could have dragged myself away and plunged elsewhere into the star spew of ice and glittering dust. But I didn't. I let myself be drawn along the unknown path. We gathered speed, the stars blurred, ripped the darkness and all sensible thought was lost until we fell into the ring of stones that I'd left in the Annurashi's keep all those years ago.

I was back.

As I hit the warmer air my wounds began to bleed. The Mage Lord woke and groaning, fought to draw air into her frozen lungs. Being transported across the Void seemed to have affected her more than me. We tumbled from the stones and came to a halt on the narrow rim of the platform which was suspended on chains near to where the Eldest of the Annurashi was standing, staring at us spoon-eyed with surprise.

"Ah, Breed. It's about time. And you brought a friend. How nice." The crone flashed her raptor smile. I recognized it then, the subtle yet powerful compulsion that had dragged me back to this place.

Darzka's eyes grew wide in terror. She clawed at my shirt. "What have you done?"

"What have *I* done? You're the one who imprisoned me and tried to have me killed. I fought back, I defended myself."

"You lied. You said you weren't in league with the Annurashi."

I had indeed said that, and at the time it was true, but times change, like now, with the Queen of the Annurashi paying close attention to our conversation. "And you believed me? You fool." I laughed.

Darzka's face twisted into a mask of hellish fury, and a tendril of darkness slapped me off the platform. I fell about thirty feet, hit another ring of stones, bounced off, and landed on the chamber floor.

The Annurashi set her throne down. She ignored me and focused on Darzka. The temperature in the chamber increased. The chains mooring the stratified platforms of angle gates rattled. "Welcome home, Mage Lord. I have so many questions."

The air thickened. Darzka swathed herself in shadows. "I will not submit to you, Annurashi. I will never submit!"

The Eldest sighed. "Yes, you will." Lightning raced across the ceiling, shattering glowstones before arcing towards Darzka. Tendrils of darkness whipped up and caught the white fire. The smell of burning fingernails filled the air.

About now seemed like the perfect time to absent myself. To avoid losing my head to an errant blast of magic, I crawled towards the door. My progress was painfully slow because I kept slipping in my claret, but where there's a will and a pair of dueling sorcerers tearing into each other, there's a way. The door handle which was made of silver and shaped like a slender leaf, curled away from my touch as I reached for it. The ground shook as another bolt of lightning arced across the room. One of them, probably Darzka, screamed as the door swung open without my assistance. There, standing before me, was Rowan.

"Breed?"

"Rowan."

"You look terrible. What's going on?"

"Best ask your mother. I'm just going to lie down here for a while."

***

Troubled dreams, full of empty-eyed dead laughing at the living resolved into the sound of hard boots pacing on a stone floor. I was reluctant to open my eyes, although I was grateful that I could, that I was alive. On first, blurry inspection I discovered that I wasn't only alive but also in reasonably good condition, my various wounds having been expertly tended. I lay on a bed in a chamber as flamboyantly decorated as the rest of the Annurashi's keep. It had featureless, grey walls and no soft furnishings save for the mattress beneath me. A cold, blue fire burned silently in the hearth. Rowan was standing before it, staring into the flames with her hands clasped, strangling-tight behind her back. Her shirt sleeves were rolled up past her razor-thin elbows, the light blue silk was spotted with blood rust.

Sensing my eyes upon her, Rowan glanced over her shoulder. Like the rest of her kin she appeared more alive and vibrant than any mortal ever could, as though nature had seen fit to paint the Annurashi in sharper focus than the rest of us. She looked pensive, in the way a raptor might look with a nest of hungry chicks to feed. The planes of her face seemed sharper than the last time I'd seen her; her four-jointed fingers longer, more clawed, and her spun sugar hair not only caught the light but seemed to amplify it. She was worried, which made me worried.

I raised my hand. "Just so you know, don't try to kill me *again*, because I'm not immortal anymore."

"Give me some credit." The frown softened and a little of her old arrogance briefly pushed through. "I gathered that much when I found you lying in your own blood in the Gate Chamber."

"Much obliged for the embroidery." The stitches in my stomach were tight but not painful, the flesh of my gut cool, uninfected. "How long was I gone?"

"A few hours. Although I think for you time has passed differently? You look old."

"Yes, all right, don't rub it in." I stood up. I felt like crap and sat back down.

"Don't poke at the stitches."

"I wasn't." I stopped poking the stitches.

"Where have you been, Breed?" She snapped her fingers and the fire became a rich, golden-red blaze that instantly warmed the room. "Where did you find Darzka, and how is it that she is alive after all these years?"

"I don't know, honest. I've just been lost, mostly. Did a bit of thieving…the usual." I wasn't going to tell her where I'd been; she might decide to try and go there. "I found Darzka on some shithole world with one sun. We had a fight, I won, and brought her back here. That's it. I take it the Eldest did for her?"

Rowan turned her attention to the table and began putting away her physicking tools. "Not when last I saw her." She kept her back to me while she talked but her voice was heavy with guilt—or perhaps it was disgust, I couldn't be sure. Unlike humans, the Annurashi didn't sweat out their feelings, which made them harder to read. Her smell remained constant and reminiscent of a cold mountain stream, ice-rimed berries, and just a hint of frog.

"Where is she now?" I found my clothes in a heap on the floor and started to dress, mindful of the stitches.

"Darzka?"

"The Eldest." There followed a long pause, as though she hoped I might forget the question if she let it lie. "So, where is she?"

"Busy."

"I need to speak to her."

She slammed the bowl down hard. Bloody water slopped onto the floor. "I told you. She's busy." Her tone was suffused with iron and a hint of a compulsion spell but not enough to sway me, not now that I had my power back.

"I wasn't intimidated by you…" I almost said, 'forty years ago'. "The first time we met. So you might as well knock the angry, godling shit on the head. Either take me to your old dear, or I'm off. And where's my sword?" In truth, she'd scared me witless the first time we'd met, but I was in a lying mood.

Her shoulders dropped. She flipped a cloth off Volund's blade, which lay on the table. "All right. I'll take you. Now shut up and get dressed."

***

As soon as I was dressed and had retrieved my precious blade, Rowan led us through an unfamiliar labyrinth of passageways. What I glimpsed of the world through the irregularly placed windows showed me a landscape that had remained unchanged in…no, not forty years. Just two fucking days. I've lived a lifetime in two days. The thought made my head spin.

On the way to the Eldest's lair, Rowan twice made as though she was about to tell me something but refrained both times. We didn't see another soul as we wound our way down from the heights to the depths, to dank windowless passageways that had been hewn into the heart of the mountain. Even though the smell of freshly spilled blood hung in the air, I was confident that Rowan meant me no harm after going to the trouble of healing me. The crone was another matter. She was unpredictable, dangerous, treacherous— much like myself only more powerful.

"We're here," Rowan had brought us to a dark corner of a damp tunnel. The door before us was made of thorn wood. The planks had not been planed, and long, black thorns protruded a handspan from the face of the door. It was an ugly wood when left in its natural state and always made me wonder what kind of a person would favor such a vicious aesthetic.

Rowan made no move to open the door. A strangled cry and a wet slapping sound came from the other side, followed by what sounded like squawking. I looked at Rowan. She didn't look at me.

"Are you going to open it?"

"No."

"Sweet salvation." I flipped my sword and hammered on the door with the hilt. It opened smoothly. Glowstones set in the walls of the dank chamber flared blue, providing a counterpoint to the hellish red of the braziers burning either side of a torture rack from which Darzka's ruined body was suspended. Beneath her lifeless form, the Eldest's dragonets were feasting on a pile of slick and steaming entrails. The crone was standing before us, bloody-handed, eyes fever bright. Now I knew Shallunsard was her creature. "Like mother, like son."

Rowan shot me a warning glance, but the Eldest didn't seem to have heard me, which was probably just as well considering she'd just butchered the Mage Lord like a pig.

"Ah, Breed. Come in child, come in. You've done well."

Chapter Thirteen

"Come, child," The Eldest repeated as her dragons fought over what must have been a particularly succulent piece of Darzka's giblets.

"Er, I've just got to fetch something from somewhere." I made to leave, but Rowan grabbed my arm and escorted me into the torture chamber.

"You wanted to see the Eldest, Breed. Well, here she is," Rowan said through gritted teeth.

Darzka had died hard. Her flesh had been sliced, torn, burned, and frozen and hung in ribbons from her broken body. The final act of cruelty visited upon her was evisceration. It reminded me of what Shallunsard's demons had done to me.

The Eldest eschewed her floating throne and walked over to a table set with trays of stones and a flagon of wine. She picked up a goblet, the bowl was made from what looked like a human skull. "Drink?"

"No thanks."

With a steady, if blood-soaked hand, she poured herself a skull of red. "I thought it was a mistake sending you through the gate. I thought that was the last I'd ever see of you, that if you survived you would never go near a gate again." She raised the grim vessel in a toast. "I'm surprised and pleased that I was wrong."

"I'm not—" I said before thinking and heard Rowan draw a sharp breath. "Surprised, that is. Edolis is my home, that I would return was never in doubt." The good thing about talking to the insane godling was that she seemed to miss things, probably because the voices in her head were shouting too loudly for anything else to be heard.

"Yes. Our home. One that Darzka and her ungrateful ilk sought to abandon, taking with them the precious gifts we had given them. Gifts they did not deserve." The Eldest's spite-filled gaze turned to the body and lingered on her grisly handiwork. Rowan kept her mouth shut and her eyes on anything that wasn't Darzka, the Eldest, or me. "You did well to slay Ozbert. He was talented."

That threw me. "I...er, thank you. It was nothing really. But how do you know that I slotted Ozbert?"

She took a sip of her drink, her eyes unfocused as her vision turned inwards. "I didn't know why, but some of my old vigor returned after you left. I told myself that it was passion, that anger had enlivened me, that hope had enthused me and given me strength, but it was nothing so…esoteric." She put down the skull and brushed her somewhat darker, thicker hair from her face, accidentally anointing her cheeks with the Mage Lord's blood. "When you slew Ozbert, the power he'd stolen returned to me." She gave Rowan a pointed look.

"And might I say how well you look, but how did you find out that I'd killed Ozbert?"

"I read it in the bones of someone called Malin. His corpse preceded you through the gate by an hour or so." She had a sip of wine. "They were most informative."

"Is that…is that his skull?" I don't know if she realized it, but much depended on her answer.

"No, of course not. What a mind you have to think such a thing." She looked at the cup. "It's… I don't know who it is. I've had it a long time. Anyway, it's not important."

Had it been Malin's skull I might have got all unnecessary and perhaps have said something I wouldn't live to regret, and truth was, I didn't want to die. My old gut brain had come out of retirement, probably because my head brain was making such a fist of existing, and it wanted to live. It was where the thoasa in me dwelt. It wasn't sentimental, it didn't give a shit about my sensitivities, or my allegiances. It had one desire, which was to continue, and I liked that idea. Old me would keep newer me in check.

"I have a task for you." The Eldest's voice was *compelling*.

I knew what she was trying to do. I gritted my teeth as I tried to resist the spell that was needling my brain.

"I want you to find the other renegades and take back what they have stolen from me. You have a knack for these gates and it seems, for finding Mage Lords."

"Did you make me bring Darzka back? Only, I was going to anyway."

"I know you were, child. I know. I just guided you."

So that's both of us lying then. "What happened to slotting Shallunsard? He's the one ravaging Edolis; why aren't we going after him?"

Her face darkened. "*We* cannot. I am the only one who can bring him to heel, and for that I must be at my strongest. Slay the thieves and return to me that which was stolen. Mortals cannot wield the power of the Universe. The Mage Lords were a failed experiment, which must be brought to an end."

I knew I shouldn't have felt guilty over what she'd done to Darzka. The Mage Lord wasn't an angel and at the time, I didn't have any power to resist the Eldest's summons. It really wasn't my fault. I was Fate's pawn, and yet, I felt like shit.

Rather than destroy her demonic offspring who was bent on destroying the world, the Eldest wanted me to hunt down the sorcerers who'd tried to escape, who had thwarted her will. I was once again working for a gang boss, only this time the merchandise was somewhat more valuable than a shipment of pel. "I'm going to need some stuff."

The Eldest nodded. "I knew I could rely on you. It's in your blood, isn't it? To hunt, to kill without thought, without compassion." She aimed a crooked finger at me. "Mark me; I do not hate the renegades, they are only human after all, but I will have what they have taken. Do you understand?"

I shrugged. "Aye. And don't you worry none. You have my word that I'll slot 'em for you." I'd never put any weight on my word; it was such a little thing, quickly used and quickly forgotten.

She smiled like the sweet old dear she wasn't. "Give me your hands, child."

"Both?"

"As many as you have."

I recalled how I'd gained the demon mark when I'd made the deal with Shallunsard. It had hurt *a lot*, as it had when I'd gained Rowan's sigil after she'd healed me the first time. I therefore braced for a similar experience, and silently questioned why pain always seemed to feature in the Annurashis' rites. She took my hands in her unnaturally firm grip, and then I waited…

. . .and waited.

Minutes passed in awkward silence. I was about to suggest that whatever it was she was doing hadn't worked and perhaps we should stop holding hands, when the next second I fell to my knees in excruciating pain. I tried to pull away, but the old bastard held me fast. Smoke rose from my bloody, burning fingertips. It felt like my hands were on fire. I screwed my eyes shut, afraid to look at what I was sure were nothing more than blackened stumps.

"Open your eyes, Breed. I have improved you." I opened my eyes to see that my hands weren't mangled stumps. They looked much like they had before, only now my claws were flecked with star steel. Oh, yes and my fingers throbbed.

"Now if you lose your pretty sword, you will still be able to kill Mage Lords."

I felt violated but I also didn't want to feel dead, so I kept my mouth shut.

"Now leave us. Darzka and I still have matters to discuss."

Confused, I looked at Darzka. Her remaining eye blinked. "Sweet salvation, she's…she's still alive."

Rowan took me by the arm and hastened me to the door. The Eldest's dragonets squawked as they tore at the Mage Lord's giblets while Darzka watched them. When the door swung closed on Darzka's nightmare and my eternal guilt, Rowan returned my sword, which I'd dropped while the Eldest was 'improving' my claws.

"I'm sure my hands feel heavier."

"It's just your imagination."

I also felt dirty, and for the first time in my life, ashamed.

"Are you well?" Rowan asked. She sounded more curious than concerned.

"Aside of having my claws melted and remade? Oh, aye. I'm in the rudest of health. Did you know what she was doing to Darzka?"

"Yes." Not a flicker of emotion crossed her face.

"And, you didn't try to stop her?"

"No. Come with me." She marched down the corridor, leaving a compulsion spell trailing in her wake. I could tell that Rowan was locked into her own, private hell and that she knew her mother was the monster. I also knew that she wouldn't do anything to stop her.

"Where are Malin's bones now?"

"I think they're in the ossuary."

"Take me there."

***

The smell of old bones and cold stone greeted us as we approached the ossuary. At the end of another, plain, grey corridor Rowan forced open a pair of verdigrised, copper clad doors. Inside was a courtyard. It was open to the elements, and a flesh-stripping storm raged in the mountains above, but down here, the icy wind sang a soft, almost mournful lament, and snow flurries dusted the bones on their plinths with a feather's touch.

"Who are they?" I asked.

"Fallen Annurashi, honored Mage Lords. Some are... I don't know. Human servants, maybe." She waved dismissively. "I am not the Keeper of Tombs."

"No of course not, perish the thought. What is it you do again?"

She gave me the side-eye. "What do you mean by that?"

"Nothing. Is that him?" While verbally poking the Annurashi I'd let my gaze roam across the vast, sky-lit chamber until I spied an embroidered quilt I recognized.

"I believe so." She preceded me across the chamber, her footfall softened by the snow. It was bitterly cold out here, and either by magic or clever design, the storm raging around the peaks didn't tear through the room and scatter the crumbling remains. "The first I knew about him was when the Eldest told me to bring the remains here."

I peered inside the blanket. I didn't know what I'd expected to see. What I saw was not my... It wasn't Malin. "They're just bones."

"What did you expect?"

"I don't know. That his skull would be missing. What? Don't look at me like that. I've seen what your mother is capable of. I wouldn't put lying past her."

"How dare you." She advanced towards me, hands wreathed in ice.

"Oh, please. We're beyond this, are we not?" I felt the faint flicker of sorcery stir within me. "Are you sure you want to do this?" She pulled up, perhaps surprised to see flames light upon the edge of my hands, or perhaps her heart wasn't it in, either way I was relieved. I was out of practice, but she didn't know that. "I've learned a lot since we last met."

The ice around her fists dissipated. "I will let it pass, this once. You are confused, angry."

"I'm not angry." I was more disgusted than angry.

"The situation is more complicated than you know. Not even I know the whole of it."

"I believe you. But a couple of days ago we were set to destroy Shallunsard. So what happened?"

"Everything changed when you slew Ozbert. The Eldest felt him die, and his power return to her. She took it as a sign." Rowan put her hands on Malin's plinth. I say Malin's plinth, but his name wasn't carved into the stone and no stirring lines of poetic verse memorialized his life and achievements. He was anonymous in death, something that I think he would have liked. "Nothing is as simple as you would like it to be."

"What *I'd* like it to be?" *You have no fucking idea what I would like.*

"Yes. You. I've known hundreds of humans and warspawn. I've seen countless mortals take their first steps and draw their last breath. I know your kind."

Bollocks. "As far as I'm aware there's only one of my kind. But have it your way. I've a job to do. As the Eldest pointed out, that's all I care about."

"I don't believe you."

"You mean you don't want to believe me."

She laughed softly. "Perhaps that's it, aye. Perhaps I want you to give a damn, to grieve, to feel sorrow, guilt, revulsion."

"Because you don't, right?"

"Because I cannot."

"I'm sorry to disappoint you, but I don't either. Your mother's right. It's not in me."

A flurry of snow corkscrewed out of the sky and scudded between us, carrying away the last, bitter dregs of conversation in a blinding swirl of icy particles. When it cleared, Rowan was halfway to the door, her white hair clawing at the wind like some mad, flailing beast.

"I'm sorry you ended up here, Mal. I thought we could just…disappear, together— that's not an invitation to come and haunt me by the way. I've just got rid of a host of ghosts. You stay wherever you are, prepare a space maybe, for an old friend." I covered his bones and jogged after Rowan. "Oi, fustilugs, wait up. It's bloody freezing out here."

***

"Are you sure you want it?"

I jumped up and down to settle the maille shirt. It was a good fit and made of steel light enough to wear for an extended period of time, yet sturdy enough to turn a blade. "Yes, I'm sure. I'm not as fast as I once was. I need all the protection I can get."

"Just don't call lightning while wearing it."

"I've done a lot of spellcasting since I left, you know."

"Forgive me." She sat on one of the benches in the cluttered armory. "It was only a few hours—"

"— Since I was forcefully shoved through the gate?"

"Since you left the keep. How long has it been for you?"

I opened my arms. "Long enough for my hair spines to turn grey. I don't know, I don't keep track."

She waved her hand and color returned to not just my hair but to my entire body. I was once again vibrant orange and red, and my humanish skin was fresh, plump and pink. "Don't get excited, it's just a glamour."

"I wasn't, and I know." I still felt like I was about to crumble to dust at any minute, but at least I didn't look like it— and that mattered.

In my old role as a Guild Blade, front was important; you couldn't drop your guard or look weak no matter how shit you were feeling. One slip and some ambitious bastard would close your account and use your corpse as a stepping stone on their way up the greasy pole. *Ah. The good old days.* I'd cadged a beautifully tooled scabbard for my sword and acquired a couple of long knives and a bow. The fletching on most of the shafts in their armory was moth-eaten, but I found a dozen arrows that were fit for purpose, whatever that purpose might be. My talons were going to take some getting used to. They were the same shape and length as before, but now I could see living flecks of star steel in them. "I'll have to be careful when I wipe my arse, eh?"

She raised an eyebrow. "I see you're just as vulgar as you ever were, despite being away years."

"It's part of my charm. So, what do you think, do I look like a deadly mage killer?" I checked my reflection in a dusty shield boss. *Do I look like I can kill an Annurashi?*

"You look like you."

"I'll take that as yes. Shall we go see if your beloved mater has finished torturing Darzka?"

Chapter Fourteen

Rowan led me through the sprawling keep to gather supplies. I say keep, but the home of the Annurashi was more a citadel than a mere castle, spread along the spine of a mountain range like barnacles upon the back of a kraken.

It was an inhospitable place to settle, a place where the elements waged constant war. And then there were the dragons, moved for whatever reason to hunt these desolate reaches, where nothing but the deathless godlings dwelt. All I'd seen of these deadly, icy leviathans was caught in the momentary flash of sorcerous lightning; a reflection of pale scales and the spear sharp gleam in a diamond eye when one came too close to the keep and was repelled by the Annurashis' wards.

I recalled Druk's mother, her vibrant, jewel-bright scales and elegantly powerful serpentine body. These things were very different and wove gales of snow and ice around their spiky grey and white bodies. I saw the tip of a bony wing spine, the flick of an icicle barbed tail but never a whole beast.

"You invaded their turf," I said to Rowan's back.

"Whose turf?" She stiffened but kept walking.

"The dragons. They don't like you. They keep flying close to your wards like they're looking for a weakness."

"How very observant. They used to breed here before the Eldest came."

"Nicely distanced."

She stopped. "It is simply what happened. Not an attempt to distance myself from the deed. I am Annurashi. We are as one."

"Well, except Shallunsard, surely?"

She made fists. "Do you want to fight me, is that what you're after? Is this your heavy-handed attempt to goad me into killing you?"

I raised my hands and tried not to smile too much. "No, I'm just trying to understand you lot, seems only sensible now that we're partners. You'll have to forgive my bluntness; old folk lack patience."

She canted her head much like a dog trying to fathom a noise. It struck me again just how unlike mortals these coves were. "Mind your tongue, Breed."

"Or you'll what, kill me? You've already done that once, remember?"

"Of course I remember. It wasn't that long ago."

I shook my head. My neckbones creaked. *It was forty years ago for me.* "I don't know if I'm ahead of the game or behind it. So anyway, these dragons. Why build your stead where dragons roost?"

"It is the most remote place on Edolis and…"

"Let me guess, star steel?" It all made sense now. "That's why the humans are all so sickly here."

"What do you—?"

I raised my hand to cut her off. "Not a criticism, just an observation. She built her lair over the star steel, just like the Mage Lords. Your human acolytes are all sick because raw star steel is poison. I get that, I've seen its effects many times."

"It isn't poisonous to mortals when it is refined. Mage Lords know how to do this."

"I know," I said. *I've done it. I've transformed it within myself. Now there's a trick you don't know, Annurashi.* "But in its raw state, like here under these mountains, or say, when arrogant Mage Lords use it injudiciously to shit out poorly crafted, but ever so explosive spells, it corrupts, and twists nature out of shape. But you know that, have always known that, eh?"

She blinked.

"My guess is that dragons, Mage Lords, and other elemental beings like you lot are immune to these ill effects. Your average sellspell gets around it by obeying their paradox and not casting anything too powerful."

"And how do you get around it, Breed? For it seems you are also immune to the adverse effects of the injudicious use of star steel magic."

"I stay within my paradox."

She turned to the window and like an echo of the Eldest, gazed through the beveled glass into the icy spindrift cascading from the nearest peaks. "Alas, no creature, no matter how ancient or irreverent, is immune to the all-consuming hunger for power. Oh, they might start out with the best of intentions, but it's never enough and eventually, the ache, the need for more warps those intentions, blinds them to the damage that they do to others in pursuit of power."

"If you say so. I've rarely started anything with the best of intentions." I waited for an answer or for her to continue but the silence extended as her thoughts spiraled inwards.

"Come on, Rowan, we don't want to keep your mother waiting."

As was the way with the Annurashi, she didn't venture anything more by way of conversation and I'd lost my appetite for discourse, being as I was experiencing a rare moment of self-doubt. Was I sure I hadn't been injudicious? No. I hadn't. I transformed the poison of raw star steel and taught others how to do the same and I'd never... hardly ever, craved more power than what I had. Obviously, there were times when I'd wished I could do more, but that was not the same as Ozbert or Darzka or the fucking Eldest, I'd wager. I wasn't like them. "This is stupid."

"What did you say?"

"Uh? Nothing." I had enough to worry about without questioning myself because of some maudlin godling's wittering. "I'm tired, is all."

"What?"

"I said I'm tired, bone weary." The rush of energy I'd felt when I'd taken back my power and when she'd healed me was fading fast. Even with the power of star steel once again flowing in my veins, even though the Eldest had given me claws laced with the stuff, it didn't feel like enough to sustain me. *Oh, fuck.*

***

The Eldest was waiting for us in the Gate Tower, and by the sound of it, she was not alone.

"It sounds like a party in there," I said to Rowan, who hadn't opened her mouth since our little chat about the nature of power. She didn't look like she was expecting a gathering.

"The tower is forbidden to all but the Eldest."

"Was."

She frowned.

As we approached, the opaque, crystal doors swung open. It looked like all of the Annurashi were within, along with their human acolytes. Jeo scowled when he saw me, before falling into a fit of coughing. After years of practicing their arts, I now saw the not-so-subtle artifice the Annurashi employed to distinguish themselves from each other. They were all of a height, only some wore elaborate headdresses or intricate hairstyles or indeed sported no hair at all. Some wore armor, others robes, but aside of these affectations and liberal use of the same glamour Rowan had cast on me, they were eerily, unpleasantly alike.

The Eldest was standing by the ring of stones that I'd thought destroyed when she and Darzka fought. They appeared whole now, and I could hear the gnat buzz of life emanating from the keystone, which filled me with relief and trepidation. I was eager to be away from this nest of madness, but I didn't want to face another Mage Lord after the last one had almost done for me.

"Ah, here you are. Come, child, come."

I half expected her to say 'destiny awaits' or some such drivel, but she just patted the stone nearest to her like it was a beloved pet. All eyes were on me as I made my way through the crowd. For the most part the Annurashi looked at me with the same, amused disdain with which they'd regarded me years ago.

I was about to take issue but then remembered that for them only a day or so had passed, and back then I had been an ignorant shit. I was still a shit, but I'd learned a few things in the last forty years. In light of recent revelations, I noticed that some of them looked at me the way hungry vultures looked upon the ripening corpse of a dead urux. The yearning in their many-hued eyes was almost palpable. They wanted star steel. Like Darzka and Ozbert, they hungered for it. I imagined that they were forbidden from taking it from each other, but I probably looked like the first course of a banquet. Or if I'm honest, a light supper. *Well you can all fuck off. What's mine is mine.*

I looked at them now with the experienced eye of a practiced sorcerer and could see that some of them looked decidedly wan, while others seemed robust and full of life— no doubt they were the ones the Eldest favored, with Rowan chief amongst them.

"My children." The Eldest's voice brokered silence. She smiled benevolently at the attentive crowd. Her tiny dragons swooped and tumbled through the graveyard of silent gates, their bellies fat after gorging on Mage Lord. "My friends. Today marks a turning point in our evolution. The battle will end. Harmony will be restored, and through power we shall have peace."

Wild applause and cheering followed the incomprehensible speech. A few of the company exchanged dubious glances, but for the most part they were enrapt and hung on her every word, words which had been sweetened by the honey of a compulsion spell. *She doesn't even trust her own offspring.* That concerned me in so far as I didn't understand what game she was playing. Surely, she could trust her own kin? She slapped her hand on my shoulder. I flinched.

"Don't be afraid, Breed." Her bony fingers dug into my shoulders. "I have faith in your abilities. You will find the renegades, you will triumph, and you will restore unto me that which is mine."

"Er, yeah, sure." Her smile faltered, and her face darkened. I cleared my throat, sketched a formal bow. "As you will it, Eldest." The smile returned. I know it was fawning to pander so, but I would have kissed her shriveled wot nots if it got me out of here sooner rather than later.

"Open the gate, my child."

While trying to keep an eye on the old crow and her get, I found the keystone and turned it. A slit in space opened within the circle and a gust of icy wind blew across the room. I would have stepped through then, happy to be anywhere but here, but the Eldest held me back.

"A moment, Breed." She turned to her nervous looking kin. "Which of my children will accompany Breed through the gate?"

Damn. It seemed that the wily old cove didn't trust me after all. Surprised murmurs ruffled the crowd until Jeo stepped forward, curling the hem of his robes in his hands as he summoned the courage to speak up.

"Might I—" was all he managed before the Eldest cut him off.

"No. Not you, mortal. Which of my offspring will go with Breed?" The room drowned in a tsunami of awkward silence. Red-faced, Jeo stepped back amongst his peers. The Annurashi eyed each other suspiciously.

"I'll go," said Rowan, as weary as death.

The Eldest shook her head. "No. not you, my dear. Azmorda, you go."

Azmorda was of course the same height and build as Rowan but had cascading blue hair that fell past his waist. He was wearing layer upon layer of violet and blue, silk robes. His skin had the appearance of fine alabaster, and he smelled of stone, probably from the finely powdered mineral dusted on his face and hair that sparkled in the scant illumination.

He smiled nervously. "I don't think I'd be much use."

"We shall see."

Azmorda scanned the faces of his brothers and sisters, searching for support. Few met his gaze. In desperation he looked to me, as though I might save him. I shrugged. There was nothing I could do. I wasn't even sure I could save myself from whatever I might find on the other side. The very air might be acid and dissolve me into a puddle of slime, and that would be that. *Fucking Delgaro. I should have just let her die and kept my immortality.* Even as I formed the thought I knew I didn't mean it. "After you." I gestured towards the slash in the air that was singing with the breath of the Void.

"Heart of the World, I beg you, do not send me hence." Azmorda pleaded. "None of us have traveled through the great gates. We are not fitted for it. Eldest, please." His voice was beautiful, melodious but his words were wasted.

The Eldest pointed to the gate. "Consider this a test then, for the good of all."

One of several things could have happened next. Azmorda might have thrown himself on the floor in a sobbing mess and refused to go. But that pathetic ploy would fail because the murderous Elderling hadn't an ounce of pity in her. He could have challenged her, but again, I didn't fancy his chances. Given the limited options, he managed to grow a spine and accept her decree with a modicum of dignity.

After a painful hesitation, he straightened and glided to the gate. The Eldest laid her raptor gaze upon him as he reached towards the rift, plunged his arm into the slice of inky black, and took a step towards his destiny and then he stopped. A look of horror spread across his face. He gasped and flung himself away from the gate, clutching his arm. The Eldest's dragonlings shrieked and flew wild spirals to get away from the stricken godling as he fell off the platform and into the crowd.

Rowan acted first and fast and cast a shielding spell between Azmorda and the Void. Alas, her attempt to save him was in vain. Where he had touched the Void, his flesh blistered and turned ashen. He staggered towards his brothers and sisters, his injured limb extended and oozing rancid blood. I wasn't surprised to see the godlings back away as black veins crawled across Azmorda's skin.

I'd seen this before. This looked disturbingly similar to the poison Ozbert's demon had used to turn people into savage, restless dead.

The stricken Annurashi fell to the floor, his back arching painfully, his limbs rigid. As compassionate as ever, the Eldest gestured to the protective shield and turned it into a sphere, trapping him inside as his skin boiled and blackened. The Annurashi's bones snapped, his jaw distended. He clawed at his face as fangs punched through his gums and smashed his pearly whites to pieces.

I revised my opinion. This cull wasn't like one of the restless dead created by Ozbert's demon. This cull was changing into something like the demon itself. Transfixed, I watched his flesh darken to blue-black and horns begin to bud on his forehead.

One of the humans screamed. The Eldest drew a sharp breath when an extra pair of arms burst from Azmorda's ribs. She gestured again, and fire erupted inside the ward. The humans were forced back by the intense heat that bled through the shield, but the Annurashi watched without flinching even as the burning godling tried to tear his way through the ward to reach them. Again, his efforts were in vain, and within a matter of seconds, he was utterly consumed. When the flames died, Rowan waved her hand and dispelled the shield. The heat wash stank of blood, iron, and burned bone. Exhausted, she slumped against one of the monoliths in a nearby ring of stones.

"Reversion." The Eldest muttered to herself. "I thought that might happen. Oh, well. Your turn, Breed."

I was more than happy to get out of this shithole. Especially now I'd put two and two together and made demon. Of course, if the Eldest knew that I knew what she was, I'd be as dead as poor old Azmorda. Luckily for me, I was no stranger to playing dumb.

"What?" I gasped and gave her a look that I hoped said, 'are you fucking kidding me?' before following it up with, "are you fucking kidding me?" Just for emphasis.

She stroked my face. "You have nothing to fear, child. You have been through the gate before."

"Yeah, before your boy was turned into a horrible monster— no offense. I'm pretty sure the game has changed."

"Be that as it may, I still need you to go."

I folded my arms and prayed she'd compel me. The air thickened and the questing tendril of her spell slapped me in the noggin. *Thank you.* "Please. You can't...do this," I mumbled as I let my feet take me to the fissure in the gate.

The Eldest's dragons swarmed onto her shoulders and fought their way into the wild tangle of her hair. "It's the only way, I'm afraid. You must do what you were made to do, for the good of everything."

"I don't want to die!" I wailed, which might have been a touch too much of the theatricals. The last thing I saw as I leaped through the gate was Rowan giving me the side-eye.

Chapter Fifteen

My departure from the madling's shitpit was marked by the usual, icy touch of the Void, as I was drawn like wire through the eye of the universe, only this time I was not entirely alone. Like the sticky thread of a spider web, the Eldest's essence clung to me. Anger became my knife, and I severed the sorcerous link before I fell into another world.

It was hot. Not skin-peeling hot; I didn't immediately burst into flames as had happened previously, but I did start to sweat, and the metal links of my maille were uncomfortable where they touched my skin. The air was filled with gritty pumice ash that darkened the sky. Lava fields stretched in all directions and rising above the black rim of the world were gape-mouthed volcanic peaks. I coughed, pulled up my shirt collar. Beyond the ring of basalt monoliths, a path led to a black stone keep where a pair of bronze gargoyles flanking a portcullis gazed upon the burning world with flame-filled eyes. "Well, this is only slightly less shit than it could have been."

No amount of star steel could induce me to make this place my home and yet some fool had done just that. I leaned against one of the gate stones, suddenly weary. I'd had less than a day to recover from my time in Darzka's arena and yet here I was in some forsaken, burning shithole of a world at the behest of a mad demon god.

Demon god.

That was going to take some time to sink in, but I know what I saw. To think, for centuries without number the otherworldly 'guardians' of Edolis, the bringers of wonder and magic, had been…monsters. "The All-Seeing Eye didn't see that one, did it?" Shallunsard wasn't an aberration, he was just embracing his true nature.

"Well, good luck to him." And why not? He'd already killed everyone I'd ever cared about. "I've had enough." I raised my face to the cancerous sky. "Do you hear me, you old bastard? I quit. As of this moment, I've retired from the Mage Lord killing business." Even if I had the slightest moral imperative to do as the Eldest commanded, even if I held onto the hope of vengeance as the sole reason to continue on this path, I couldn't pretend that she was going to kill her renegade son. So, what was the point?

"I'm sure I can find a nice, quiet world somewhere…somehow." I searched the gate. "I'll settle down, raise animals, do what ordinary coves do and live out my final days in peace." The keystone came alive under my touch.

"Wait!" A thin voice yelled from somewhere behind me. "Please, wait!"

I turned and saw an elderly codger waving frantically from the battlements. His unkempt grey hair waved like a frayed candle wick above his scrawny body. He beckoned me. It didn't look like a trap, but Mage Lords were clever bastards and I was not immortal. I waved back. "Farewell!"

"Sweet salvation, please don't go…" His words dissolved into a fit of coughing, which doubled him over. If it was an act, it was a good one.

"Fuck's sake." I strung my bow.

The walk to the keep was punctuated by booming explosions, earth tremors, and steam geysers venting uncomfortably close to the cinder path. Nothing green or growing marred the volcanic perfection as far as the eye could see. No birds flew; not so much as a lizard scrabbled amid the clinker.

The fellow on the battlements finally stopped coughing. "Oh, thank you, thank you," he called. The chains of the portcullis rattled, and the gate began to rise. I trained an arrow on the opening, half expecting a hoard of restless dead to charge from the darkness, but I was happily disappointed.

"Come, come." The old cull scuttled along the battlement before disappearing inside. Curious by this point and keen not to be scalded by the nearby vents, I entered, making sure to keep the arrow nocked and a spell in mind.

Which was just as well.

An armored giant clad in bronze plate stood in the center of the courtyard. Upon its head sat a flaming crown of gold, a massive, two-handed sword was clasped in both his hands. The tip of the blade rested in a groove in the courtyard's mosaic, stone floor, and his head was bowed either in prayer or contemplation. I wasted no time and cast a spell of lightning before the overlarge cull noticed me.

The jagged arc struck the sword, raced along its length and wrapped itself around the giant's torso. Instead of burning it to a crisp, there was a loud implosion of air, and the whole thing vanished leaving my spell to ground itself in the floor. The mage appeared at the top of a flight of steps which led from the battlements to the courtyard. He was panting; his eyes were red and streaming from the constant rain of stinging hot ash.

"At last!" he exclaimed and flung his arms open wide. He closed his eyes. "I am ready to die."

"Eh?"

He opened an eye. "I said, I'm ready to die. Come on, get it over with."

I hadn't expected that I'd be invited to slot him, so his request quite threw me. I lowered the bow. Call me contrary, but I like to make my own decisions when it comes to who I'm going to kill.

"Why?"

He opened both eyes and lowered his arms. "It's complicated. Just kill me, would you? We're running out of time."

I lowered the bow. "No."

"No?"

"No."

"Oh, bother." He flopped down on the stairs and put his head in his hands. "This wasn't supposed to happen."

I approached cautiously in case this was an overly-elaborate trap. Up close, I could see that the fellow wasn't just old, but truly ancient. His skin was as thin as fine parchment and his muscles almost entirely wasted. His matted hair was rigid with ashen residue. His robes were worn and bleached with age. Heavy gold and emerald rings hung on his thick knuckles. Emerald earrings hung from his distended earlobes. "I thought I was old."

He shook his head sadly. "You have no idea."

One of the volcanoes growled. "Well, why don't you enlighten me? Inside, perhaps?"

***

He took me into a hall that had seen much better days. In one corner the wall had collapsed into a hole in the floor and was now being used as a privy. A bed was nearby, and a dusty throne stood alone in the center of the chamber. Unsure and agitated, he paced between the bed and the throne before eventually choosing to sit on the bed.

"What's your name?"

"Irammus."

"How the hell do you live here? The air is poison, I can't believe anything can grow here."

"It can't. There is no water, no animals. It is hell."

"So how do you live?"

He must have noticed my hand drift towards my blade and smiled. "I assure you, I'm alive."

"How?" I wasn't entirely convinced he was telling the truth.

"Magic, what else?" Another tremor shook the hall. Dust trickled from a crack in the ceiling. The old fellow waved his hand, and the crack pulled together and sealed. He was a mage, all right.

"There is star steel here, enough to sustain the many curses laid upon me." He screwed his eyes shut to aid concentration while his mouth worked on a calculation. "Seven hundred years ago, or perhaps it was twenty? Or less…I can no longer recall."

"Do you mind?" I pointed to the throne which, aside from the bed, was the only seat in the room that hadn't succumbed to decay. "My back is killing me."

"Please."

I sat down. The throne was carved from obsidian and decorated with a flight of dragons. I'd seen something like it before, but I couldn't remember where. "That's better. They call me—"

"Blake."

"Breed," I said without missing a beat and hopefully without betraying my surprise.

The old fellow looked confused. "Oh. Are you sure?"

"Yes."

"Oh. Then, perhaps you're not the one. But you fit the description…give or take a few minor differences." He rubbed his grizzled chin with painful deliberation. "I might have got the name wrong. That's the trouble with geasa, you see. The prohibitions can impair mental clarity. Not that…" He began coughing. "…The…*thing* I cannot mention cared."

"To be clear, you're under a geas that prohibits you from naming the person who cast the curse? Can you say that much?"

He looked pained. "I can't say, or draw, or write, or even dance about that. I can say that geasa are the vilest of curses. I can say that I cannot die, except by Blake's hand."

"Why?"

"I can't say."

"Fucking marvelous."

"It's not my fault." He put his head in his hands.

I had to laugh. "That's my line. What's your name again?"

"Irammus, also called the Emerald Serpent, I think. It's been such a long time since anyone called me anything. But I believe that was my name."

"What else can you tell me?"

"Trust your instincts."

"Er…is that it?"

He scowled. Green fire lit in his eyes, and the air briefly thickened. I prepared a warding spell, but the storm passed as quickly as it had risen. He sagged. The fire in his eye diminished to a sad glow as he collapsed into a fit of coughing. I waited impatiently for him to finish. "That is what I was told to tell you. That, and 'don't forget the prophesy'."

"And which prophesy would that be? I've heard a lot in my lifetime."

"I don't know; that's just what I was told to say."

"And you can't say by whom?"

"No."

"Well, this isn't annoying. You sure you can't write some of this down?"

"I told you already. The geas is as tight as a soulsoiler's ringpiece."

"Nice imagery." My gut told me to leave the old lunatic to his madness and be on my way. "As nice as this has been, I really must be going."

Panic lit in his eyes. "You can't go yet. You must release me."

I shrugged. "Consider yourself released." Curious as I was to know who'd left him here with a message for me, meeting him had convinced me more than ever to get as far from Mage Lords and the Annurashi as I could and not look back.

"You don't understand." He stood up and hobbled towards me. "I cannot leave this place."

"And? Look mate, I don't mean to be rude, but I don't give a shit about your woes. I have a ton of my own." I stood up.

He grabbed my shirt. "Please. I cannot stay here like this any longer. I can't breathe, nothing lives here, and nothing grows here."

I unpeeled his hands. "Use sorcery. Create a garden. A plethora of golems to serve you. Phantasmal concubines to service you."

"I have done all of those things and more over the centuries, that is, I think it has been centuries." Tears ran down his sallow cheeks. "I've had enough. I want to die. Please, kill me."

"I've stopped killing to order. Sorry, friend."

"Please!" He reached for me. I slapped his hand away and headed to the door. He apported, blocked my way. "If you don't kill me I will be bound to this place forever. That fucking—" He exploded in coughing and his face turned purple. I thought for a moment that he might have just granted his own wish, but he recovered, gasping for breath. "That person will never let me go. You must slay me, or I will never escape this hell." He dropped to his knees. "I beg you, end my torment."

I made to step around him, but he grabbed my leg.

"Please, have mercy, I—"

"Sweet salvation." I snapped his neck. "Happy now?" I cannot say he died with a smile on his face, but he got what he wanted.

I left the body to lie where it fell. There was no point burying him, the ash would do that eventually. There was no need for a marker, as no one was coming to mourn Irammus the... whatever he called himself. Bones don't crave dignity only the living value such things, and all the death rites in the world would not soften the blow of this cove's passing, for there were none left alive to feel the force of its pain. I did relieve him of his emeralds because I would need a grubstake in my new, quiet life and old habits die hard.

Another tremor shook the keep. Without the Mage Lord to hold the place together, the cracks widened, fissures raced up the walls, and the floor buckled beneath me. I rode it out, leaping from one unbroken piece of ground to the next until I made it outside, whereupon I sprinted to the angle gate as the towers began to fall.

Before I turned the keystone, I held in mind the avowed desire to go somewhere livable, with clean, breathable air and no Annurashi or Mage Lords. I held the image of rolling hills and sweet flower meadows in my mind and willed myself to find somewhere like that as I turned the stone and stepped into the Void.

Chapter Sixteen

*B*e careful what you wish for was the phrase which sprang to mind when I stumbled from the land of volcanoes into the ruin of the Annurashi's lair.

In the short time it had taken me to find and slay the Mage Lord, someone had been very busy. The roof had gone, leaving nothing but a ragged hole. Many of the angles gates had been reduced to rubble. Scorch marks pitted the walls and floor and the hot needle sting of schism magic prickled my skin.

And then there were the bodies.

It looked like all of the humans and most, if not all, of the Annurashi had been slain where they stood. Many were fused to the floor; some body parts had been welded to the walls. Others had been burned to charcoal. I don't know if I was relieved or disappointed that I couldn't see Rowan amongst the dead.

The Eldest was standing calmly in the midst of the carnage. I glanced over my shoulder and saw that the angle gate I'd just stepped through was blackened, and cracks ran through the stones. I was about to politely inquire as to who had done this and why, when a shadow too swift to be a cloud passed overhead. I ducked, and looked up to see the open, dagger-fanged maw of an ice dragon about to disgorge a gutful of freezing vomit on me. I cast a shield spell as it stooped to a dive.

Braced for impact, the moment stretched to hours. It was another irony that should my shield fail, I would die the death I'd escaped all those years ago, the result of which had brought me to this time and place. I looked up and met the dragon's furious gaze for about a second— before it smashed face first into nothing.

The Eldest chuckled.

I should have realized she would have thought to protect herself and her keep. I also should have noticed that there wasn't any snow inside the chamber. I forgave my failure of observation given the dual distractions of bodies and dragons. Speaking of which.

About fifty feet above me, the tip of a tooth as long as my arm snapped against the ward. The fight went out of the stunned dragon as its snout crumpled against the magical barrier. Blood and snot and icy spew delineated the scope of the invisible ward. The beast flailed. He— for such things were obvious from this angle— spread his white wings and fought to regain his balance, even if his dignity was forfeit. He roared his frustration and was answered by the half dozen or so of his kin who were circling above; agitated, dark shadows knifing through the raging storm.

To say that I was disappointed to be here was an understatement. My inability to control where I went frustrated me beyond endurance. I felt as stupid and ignorant as the first time Mother had tried to teach me how to cast a spell. The look of disgust and disappointment on her face when she realized I couldn't came back to sting me.

"What happened here?"

The Eldest sighed. "When you slew the renegade, the backlash of power through the gate killed my poor serfs."

You fucking liar, I thought but held my tongue. I might have swallowed another story— that the dragons had breached the keep's defenses, or that one of her children had made a play for power. But a fool could see from the position of the scorch marks and where the bulk of the bodies lay that the destructive force unleashed on the godlings originated from a point somewhere very close to where the Eldest was standing in a pool of rendered fat.

She picked her way towards the door. Another dragon landed on the shield and began trying to smash its way through. The Eldest remained unconcerned, being as she was both insane and supremely confident. "Go now, child, and quickly. The air here is… unclean. Go. Slay the last renegade."

There was no subtlety to the compulsion spell she cast; it hit me like an ax between the eyes. I tried to resist but the effort almost dropped me. And then I didn't want to resist. Her request seemed entirely reasonable, nay, desirable. I wanted to slay the last Mage Lord without delay.

"Of course, Eldest." Driven by the compulsion to obey, I tried to turn the keystone. It didn't move. It didn't so much as tingle. My heart sank. *No, no, no, no.* I searched amongst the other stones in case I'd got the wrong one before returning to the first one. A part of me knew that if I couldn't open the gate, the Eldest would have no use for me. With that sobering thought in mind, I pushed a little power into the gate in the hope I might shock it awake. Nothing. I glanced at the door. The Eldest was watching me, a calculating look on her face.

I had to stay calm and focus or I would undoubtedly fail to open the gate, and then I would die like the rest of her brood. This was a tempering moment, where cool logic and the hot iron of raw emotion— in this case a hefty dose of fear— met.

"Is something wrong, child?" She spoke softly but her words stabbed my brain. The air grew hot, my skin itched. I went into myself, found that calm place where a dragon slumbered. *No, not that. I don't need a dragon. I need a key.* I searched for something else; something I'd always felt lurking in my oldest memories like the dregs of a half remembered dream. The memory was hazy; something shining in the Void. The stone shuddered and began to turn. I could hear myself yelling, could taste blood in my mouth where I'd bitten my tongue. But the fucking gate opened.

***

The cold rush of the Void snatched the sorcery-fouled breath from my lungs. A moment later I fell onto wet sand. I opened my eyes and was blinded by sunslight, a second before a wave slapped me in the face. I was on a beach; two suns shone in an azure sky and a whitewashed tower stood alone atop a wind knapped cliff. I tasted the air; the fine thread of a human's scent carried on the breeze.

Kill the Mage Lord.

Ah. Yes, that was why I was here.

There was a path leading up, which cut through a narrow defile in the cliff, but it was overlooked by the tower. Rather than line myself up for an easy kill, I chose to scale the cliff out of sight of the windows and door. Wards were another matter, but I'd deal with those if and when I had to. It was an easy climb as the rock had been sculpted by wind and sea into a honeycomb of excellent holds. No roads or paths led to the tower, there was no defensive wall, gate, or guards; just ragged scrub that crept across the broad sweep of land before vanishing into a valley fringed with stunted, grey leafed trees. Cloud-dusted mountains climbed to the sky in the north and east. To the south, the land dropped away to rocky cliffs. The sea flooded the west where the ring of greened stones stood, half buried in the sand and bathed in glittering spray.

It would have been a sweet spot to idle away a few hours, maybe years, if a body was inclined to peace and simple, sea-scrubbed beauty. To my eyes the tower's isolation lent itself to murder, the crashing waves perfect for masking screams. The tower door flapped in the breeze; a slow clap mocking my quest or perhaps applauding the attempt.

I hadn't noticed how hot it was outside until, quiet as a shadow, I slipped into the cool interior of the tower. Sweat dripped from my brow, spattered the smooth, limestone tiles beside the graceless imprint of my wet feet. There was nothing on the ground floor apart from a sand-dusted hall and a spiral staircase leading up into the tower. I headed up, drawn by the sweet perfume of human, cinnamon, and star steel.

***

She was standing with her back to the stairs. Her voluminous, red gown almost filled the empty tower room. Her veil drifted, revealing dark curls but nothing of the face beneath. As she turned I felt her gaze fall upon me.

"You took your time," she said.

"Yeah. Sorry to keep you waiting."

I drew my blades.

The urge to kill her vanished with the ringing echo of her laughter. My vision blurred as the Eldest's compulsion spell shattered, and I felt a cloud lift from my mind. "I swear I will never use a compulsion spell again as long as I live." My head began to ache. The contrast between the Mage's scarlet gown and the stark white walls was acutely painful. The cloud returned. My blades felt like strangers in my hands and I sheathed them without meaning to. "You can knock that shit off."

"No. I can't. Too much is at stake, and you are too unpredictable to stand there waving steel." Like the Eldest, she spoke softly, and like the old crow, her words held weight. "And before you get all sulky, don't. We're on the same side."

"I'm not on any side but my own. But go on, fustilugs, tell me your tale."

"I knew this would be difficult. The first time I laid eyes on you, I knew you wouldn't make this easy. Listen and you might learn something." A leaf sized piece of her gown fluttered out of the window.

"What? First time? This is the first time, now, today." *Why are they always insane?*

"It isn't, and you know it."

"I've forgotten a lot over the years, but I would remember if I'd met you— and I haven't."

"Do you remember the prophesy I wrote?"

"Which one? I've heard a lot. Magic swords, ancient heroes— there are a *lot* about heroes. Some come fully formed, but most start out as shepherds or pot boys, but whichever form they take, there are a lot of them. Oh, ah, yes— there was one I heard about a mystical pair of socks that they said had been woven from the golden beard hair of a blessed hermit— that wasn't yours, was it? I only ask because the symbolic meaning always evaded me."

I sensed that she narrowed her eyes. "Are you mocking me?"

"I wouldn't—" And then it hit me. "You're Halda, the Red Witch."

She swept her arms wide and bowed, like an actor accepting applause. I recalled the time Tobias had told me about the prophesy and how at the time it had sent a shiver down my spine to think that one of the great Mage Lords had seen me from across the span of centuries. And now here we were, at last, face to veil. "You're who Irammus couldn't mention."

"Yes. I arranged it so that when you found the little piss-weevil, this shard would wake."

"This shard would what? I don't understand what you mean."

She tossed her head. I felt the eye-roll which accompanied it. "Really?"

"Aye. You must forgive me, but when I was a youth I skipped metaphysical studies in favor of pleasuring myself ragged."

"You're just like..." She sighed. "Like I imagined you would be."

"Think about me a lot then?"

"Every day."

I allowed myself a grin, leaned against the wall and folded my arms. So, she was Halda the Red Witch, so what? She didn't impress me. I was a powerful sorcerer in my own right and a fearsome Guild Blade. I was . . . *entirely out of my depth bantering with a legend.* I glanced out of the window, half expecting to see the Hammer of the North paddling in the surf, but all I saw were waves, rolling silver on the beach. "So, where are we?"

"Nowhere." More pieces of her gown tore free and fluttered away.

"Come again?"

"This place isn't real. It's a shard; the memory of a place." She pointed a gloved finger at her chest. "This is a shard; a sliver of my personality."

"I've never heard of that kind of magic."

"Because unlike self-pleasure, I am the only one who has ever done it." Another shred of her gown, *of her,* floated away into nothing. "This shard and this place only came into being when you slew Irammus. If you hadn't found him, if you hadn't killed him, we wouldn't be having this conversation. Do you understand?"

I laughed. "Fuck no. A few days ago I was fighting for my life in an arena. Now you are telling me things that sound like my life's path has been set out before I was born. No, I don't understand. I mean, how did you know that I'd kill him?"

"Because I laid a powerful geas on him, on his keep, and on the very air of the place. Don't feel bad, neither of you could have resisted my will."

"That's harsh. Why not just leave a note? Let Irammus live out his years somewhere less hellish?"

"Because sometimes only death pays the bill, and I assure you, the Serpent deserved what he got; indeed he was lucky that I let him live long enough to atone for his sins." More of the gown drifted away.

"Am I talking to a ghost?"

"There are no such things as ghosts."

"Oh, yes there are."

"No. There aren't. There are just gullible lackwits."

"Have it your way."

"Now you're getting it. I broke myself. I became nothing, to ensure we had a chance of undoing the terrible wrong that had been done." She leaned against the window, shafts of sunslight stabbed through the red gown. "I scried, read every sign, and planned for as many possibilities as I could envisage." She laughed, it was a dry, hollow sound. "So many pieces of me will never be found, but even so, it was not a waste because you found your way here in this fleeting moment and this impossible place."

"Did I find my way here or did you lead me here? I've always felt that I was Fate's pawn, but I was wrong, wasn't I? I was your pawn."

"No. And I've already told you, don't sulk. You are not a pawn. The fate of millions rests in your hands."

"No. Let me stop you right there." I backed towards the stairs, quite certain that I would throw myself down them if she tried to put the 'fluence on me again. "This is too much. I'm just a half-thoasa, half human, fucking thief. You can't lay all that 'fate of millions' at my feet. I won't have it. I won't. None of this is my fault."

"No, it isn't. It is mine, the Annurashi...Shallunsard. It is not your fault, child. But you are the only one capable of saving everything. Only you are attuned to the power of the stars."

"Fuck off." I laughed so hard that I almost puked. "You had me going then, right until the 'power of the stars'. I mean, really? I'm cringing for you. Is that the best you could come up with? Have you never read a story? Heard a myth?"

The shard put both not-hands on its hips. "Whoa. Now you just shut your yap hole a minute or by the gods I'll fucking slap you from one end of this beach to the other. And yes, for your information, I was very well read. There's a shard of me in the Great Library of Valen, just in case you'd decided to pick up a quill instead of a fucking sword. What a waste that was, eh?"

"A quill? Do I look like a...a scholar?"

"No. but you could have been."

"Really? I was born in a sewer."

"Oh, please. Enough of the self-pity. You must go back to the Annurashi, find the gate that will take you to Old Valen, and slay Shallunsard. Don't let them imprison him this time." The shard swooped towards me and floated a few inches in front of my face.

I raised my hands. "Sorry to disappoint, but there isn't a gate to Old Valen. There's just the one that brought me here. All the others are dead."

"It isn't dead it was just dormant. It will wake now. If you do not change the past, everything will have been for nothing. You will die. The world will die. Your friends will die."

I stepped back. "My friends are already dead. Shallunsard put their heads on spikes."

"You can save them."

"Your scrying was wasted. You got it wrong. I'm not the person you think I am. I wish I was; it would be nice to have that power, but everything I touch, I mean *everything,* turns to shit."

A strong gust of wind tore at the shard, ripped away her veil, revealing nothing. What was left of the animated gown sniggered.

"What's so funny?"

"Your face. Now go and kill Shallunsard. You know it's the right thing to do."

"I beg Your Ladyship's pardon, but you can't just demand I kill a demon who has had the better of me two of the three times we've met. Also, that small detail of returning to the Annurashi? You're probably not aware, given as how you're nothing but a rather garish and slightly-too-literal-for-my-taste fucking gown, but the insane, god crone Eldest of the Annurashi has already slain her entire brood. If I go back without having slotted you, she'll kill me before I get anywhere near any gate to Old Valen."

"You have to go back, no matter what. This place has served its purpose; it will soon cease to exist. If you stay, you'll die."

"If I go, I'll die."

"I would feel sorry for you, but as you've just so eloquently pointed out, I'm just a fucking gown."

"Why don't you do it? You're clearly powerful, even for a dress. Why don't you get the rest of yourself together and go settle her account?"

"You're lucky that this is one of the nicer pieces of my personality." There was something familiar about her voice but as so often happened these days, my memory failed to recall what. "All of my shards are stuck where they are and have been since I split myself. It was the only way I could do what I have done. You are the only being who can go back, who has a chance of slaying Shallunsard before the Annurashi imprison him."

"Can't you send me to Old Valen from here?"

The phantasm froze and slapped its forehead. "Of course!"

"Really?"

It gave a hard stare, no mean trick for something without a face. "No. For fuck's sake." The memory of thunder rumbled in the unreal distance. The light of the perfect suns began to wane. "I might not be the greatest Mage Lord who has ever lived— well, I probably am, but what is certain is that I'm not a lackwit. If there were a way to send you back from here, I would have done it. The only way to then, is through the gate, which the Annurashi stole and took to their lair."

"Ah yes, about their lair."

"What?"

"It's got a bit of a dragon problem. The lair might not be there when I get back."

"It's a risk you'll have to take."

"That's very generous of you."

The gown began to fade. "You have no idea. Now go while you're able and good luck. I hope and pray you can save us."

I've never had much use for prayer, and as my dear old mother used to say, 'hope is for fools'.

Chapter Seventeen

S oaking wet and freezing cold I stepped from the angle gate into the waiting arms of the Eldest. I say *arms*, but it was actually just her hand, with which she grabbed me by the face.

"Why haven't you slain the last renegade?" she asked in that unnaturally calm way that insane evil bastards speak when they are murderously angry. "It was a simple request, why didn't you do it?"

"See washent yere."

The crone frowned and slammed me against one of the stones. My jaw popped. She drifted around the circle, glaring at me like a malevolent raisin. "Did you say, 'she'?"

"What? No. I said 'they'." *Shit, shit, shit.* "They left a decoy, a phantasm of sorts, but I found out where they really are."

"How do you know where they went?"

That's a very good question. My mind was momentary, dangerously blank. I stood up, dusted myself down and tried to keep her in sight as she stalked me around the stones. It was night; the sky was dark, depthless grey, storm-laden. I couldn't see any dragons, only snow crashing against the ward in explosive plumes, but that didn't mean they weren't out there somewhere, waiting for another, better opportunity to attack.

"I twisted the phantasm's metaphysical arm and it told me where he'd gone." I wasn't sure if it mattered that she knew the last renegade was Halda, but as Mother was fond of saying, 'when in doubt, lie'. "Apparently it was a shard of the original personality or something? I didn't understand much of its prattle." I shrugged. "Oh. You don't mind me lifting the odd bit of chink while I'm inhuming these coves, do you?" I affected the air of a jut-jawed bravo, rough enough to convince her that her godly machinations were beyond a simple cove like me. Her pucker tight features relaxed as her hubris got the better of her suspicion.

"I don't mind in the slightest, child. Take all that they have, fill your pockets with the profits of their treachery. Strip their bones bare."

"Thank you kindly, dame." I guessed she meant that literally. I smiled innocently and with a measure of enthusiasm I did not feel. The ground continued to shift beneath me; the rules of the game changing with every hand. The Eldest's tiny dragons, their bellies fat from their feast of Darzka's vitals, crawled amongst the dead Annurashi who still lay where they had fallen. The Eldest cooed to the nearest creature, which flew to her shoulder and coiled its whip-like tail around her neck. She appeared to have lost interest in me, which was all to the good, as I set about finding the gate that would apparently take me to Old Valen.

Just as Halda's shard said, I could hear the gate. I stood a moment, pretended to adjust my maille while I tried to peel the low hum from the distant roar of the storm. Muttering, the Eldest pottered through the wreckage and clucked over the dead like a sorrowful grandmother lamenting the loss of loved ones, proving the adage that looks can be deceptive.

It took me less than an hour to find the newly awakened gate. It had six uprights, all of which were about as tall as me, give or take. They were slender and at some point, had been exposed to a high temperature, giving them a flamed finish and making them rough to the touch. I sought the keystone somewhere amongst them. Until now it had never occurred to me that I alone had this ability or how I'd come by it, but I'd bet a sack of gold that Halda knew.

"What was that?" Eldest called.

"I didn't say anything." I'd thought something, but she couldn't read my mind, could she? I put my hands on the fourth stone. It tingled; my palm itched. I looked up to see the Eldest make a claw hand gesture at a pile of flesh and bones, a look on her face that was part curious, part amused, and entirely wicked. The bits and pieces quivered, slid together, and resolved themselves into something roughly approximating a biped made out of mangled body parts. The Eldest cast her gaze about the carpet of fleshy detritus and more mounds of parts began to jerk and spasm and pull together. I turned the stone.

"A moment, Breed." I stopped, fixed in place by her power as the air folded in upon itself within the gate, and a slice was cut into this grim reality. The blackness of the Void was tantalizingly close, I could almost taste it but frustratingly, couldn't move an inch towards it.

"Shouldn't I go slay the renegade?"

"No, child. I've changed my mind. Halda— it is Halda, isn't it?"

I chose silence, which was answer enough.

She smiled. "She is difficult. More treacherous than the others. More cunning."

"You mustn't worry about me, dame. I can handle this Halda person," I said while straining with every fiber of my being to move, to at least fall towards the gate. It was of no use. My limbs would not obey me. Meanwhile, more golems were forming and rising from their graves.

"I'm sure you can, child. That is a battle I would like to see." She apported beside me. "But I no longer need your unpredictability or your skill at finding gates. I just need to send something through that can rip her to pieces, which won't be destroyed by the scathing power of the Void."

"That's me. I'm fine in the Void; it's like a second home."

"Yes, I know and that is a mystery I would love to unravel. Alas, I cannot send something with a mind that can be manipulated by the witch, something she could send back to harm me." I heard a blade slide from a sheath.

"Honestly, I barely have a thought in my head worth manipulating." I caught the warning flash of steel out of the corner of my eye.

"Yes, child, I know."

"You murderous old fuck."

"Yes, child, I am."

In an instant, the air grew heavy with the smell of storm born petrichor. I closed my eyes as lightning flashed and smashed the Eldest off the platform. Her knife flew from her hand. I stumbled, free from her power. Rowan was standing in the doorway, spikes of wildfire coruscating around her.

"Go!" she shouted needlessly, as I was already diving through the gate.

***

I arrived on the other side, scrambled to the keystone, and turned it in case any of the Eldest's latest creations decided to follow me through. I was panicking unnecessarily. The stone didn't move, the rift remained closed, and the unwholesome conglomerations of animated body parts did not march from the Void. I lay in the dust and took a moment to catch my breath. Above me was a stone slab set at a jaunty angle upon six columns. "Thanks Rowan." Beyond the stones a faint rind of violet hung over tent ridges and framed the listless silhouettes of pennants and tattered battle standards. I'd been here before, amid the rubble of a once great city. I was in Old Valen, seven hundred years earlier than my first visit.

"You shouldn't be in there." The cove who spoke had a tray of oddments slung around his neck and a small wooden chest strapped to his back.

"You've got that right, friend."

He peered at me from behind a fringe of lank grey hair. "Which banner are you with?"

"That is a very good question. Not the best I've been asked today, mind you, but it has its merits." I stood up. My back complained, as did my right knee. "Death by a thousand sprains."

"Ah. I have just the thing you need, my thoasan friend."

"Close enough."

The fellow set his cap back on his head and sorted through his tray of charms. Around us, the camp was beginning to wake. The air bubbled with coughs and farts and rang with the clatter of pans and plate armor. It was a familiar liturgy, one I'd never been particularly fond of.

"What have you got there?" I asked as I stepped under the stone-roofed angle gate that would at a push, make do as a bier for a hero.

The peddler held up a single, blue bead threaded on a silver chain. "Only the finest charm against the pain of arthritics this side of the Great Ocean."

"So, they have better charms in Shen, is that what you're saying?"

"Er…"

"How much?"

"Two copper druk. What's so funny? That's a fair price."

"I'm sure it is. I know a dragon called Druk is all."

The peddler gave a toothless grin. "Do you now? Invite it to Valen. We could use a dragon this day."

I fished the tarnished, Black Penny coins from my pocket and tossed them on the tray. "He was just a small dragon. Now, his mother, she's quite something."

"Ah. You're a storyteller, eh?" His face darkened. "You give me silver? Are we in such bad shape that you're paying…ten times what I asked?"

I took the bead, stuffed it into my shirt. It felt warm to the touch. "Today is not a day to bargain for good fortune. Today is a day to pay what it's worth, or near enough, eh?"

The fellow's hand swept over the tray of beads and the coins vanished. He tugged his cap down over his eyes, either in respect or to hide his amusement. "Indeed, one cannot put a price on good luck. And mind how you go. They say funny things happen to folk who loiter among the sorcerer stones."

"I'll bear that in mind." I waved him off, watched him clamber over tent ropes while trying to balance the chest on his back and the tray on his chest. He didn't look like a starveling, but he was wearing odd boots and a patched doublet; a true reflection of the efficacy of his charms.

One thing was certain; his luck would change today one way or the other. *You're talking to a corpse walking amongst the dead-who-don't-know-it.* Hundreds, perhaps thousands would die today, even if I was successful and slew Shallunsard. With that joyous prospect rooted firmly in my mind, I set off in search of the Hammer of the North— for wherever he was, the demon was sure to follow.

I passed regiments of humans, thoasa, arrachid, and amphibane. Those who noticed me at all regarded the aged, half warspawn, half human with disinterest, some even shook their head in pity which, I must confess, wounded as much as a blade. I hated my inadequacy and wanted to explain to anyone who made eye-contact for more than a second that I hadn't always been the decrepit husk they saw before them. I wanted to explain that, not only was I a powerful sorcerer, but I had also been a Guild Blade, a deadly and, some might say, romantic figure that people might envy if not entirely respect. But I refrained because that would make me sound like a boorish old twat, which was exactly the kind of person who would think such an explanation was warranted.

My thoughts drifted from the past to the present as I wandered, and I wondered if the many paths I had taken in my life had all been leading to this time and place. I didn't like that idea. That thought dogged my every step as I passed through the tents that had colonized the ruins of the first Valen like fungus spores on a dead tree. Had I been entirely human I might have lamented the pain in my back and knee, the destruction of what had until recently been a great city, the epic scope of the grave pits, and the amount of dead still to be buried. But I wasn't anywhere near human and never would be. What struck me was that all around me warspawn of every stripe were gearing up for war, shoulder to shoulder with humans.

I know I was only seeing the narrowest slice of the cake; knew that war and necessity make strange bedfellows, but the easy camaraderie on the dawn of this most bloody and inglorious day was good to see— even if it wouldn't last. I alone knew what went wrong, what lies and misinformation had been spread to assuage the fears of the Annurashi and the Mage Lords. I also knew something else. That I could change it. The thought made my head spin. Not for the first time, I wished that I was forty years younger and somewhere far from here.

I entered an open plaza that was now packed with tents. A giant statue that had once dominated the square now reclined in pieces, a puzzle in stone I was not inclined to solve. The statue's legs were still attached to the plinth and framed a view of red tents on the far side of the plaza. The tents had been erected in the exposed guts of what had been a magnificent, columned building before someone had burned it to the ground. A scrapling child sat upon the fallen torso of the statue, eating a piece of bread and staring sullenly down the gullet of my glance.

"Good day, to you, young fellow." I smiled at the child.

"Fuck off, lizard," the brat shouted, before sliding down the giant's backside and running off laughing. I leaped onto the plinth and growled, which made the impling screech with fearful delight before he disappeared into the canvas city. It was a relief to know that even in the age of heroes, little shits were still little shits.

From my vantage I could see the fear wrought sigil of war engraved on every pensive face that dared the chill air. Lovers lied to each other, the too young and too old gazed wet-eyed at kin preparing to join their units. Every cull was consciously, painfully aware of every breath. Every moment that would normally pass without the slightest attention being paid to it was sacred. Every precious second shone like gold in the breaking dawn.

I made for the red tents, where purposeful activity was concentrated. When I got there I saw that the guards posted on the steps of the hollowed-out building showed no signs of being alarmed by the shouting and screaming coming from somewhere within the tents.

"Don't be a cunt, Ruben!" A woman yelled; the pitch of her voice painfully sharp.

"Halda, please—"

"—and you can shut your yap-hole."

"Please put that down, it's very valuable…"

Something smashed.

"That was just petty…"

Something else smashed.

And on it went. I approached the steps, nodded to an armored amphibane and her arrachid companion, who were leaning on their halberds and trying not to look like they were paying attention to the raging argument. They were so engrossed that I made it up six steps before they had the wit to stop and question me.

"Just a minute." The arrachid sprang up beside me. "What's the watchword?"

I folded my arms. "I'm not sure I should tell you."

"Eh?" She looked at the amphibane, giving me time to prepare a compulsion spell. However, before I could cast it, there was a flash, and someone appeared on the steps. She smelled of fire and incense, hot iron, blood, and magic; but the clothes and the veil were enough to tell me I was meeting the Red Witch for the first time—*for her*.

"Halda—" was all I managed before she gestured towards me.

Chapter Eighteen

"Get out of my fucking way," she yelled, and a blast of air punched me in the chest. I stumbled back, my knee gave way and I fell. The mage apported mid-stride. Being somewhat nimbler than either of us, the arrachid leaped out of the way to the top of a broken column.

"Halda! Wait. Please, love." The thoasa charging after the Witch didn't look like the kind of cove who was given to calling people 'love,' but the words were still on his lips when he ran to the top of the steps and scanned the tents for Halda. He was scarlet and blue and almost seven feet tall. Copper bands shone amongst his crimson hair spines, and he wore mismatched bronze armor, more mended than whole. His seven-toed feet were bare. At some time in the past, his tail had been broken and it kinked to the right. There were scars, but he was a fighter; there were always scars. The last time I'd seen him he'd looked less impressive for being dead and also less feckless and distraught, but the Hammer's hammer hadn't changed.

"Oh, shit. Are you all right, Elder?" He had a honey and moss scent signature, with a touch of hobnail and stone, something else I hadn't known because a thoasa's scent signature doesn't linger long after death.

I looked around for this 'Elder'— and then realized he was talking to me.

"I was until a Mage Lord knocked me on my backside." *The same one who sent me here in the first place.* In a single bound he was beside me, casting fretful glances across the sea of tents as he picked me up. My knee creaked to lend voracity to the title he'd bestowed upon me.

"You mustn't think badly of Halda. She's not been herself lately."

"Who's she been, the avatar of pissed off?"

"What? Oh, aye. She does have a bit of a temper, but her heart's in the right place." He grinned sheepishly. "I should know; I listen to it every night." He stood a moment in smiling contemplation then shook his head, adopted a more sober mien. "It er, helps me sleep." He sat on the steps and rubbed his eyes. As my knee was paining me, I joined him. "I don't sleep well; too much stuff on my mind, you know?"

I shook my head. "No, my friend. I sleep like the dead." *Quite literally sometimes.* "Are you and her... you know?" I made the universal hand gesture for 'lovers'.

His smile met my own. "She's quite something, you know? She can fight infernals all day and then fall into bed and straight off to sleep." He clapped his hands. "Just like a baby. Like she hasn't got a care in the world." Another, soppy smile crept across his scarred muzzle. "She's beautiful when she's asleep. She's beautiful when she's awake, mind, but she looks *peaceful* when she's asleep."

"I'll have to take your word for it on account of the veils and all. Why is she in such a mood?"

"We argued." He spat in the dirt and put his elbows on his knees like a great, sulking child. "She most often knows best, I heed her counsel more than that of any other."

"But not today?"

"No."

He had the air of someone who wanted to talk, and I was keen to listen. He was the Hammer of the North, who wouldn't want to listen to a legend? He rubbed the spit into the dirt with his heel. Although similar in shape, side by side, his feet were twice the size of mine. "This goes no further?"

"You have my word, son."

"She wanted us to leave. To flee this fight. She says no matter the outcome we will lose. It's that Annurashi, Rowan. They talked and ever since, Halda's been in a mood. Between you and me they make my flesh crawl."

"I agree, and your woman's most likely right."

He nodded. "She often is. But leaving would still be wrong."

"Are you sure? Don't look like that; it's a reasonable question."

An earnest expression muscled its way onto a face not fashioned to show emotions beyond rage and base pleasure. It was a cruel and arrogant omission on behalf of the Mage Lords but one that most thoasa managed to overcome with strength of character.

"I can no more leave these people than I can leave my shadow. This is where we will stand or fall. These people cannot flee, and even if they could, the demons would keep coming. They will not stop unless we stop them."

"Yes, but if you all ran, it might take the demon horde a long time to find you. Long enough perhaps for a thoasa to live a full and happy life." *And not fight battles for ungrateful Mage Lords and mad gods.*

He smiled one of those stupid, resigned smiles that encompassed an acre of meaning. "It would not be a happy life."

"Has anyone ever told you, you're very sentimental for a thoasa? Nice hammer by the way. I used to have one just like it."

"Yes, they have, and no, you didn't." His smile was patronizing but not unkind. "Halda made it for me. Mage Lords must craft something out of star steel; like a magician's 'prentice piece. They say they put a piece of themselves into whatever it is that they make to give life to their magic." He untied the loop of leather holding it in place and held it in the light. "If you turn the shaft, like so." He slowly turned the hammer. "The pattern in the star steel looks like a dragon prowling towards the head."

"Fuck me." I couldn't believe it.

"What's wrong?"

What was wrong was that I'd never cared to examine it closely. I'd never noticed the subtle pattern of the star steel that the Red Witch had folded into the shaft, which when it was turned in the light, looked like a ghostly dragon. I'd only ever cared about its power, and how I could use it. "Nothing. It's just…very beautiful. She must love you very much."

He shrugged away, as coyly as a giant made of muscle and claws covered in armor could. "I don't know. Sometimes I think she hates me. She's got a wicked tongue on her, not to mention the fire and lightning. See this?" He pointed to a scar on his bicep.

"If I hadn't put my arm in the way she would have taken my face off."

"Some people show their love in funny ways. My Mother cared enough about me to put a bounty on my head."

"That is…an unusual display of affection. When Halda attacked me she was furious."

"Aye, well my mother is a complicated cove. I've never really understood her, to be honest."

"I'm sorry."

"Don't be. I'm not."

A horn blared and was answered by a dozen more. The blasts ranged near and far, spreading a net of sound across the embattled city. The Hammer stood up, shadowed out the sunlight filtering through the fog of dawn and campfire smoke. "I've got to find her. You're a warrior?"

"What gave it away? Was it the maille or the two swords?" I thought he was going to ask me to help him look for her.

"Only, the fight will be hard today. You should stay in camp."

"I'd love to, but there's a demon with my name on it."

The gentle smile was replaced by a wolfish grin. His scent signature changed, became steel and bone. "Aye, there's one for me too. A really fucking big one." He slung the hammer— *our* hammer, over his shoulder, tied it in place, and offered me a hand. I took it, and to my credit, resisted the urge to cut the purse that was swinging from his belt like a fat bollock.

"Thanks, son."

"The camp will need defending. Strong warspawn with wit and strength and—"

I drew the sword I'd bartered from Volund, light lit along the edge of the star steel blade. "This isn't my first battle, and I don't intend for it to be my last. My place is on the battlefield." *Right behind you.*

A sudden burst of laughter rose from deep in his gut bag. It was a good sound. He'd never been my hero, I don't go in for all that nonsense, but he was a hero to many, so I was glad that the Hammer of the North wasn't a prick.

"Farewell, Elder—"

"For fuck's sake, my name is Breed. All this 'Elder' bollocks is making me feel old."

"I thought it was a polite form of address."

"Aye, well polite isn't all it's made out to be. I know some proper bastards who are insufferably polite and some wonderful coves who have the manners of swine." The image of Bolin the Boar came to mind.

"Fair enough. Well then, *Breed*. Farewell. If you need a sword mate, I fight under the banner of the Crimson Vanguard."

"I'll bear that in mind."

The Hammer nodded, flicked out his bifurcated tongue and tasted the air. I guessed he was searching for Halda, trying to unpick the knot of smells roiled up in the plaza and find the thread of her scent. When he was sure of a direction his nostrils flared and he made to head off.

"Oi, Hammer, hold up."

"What is it, Eld— Breed?"

I sheathed my blade and fished the blue bead necklace from my pocket. "I have something for you. It's for luck. I wouldn't put too much faith in it, but you never know, eh?"

He smiled and took my offering. It looked small in his hands, the chain hung between his claws like dew on a spider web, but he deftly fastened it around his neck. "It is a gift well meant, which is luck enough for me. May your gods guard you, and may the suns rise on the morrow in your still living eyes." He musked the air with the smell of blood and stone, moss and steel. Not for the first time I wished I could return the gesture, but I couldn't, so I just waved, unsure if the next time I saw the hero he'd be dead.

The arrachid guard scuttled down from the broken pillar, and the amphibane crept from behind the pile of garbage where she'd been casually earwigging on our conversation. They looked like they were about to ask for the password again when someone else bounded from the red tents. I knew this fellow too; a strapping cove a hand span over six feet, with sky blue eyes, a mane of wavy golden hair, and a pearl white smile which he flashed upon seeing me and the guards. The last time I'd seen him looking like this had been in a painting in the Hall of Heroes in New Valen. They'd lied then, called him the Hammer of the North, but I knew him by a different name.

"I say." Ruben's gaze swept across the three of us like suns light. "Did any of you happ—"

I punched him in the face. My old hand bones made some interesting crunching noises, but I'm quite the expert at fisticuffs and hit him square, spreading the load across the whole of my gavel. He staggered, gazed a moment in stunned surprise before the blood began to pour from his nose. Both hands flew to his face. "What the…Who the hell are you?" he mumbled as he stumbled away, trying to put distance between us while staunching the flow. "Oh, for…This doublet is Shen silk…It's bloody ruined…"

The two guards leveled their weapons at me unsure. I raised my hands. "Before this gets unnecessary, this tosspot has it coming."

"I What? I do not!"

"Yeah, well, you will."

"All right." The amphibane got between us. "Tell that to the magisters." She reached towards me.

"And he doesn't like warspawn. Doesn't think we're good enough." *To have a hero of our own. That's why you're going to lie about the Hammer, isn't it, you prick?* The guards pulled up, shared a questioning look before withdrawing.

"That is an outrageous claim. One of my closest comrades is a warspawn. All know this."

"So you fight with the Hammer. Who else?"

"What?"

"How many other warspawn do you know personally, Ruben, or is he the exception?"

He blushed. "Don't be ridiculous. I know plenty of warspawn."

"Name one. Name him, what's the Hammer called?"

"I…" He stammered. "I don't have to answer to you— who the hell are you anyway? And what are you, come to that? You're no thoasa. In fact, you don't look like a warspawn at all." He swiped his face with the back of his hand. "You have the stink of the infernal about you."

The guards shuffled uneasily.

"Oh, fuck off. And you two don't listen to him; he's just trying to deflect."

"I am not, *demon*."

That was one barb too many coming from this soon-to-be traitor. "That's it." I took a step towards him. He swept his blade from its scabbard, a murderous gleam lit in his eye.

"All right, all right. That's enough," said the arrachid as she got between us, one leg holding me off, another holding Ruben at bay. "I don't care who either of you are. With respect, citizens, the enemy is out there. Go fight them, not each other."

Fuming, Ruben slammed his sword back in its scabbard. "So help me if I ever lay eyes on you again..." Implied threat made, he stormed back towards the red tents.

"Seriously. He's a proper prick."

"We've got eyes," said the amphibane. "But you can't go around antagonizing the Hammer's bannerman. Now go on, be on your way."

I tipped them a nod and ran off into the tent city, just to prove I still could, until I was out of sight, at which point I slowed down and caught my breath. My knee was aching, and my knuckles had started to swell, but it was worth it to have punched that pitcher-faced nutlouse in the snotbox. Unless of course, I managed to swerve Fate from its course, then my assault on Ruben would be nothing more than the attack of an aged lunatic.

Unless. Such a small, pebble of a word upon which a mountain, nay, a world, balanced. Why I couldn't have come to this point when I was nineteen and full of vigor was a rum jest, but there it was. I hobbled towards the center of activity. On the way there, something small and squalling crawled from beneath a tent flap before me. Entirely unaware of what a momentous day this was, the child quested for the wonders of the world which, apparently, lay within every handful of gutter muck it grabbed and scrutinized. It was about to sample not only the visual, but the oral delights of a fistful of mud when its tousled haired mother burst from the tent in a panic and snatched it from the dirt. After checking for injury, she wiped its paws, and latched it to her grubby breast while casting a warning glare in my direction.

I walked on; the leaden weight of responsibility turned my aching knees to water. drowning in maudlin thoughts, I got caught up with a cohort of troops who were marching in disorderly fashion to their muster point. I didn't know who they were, but according to their chatter they were headed in a battlewards direction, which would suit me well enough and so I stayed with them.

"Get a shift on, will ya?" A youthful amphibane bounded up behind me. As he seemed in a hurry to die, I tried to step aside but the way was too narrow for him to pass. "Holy Eye! What's wrong with you, are you lost? ARE YOU DEAF?" the amphibane shouted in my face. "I said, get a shift on, not stand still." He squeezed past me, shaking his head.

"I'm doing all this to save pukelings like that?" I asked myself, as the cocky halberdier bounded down the narrow, canvas alleyway. "I'm not entirely sure it's worth it."

But here I was. I could still walk away, build a new, albeit short life, watch the Hammer be erased from history and kinchin coves born with tentacles drowned or mutilated at birth. Or, I could try to slay Shallunsard. But did these coves deserve saving, and who was I to make that decision? At heart I was a thief and a killer was I really in any position to be the moral arbiter of an age? And as for the Hammer, he didn't strike me as someone who would give a shit whether he was remembered or not. Although he did strike me as someone who wanted Shallunsard stopped. Just thinking about it made my brain hurt. To distract myself I decided to teach the pukeling amphibane a lesson. Because warspawn weren't supposed to be able to use magic, I surreptitiously cast a knot of air about his feet and caught him mid-leap. He stumbled, fumbled his halberd and went sprawling in the dirt, ripping a hole in a tent as he tumbled. Petty, I know, but it was also amusing on a day short of laughs.

"What are you doing, you clumsy fuck?" A thoasa bounded past me, grabbed the amphibane by the back of his padded jack, and stood him on his flippers— much to the amusement of his comrades.

I gripped the hilt of Volund's sword. The star steel within the blade answered my touch, made my palm tingle. The alley widened. Ahead of the rough crew of thoasas, amphibanes, and humans a phalanx of arrachids encased in plate armor, hammered the ground with their steel-shod claws. Ogren war machines followed behind us, dragged by uxatzi the size of houses, their horns hung with banners. Drums boomed and beat out the marching time for the army as it formed up outside of the ruined city walls.

I was swept along in the flood of thousands gearing up for war. The thoasa who'd picked up the halberdier was counting the crew I'd fallen in with through the gate. He stopped me as I passed him.

"Are you lost?"

"Still no. And I'm not deaf either, and I know the camp needs defending, but my place is out there, fighting demons, something I've done for many more years than you've been alive."

"Easy, there." He raised his hands. A smile creased his grey and black marbled face. "I was just going to say that if you're not lost, you're welcome to fight with this crew, but we don't take no snivelers or runners, so if you're inclined to either, best step out of line now."

I gave him a dead-eyed stare.

"All right, all right. Save your ire for the demons."

Dawn broke clear over Old Valen. The suns' light rebounded off a sea of armor and weapons raised like wave points. A thousand drums hammered thunder into the sinews of the morning as regiment after regiment formed up outside of the city's walls. I'm not a cove to be moved by martial pomp and all that bollocks but on this rare day, even I had to admit it was an impressive gathering.

And then I saw Shallunsard's army in all its infernal glory. As mighty as the mortal force was, I struggled to conceive that it was a match for the renegade Annurashi and his horde. Clouds of winged things flocked over the tumultuous ranks of demons and painted terror on the sky in dark and darting murmurations. The earth rumbled, and fissures raced across the ground from which crawled all the horrors of the underworld.

"I'm not sure I can do this."

Chapter Nineteen

"**O**i! where do you think you're going?" The thoasan lieutenant barred my way with his halberd.

"To indulge in a pre-fight shit. Is that all right?"

He gave a crack-toothed grin. "No one's gonna mind if you shit yourself. Remember what I said about runners?"

"Remember what I said about fighting demons before you were born?"

"Just fall in, Tailless."

My initial panic was subsumed by irritation at the young cull's presumption, but I fell back in line behind the banner of the 4th Murdoon Rangers. When we were outside of the walls, our regiment split left. A company of arrachids and horse-mounted humans charged past and raced to the distant flank where dozens of others were waiting. A skinny human standing beside me began to choke on the dust cloud they'd raised.

"Steady on now." I slapped his back. "You don't want to cheat the butcher now, do you?"

He stopped coughing and wiped the snot from his lank mustaches while casting a rueful glance at the gloomy horizon. "Better to choke to death than getting torn apart by a demon."

"You won't get torn apart by a demon," I said with confidence.

He brightened like a drowning man who'd just been thrown a rope. "How d'you reckon that then?"

"I've seen it all before, my friend. No, you'll most likely go down in the initial charge and be stomped to death by your comrades." I leaned in. "You know what thoasa are like when their blood's up." I mimed great, stomping claws with my hands to illustrate my words.

He paled and nodded. "I do. They're really fierce and quite determined once they get going."

"Exactly. And if you survive the initial charge, you'll most likely be taken down by a swarm of spew maggots or ripped to shreds by those kirujo before you even get within spear-thrust of a demon."

"What the fuck's a kirujo?"

"See them winged horrors flapping about over there by that village?" I pointed out a cloud of kirujo gathering like gnats on the right flank of the infernal mass. "I believe the demons call them, 'flying knives' on account of their talons, which can tear through imperial plate like it's paper." He looked at the studded leather jerkin he was wearing and swallowed. Warming to my subject, as old folk with too much knowledge crammed in their noggin often do, I continued despite his wilting expression. "Now, if by some miracle you do survive long enough to come up against an actual demon, it'll most likely bite you, then infect you with a poison that will turn your guts to putrefying liquid while its chewing your face off. Then if you're really unlucky you'll come back as one of the restless dead and murder your friends."

He did not return my comradely smile. He gripped the hilt of his sword like he was trying to strangle it. "That isn't going to happen. The Empirifex, the Mage Lords themselves have said that we will triumph this day."

I laughed. "*They* might triumph, old fruit. But you're most likely crow food," I almost said 'because I've seen it. I've seen the bodies piled five-deep in a frozen piece of this field that was so polluted with dead and dark magic it had to be locked away forever.' But that would have ruined his day, and I'm not a monster. "Or not. See how it goes, eh? Maybe you'll get lucky."

"Fuck you, doom-monger. Do you see this?" He jabbed at a badge sewn on his greasy doublet. "These are my colors, and these are my family." He scanned the ranks of the 4th. "We will save each other, the Empirifex, and our country, and then we are going home to our kin." His voice trembled, he set his face in an angry grimace, most likely to stop it falling into tears. I laughed even harder, prompting him to push his way through the ranks to escape my mockery.

'Save our country' the Empirifex? Fucking idiot. As a Guild Blade I was paid to protect Mother's interests and keep her wealthy, much like any soldier fighting for any 'legitimate' noble. But I was under no illusion that I was a hero for doing so, or that I was fighting for a worthy cause or sainted leader. Now, the kings and queens of the Daylight Court had pulled a bit of a swifty on their devoted subjects. They'd made sacred the act of protecting wealth; made noble— even holy the defense of arbitrary and imaginary boundaries between one gang's turf and another's. It was genius. This was a fight for survival, nothing more. The lying, the betrayal, the sermonizing and finally the theft of glory would come after, unless.

***

I'd forgotten how boring it was waiting for battle to commence. Something I remembered about two hours after taking my place with the 4th. We waited another hour and a half for the remaining regiments and engines of war to trundle out of Old Valen's shattered gates, by which time Shallunsard's force had swelled like a drowned pig to twice its original size.

"Why the fuck didn't they attack him in his keep?" I threw out the comment.

"They did," my nearest comrade, a stout human woman called Gladwyn answered. "Bastard broke out, killed one of the Annurashi, a couple of Mage Lords, and flattened half of Shadowspite Mountain, so they say."

"Swords! Form up behind the shields, either side of the halberds," Lieutenant Ghanul bellowed, his tail swishing in time with his words. "*Shamak*! For fuck's sake. *Nerrush vatun ya*! I said, pick up the pace that means you too smooth-hides. Let me see those skinny, chicken sticks moving. Come on, close up, damn it." His amber gaze fell on me. "Tailless! Why the fuck are you talking when you should be listening to me?"

"Shallunsard," I said. Heads snapped around. Glares rained upon me from all within earshot. Fingers were crossed, amulets clutched. Ghanul spat before making the sign of the horns.

"Do not speak of demons, lest they hear ye, and come a-calling," a one-eyed cove called Wink sagely proclaimed. His words were followed by a chorus of mumbled agreement and more angry glares cast in my direction.

"Am I the only cove who sees the irony of that statement?" I pointed to the far side of the field where a village was burning behind the pole-spitted inhabitants who had been too slow to flee the horde.

"Now, I'm no expert on demons, but I'd say that he and his crew will be paying us all a little visit soon enough, whether I say Shallun-Fucking-Sard or not."

Ghanul stomped over, in an uncanny echo of my earlier mime and stopped inches from my face. "If you're going to stand with the 4th, you will do as you are fucking told and refrain from saying naughty demon names. Now, draw your fucking swords, and form up in front of the halberds. DO YOU UNDERSTAND?"

I wiped my spit washed face. "Yes, Lieutenant, you are to be applauded for your excellent erudition."

He growled. Despite his confident demeanor, his gaze continually tracked to where a tornado of kirujo spiraled in the lightning-veined sky. I found a gap and squeezed into the rearmost of four ranks of sword-swingers who were standing behind two ranks of shields. Behind the swords were five ranks of halberdiers.

"That's the spirit, elderling," said a hulking ogren behind me leaning on his halberd. His single pauldron was tastefully decorated with demon skin, and a necklace of serrated fangs hung around his thickly furred neck. His boiled leather armor was heavily scarred, and yet he had the air of a cove without a care in the world. I was about to tell him that if he liked his own teeth he'd better not call me 'elderling' again when a mighty cheer went up.

"'Bout fucking time they showed up," said the ogren.

All heads turned to a platform before the gates, where a portico had once straddled the main road into the city. It was to this platform that the Mage Lords apported. Having been a dragon mage for almost forty years, I was used to such spectacle, but my neck spines prickled when Darzka appeared, resplendent in midnight blue and silver robes.

"I'd do her in a heartbeat," the ogren's boast was met with laughter and applause.

"She'd break you, Gizzy."

He cupped his nethers. "Can't think of a better way to go."

"Old age!" someone shouted.

Ozbert appeared next. He looked taller than I remembered and was wrapped in a cloak of shadows but his punchworthy mug hadn't changed.

"I don't like that one." Gladwyn elbowed me and chinned towards Ozbert. "Look at him, waving like the battle's already won. Proper wanker."

"He certainly will be." The urge to transform into a dragon and murder him and Darzka was almost too much to resist. *Remember Sketh?* I resisted the impulse. When the visceral heat of my furious gut reaction passed I realized I was judging them for things they hadn't done, which was strange even by my standards. While I pondered those things that I didn't understand, Irammus appeared clad in scintillating, tasteless, emerald green robes with serpents of smoke coiling around his brawny shoulders. Another half dozen Mage Lords followed him. I recognized some from paintings and statuary, others were entirely unknown to me, their names and faces lost in history's fickle maze.

The still heat of a storm weighted the air as the sorcerers of both camps drew down power, ready to turn the field into a blasted, poisoned wasteland and every living thing upon it in to a corpse.

Finally, Halda appeared. She raised her veil just enough to uncover her mouth and promptly threw up.

"I know how she feels," said Gladwyn.

It took a while for the Mage Lord to stop heaving. Ozbert made to help her mid puke but was rebuffed in no uncertain terms. When she was done she wiped her mouth on her veils and raised her hands. Pikemen pushed the crowd away from the podium and made a clearing as big as a town square. The Mage Lords gathered around the Red Witch to lend her their strength, and then the storm broke and lightning ripped the sky asunder.

"Demons!" The tornado of kirujo swarmed and arrowed towards us as Halda did something I'd never seen done before or since and summoned the Hammer of the North and the Hammer's regiment, the Crimson Vanguard.

"Now that is a neat trick," I said. My comrades evidently agreed and split the air with wild cheering. The sight of all the thoasas, ogren, arrachids, and humans appearing in formation around the podium stirred even my cold, old heart as it was no doubt designed to do. The sudden cheer as they appeared was so great that the demon advance faltered, unsure as to the cause. The flying knives broke formation and gusted about, stunned by the wall of noise that hit them. Banners aloft, the scarlet-clad warriors marched through the army and took the center of our force; a red spear of battle-hardened bastards with the Hammer at the head. I craned to see more, Halda rose into the air, her red gown fluttering like wings.

Like the rest of the army and indeed the infernals on the other side of the field, I fell silent as the Vanguard flowed like blood across the plain followed by the rest of the army. A new confidence filled those around me. The acidic, vinegar stink of fear and anxiety vanished. Horns blared, magic bloomed. The Mage Lords were real and, in this moment, bound to a single, unifying cause. Such a gathering would never be seen again, not in any world, let alone Edolis.

But Shallunsard was a long way from being beaten or cowed. The ground beneath his army blackened and turned to ash. The mountains behind the dread gathering bled rivers of lava, and the sky above them sickened to a sulfurous yellow. All life, all hope died where the demon's shadow fell. If nothing else, he was thorough.

"Shields up!" an officer shouted as she rode behind the lines, fighting her terrified mount. Before us, sorcerous lightning blazed across the field and lit up the giant wards that had been set before our army. The Hammer raised his hammer. Halda cast a coruscating bolt of lightning at the weapon. The dragon I'd never noticed when I'd owned it glowed, and the Hammer led the charge, his regiment behind him. Units of fleet-footed arrachids and horse warriors swept along our flanks and were the first to engage ravening packs of six-legged, wolf-headed infernals. My palm burned. I needed to get close to the Hammer, but he was almost half a mile away.

A dozen Mage Lords cast their wards. The powerful backwash of their spell almost knocked me off my feet. The whole army reeled as the air was drawn and bound into great, roiling walls before the front rank of our advancing army. I had to get nearer to the Hammer, but I wasn't keen on apporting into a ward-shrouded mass of moving bodies. I could turn into a dragon, but odds were I'd have to fend off a dozen Mage Lords' attacks because they wouldn't know who or what the fuck I was and would most likely blast first and ask questions later. I could do it the hard way and try to fight my way through to the Hammer, but that would mean battling my way through half an army. "Apportation it is then."

I plotted my route, tried to take into account all the many variables that made apporting into a moving army a really bad idea. In the main, apportation is a forgiving spell; it has to be or else mages would be forever picking blades of grass, and grit out of their feet or worse, becoming one with flying insects and a host of other things you don't want to become melded with, like walls or people. Every sorcerer knew the apocryphal tale of the mage who apported into a solid object, but most often the spell would swerve you around any solid objects in your path. With confidence in this innate benevolence and a deep desire not to have to shove my way through an army, I cast the spell.

Nothing happened.

I sighed. The more spells the Mage Lords cast, the more the air turned to needles and took on a yellowish hue. We moved forwards through it, slowly gathering pace as we went. The Mage Lords were in the vanguard of the army and with their combined power, reduced wave upon wave of spew maggots to pools of rancid, burning slag. Clouds of flying knives descended and were smashed from the air like moths caught in a storm made of blades, ice, acid, and fire.

While the sorcerers' of both sides conducted long range warfare, the two fronts crawled inexorably towards each other. A space open up between the Crimson Vanguard's command unit and the rest of the regiment when something with too many arms and too many heads smashed through the ward and shield wall. The Hammer's weapon blazed turning whatever it was into a roaring fireball. I again tried to apport and this time, it worked.

Chapter Twenty

As I said, apportation is a forgiving spell. Magical wards by their nature are not. It should have occurred to me that both sides would have protection in place to prevent either side getting behind.

But it didn't.

I apported and appeared, not where I'd intended, which was behind the Hammer, but out in the open in the middle of the battlefield between both armies where no wards had yet been placed. My sudden appearance halted both sides' advance, which on a level was flattering. I looked to the Hammer, who looked as surprised to see me as I was to be here. I looked at the infernal horde and Shallunsard, who was staring at me, head canted to the side.

I looked at my feet and sighed. "Fucking, fuckety, fuck." Silence fell like a stone.

I could have tried to make it back to the 'friendly' side. I could have tried apporting again, but that was unlikely to work due to all the bastarding wards. I could have tried to run; equally unlikely to have a positive outcome, because I was old and more than a little bit broken. The awkward silence was followed by mumbling and murmuring from both sides.

I rolled my shoulders, tried to work a few kinks from my neck. I probably couldn't do this, but what the hell, I was here now.

"Shallunsard!" I bellowed. "I challenge you to single combat." I was unlikely to survive whichever path I chose, but in truth, a part of me was relieved that the end of a long and painful journey was in sight. There was a collective intake of breath from the mortals. The infernals appeared confused.

"I was going to do that." I heard the Hammer say. Halda the Red Witch was floating behind him. I couldn't see her face, but I could feel her staring daggers at me.

"Well?" I rested my swords on my shoulders. "I haven't got all day, you—"

"I ACCEPT." The ground trembled, as he strode through the ranks of his troops, but I was used to his delicate tread. My only advantage was that I knew this bastard far better than he knew me. He walked towards me, spectral cloak flying dramatically in the sickened air.

Shallunsard the demon hadn't changed much in seven hundred years. He was perhaps a little taller in the full flush of his power. He had two pairs of sweeping horns reminiscent of the demon thing that Azmorda had become. A mane of black hair hung between his scaled, spike-winged shoulders, and he was clad in shining, silver maille. I noted with interest that he was wielding Dawnslight, a sword I'd break in about seven-hundred years, unless Fate was on my side and I broke it today. He completed his ensemble with a cloak of writhing shadows, which I thought somewhat over-egged the, 'I'm a terrible demon lord' pudding but it was in keeping with the Mage Lords' sartorial crimes.

When he was about twenty feet away he stopped. "Who dares challenge me?"

I glanced over my shoulder at the mortal army. "Er…is that a trick question?"

"What?" He narrowed his perfectly black eyes. "Not them. You. Who are you?" He looked to Halda. She shrugged and folded her arms.

"I'm Breed."

"Have we met?"

"Ah, now, funny you should ask that. No, we haven't, yet. It's very complicated."

"No matter, I will eviscerate you slowly and set your still living head upon my battle standard to scream for eternity." He strode towards me, fists wreathed in blue fire.

"Yeah, you've already done something like that to me, or rather you will," I said as I danced back. "Between you and me, all that evisceration and still living head screaming for...blah, blah, is getting old." I smiled sadly, enjoying the fury building in his craggy face. "I suppose it's like your mother said. You lack imagination."

He stopped. The fire faded. "Who are you?"

"I just told you, keep up. And I understand your anger. I've met your kin." I shuddered. "And I also have a difficult relationship with my own dear progenitor. You're angry, you feel betrayed and you have been, but you're directing your ire at the wrong people. If you want to blame someone, blame the one that made you something that you aren't."

He drew himself up to his full height. His face once again became an impassive mask. His sepulchral scent was unchanging and gave no clue as to his feelings, but for a few seconds I would swear that he considered my words. And then the fire returned.

I aported behind him just before he burned the air where I'd been standing. When I appeared, I ducked, as I guessed he would anticipate the move.

I swung at his legs, scored the tiniest scratch on his greaves as he stepped back and pivoted away. He swung at me. Dawnslight sang scant inches above my head. I apported again, this time half a foot back from where I was standing. As I vanished, I saw Shallunsard begin to turn; ready to cut me down as though I was stupid enough to try the same trick twice and apport behind him. While his back was turned, I leaped forwards and aimed a blow at his neck. He wasn't fooled for long. As he turned around to face me he raised his hand. I saw what was coming and changed my stance from one of attack to defense as he loosed a gout of cold, white fire. Volund's blade deflected the freezing, burning flames.

Up to this point I'd been doing well, so naturally, I had to go and spoil things. I attempted to return the compliment and excoriate the fucker with my own, sorcerous might. My fiery attack rebounded off the ward that he'd had the foresight to cast upon himself, giving him the opportunity to do to me what I had done to him. The fulgid backwash of my failed attack momentarily blinded me, and so I didn't see him apport behind me.

The soft implosion of air was my only warning of where he was. I turned and raised both swords almost accidentally blocking Dawnslight. The impact numbed my arms, I was pushed back. Volund's sword rang furiously and gloriously as though it was enjoying the fight. The other blade shattered like glass. Encouraged, he swung again. I hollowed around the strike. The tip of the blade opened my maille. Steel links split and flew apart like sparks. The mortals raised a cheer about a second before he grabbed me by the throat. *Again*. His fingers burned. I raised my now empty left hand to try and free myself from his grasp before he could run me through or turn my head to charcoal. He saw his sigil in my palm and froze.

"How is this possible?"

"Like I told you, it's complicated." I kicked him in his armored nutsack. He winced, and a few thousand warriors winced with him, and then he slammed me into the ground.

My sword flew from my grasp as the air rushed from my lungs. He took a two-handed grip on Dawnslight. The air thickened around me. Someone, probably the Hammer, shouted a battle cry. The sky above Shallunsard darkened. Lightning coruscated through gravid clouds that were the color of blood.

With a yell the demon brought his blade down. I watched, grimly fascinated as the tip struck a ward that some kind soul had cleverly slid between us. It didn't stop the blow, but slowed it. I squirmed back so rather than stabbing me in the chest, he skewered me in the gut. Before he could pin me to the ground, something big and red and angry vaulted over me, taking Shallunsard with him. Leaving me a bystander to the fight I'd been vain enough to think I could prevent.

The Red Witch drifted above me. "That was a brave effort," she said. I couldn't find the voice to answer her, and then she was gone, rushing to the Hammer's side followed by the Crimson Vanguard.

"Now, Ludorius!" I heard her cry.

I couldn't see who she was talking to through the press of bodies, but I felt the ground heave and walls of earth and air rose to cut Shallunsard off from his horde. Whether they could keep him isolated was another matter, but that was no longer my concern. I had failed. One of the Crimson Vanguard's physickers knelt beside me, began fussing over my wound.

He peeled back my arming jack. "You'll be all right." He grimaced.

"No I won't."

"Lie still."

I shoved him away, sat up and coughed. A combination of blood and the infectious brume of schism magic planted thorns in my throat. The renegade's army swarmed across the field and were met by the Hammer's crew. The Hammer was toe-to-toe with Shallunsard. Ruben, Halda, and another cove were behind him doing all in their power to support the thoasa. Halda shouted something at the skinny cove levitating beside her. He had a shock of white blonde hair and was clad in sober black, eschewing armor or fancy robes in favor of a simple, quilted jack. He carried a plain, ironwood staff. I felt sorcery flow across the battlefield as an expanding, concussive wave felled hundreds of infernals. Hundreds more took their place, clambering over the fallen, smashing through and climbing over the barricades created by the Mage Lords.

Shallunsard bellowed and lightning arced from his blade. The Hammer raised his weapon and intercepted the effulgent strike. Warriors closest to the battling giants were hit by the wash of cold fire and fell, scorched, burning, screaming. Halda and Ludorius continued to raise walls of earth, air, and fire. The Hammer's hammer glowed, and he hurled Shallunsard's lightning back at him. The demon split the incoming bolt with Dawnslight, killing dozens of his minions. Monstrous golems exploded, became flaming kindling.

Panic infected the warriors around me as the infernal horde surged forwards, desperate to fight their way to their master. Out of nowhere, the physicker tending me caught a blade in the face. Blood sprayed, and he fell back. A hoof caught me in the side of the head. I had to get up. I struggled to rise as the mass of fighters rolled over me. Some great oaf stood on me, which didn't help. I gasped, choked on dust. After everything I'd survived I was going to be crushed in a melee.

From nowhere a meaty paw reached down and grabbed the back of my shirt and dragged me to my feet. I didn't see my savior, as I was carried forwards with the counterattack. Another bolt of crackling energy lanced towards the Hammer. Again, he caught it on his weapon and hurled it back at Shallunsard only this time he leaped forwards and caught the demon in the chest with a resounding blow. Shallunsard was lifted off his feet and smashed into a wall of earth in which one of the Mage Lord's tried to enfold him.

An infernal with a featureless, grey face charging from the horde riding a wave of animated hands. It smashed into the shield wall. A mouth-like tear opened in its blank face and the thing vomited ichor on the warriors holding it at bay. Those it caught by the puke fell back with maggots pouring from dozens of tiny, thorn-lipped wounds. Heedless of the danger, more warriors ran forward to fill the breach. Mage fire arced above their heads and hit the infernal and spears were thrust into its pus-filled body. The thing went down wreathed in flames, its chariot of hands writhed and twitched as they burned.

Catapults sang and lobbed mundane fire into the nightmare mass of undead and abominations. There was a flash, an inhuman cry and Dawnslight pinwheeled through the air its diamond-encrusted hilt sparkling in the mid-morning suns' light.

I spied Volund's sword amongst the dead and fought my way towards it. A deafening cheer rose from the ranks of mortals, matched by howls of dismay from the monstrous horde. The Hammer raised his weapon. Shallunsard cowered. The space around them widened as the Vanguard rallied, and the demons fell back in disarray. The thoasan hero closed in for the kill. My heart thundered. *This is it.* I picked up my blade. Shallunsard half turned from the Hammer and Dawnslight appeared in his hand, the magical trick unseen by the thoasa.

I yelled a warning as the Hammer swung at Shallunsard, but my shout was lost amid the tumult. A sense of dread filled me as at the last minute the demon swayed away from the blow and slashed the thoasa from groin to forehead. Time froze. Or perhaps it was just me. A woman screamed. The Hammer took a two-handed grip of his weapon and brought it down in a crushing blow. Shallunsard raised his sword to block. Dawnslight didn't break. The demon's arm broke. He dropped the blade as the hammer smashed into his shoulder. Splinters of bone speared from the dead white flesh, black blood sprayed. The demon fell to his knees. The Hammer stood a moment longer before he too went down.

I have to do it now. I told myself, but I was struggling to concentrate, to breathe let alone slay the demon lord.

The Red Witch apported to the thoasa's side. Shallunsard recoiled as she unleashed her fury upon him. He raised his one good arm, the skin blistered, blackened, and burned under her onslaught. He bared his fangs, screamed in pain, something that warmed my cold, thoasan heart. Ruben stumbled from the ranks, blood pouring from a head wound. He knelt beside the Hammer.

Ludorius joined the Red Witch and attacked Shallunsard with a storm of black glass blades. On seeing their lord fall, the infernal advance stalled. The acrid taste of sorcery stung my throat, made my eyes water. I looked around. Corpses lay twenty deep in all directions. The poisoned earth ran red.

"I yield!" the demon roared.

"No, bastard. You die," Halda screamed and redoubled her efforts.

"Warrior," Shallunsard reached towards the Hammer with his blackened hand. "I beseech you, on your honor, accept my surrender."

The Hammer's amber eyes flickered open. "Halda— stop." Blood bubbled on his lips as, with the help of Ruben, he sat up. "Love, he has asked for quarter."

"No!"

"Halda." The Hammer reached out and took hold of her fire-wreathed hand. "He has yielded. We've won, love. We've won."

Her fire died as the Hammer fell into her arms.

Like everyone else, I was captivated by the tragedy and therefore didn't notice when Rowan arrived.

"He spoke the truth, child." She turned to address those closest as the infernals retreat turned into panicked flight. "You have won. Humanity, and its allies have triumphed over the forces of entropy."

I knew how this would turn out for the warspawn, but it was interesting to note that the Annurashi couldn't even bring herself to use the word 'evil'. But then, he was her brother, cast from the same, twisted mold.

Rowan looked exactly the same as the last time I'd seen her; pale, detached, unreal. The only difference was that she was wearing a suit of poncy looking armor, although I doubt she'd ever fought a battle in her life. Now that the fight had gone out of the infernals, more Mage Lords began to gather around Halda who still held the Hammer cradled in her arms. I noticed that some of them struggled to hide their disdain for the sobbing woman and her dead warspawn lover. Others— Ludorius amongst them, could hardly contain their fury and cast bladed looks at the demon and his sister, not that they knew Rowan, the wise Annurashi, was the demon's sister. I felt faint, my vision swam.

"Friends," Rowan spread her arms to encompass the mortals. "Though we will celebrate this victory, we will never forget those who have sacrificed their lives here today."

"Yes, you will." Like Halda's tears, my words were lost in the resounding cheers that rang across the bloody plain. I knew how it went from here, how Rowan would 'convince' those gathered to hand Shallunsard over to her for punishment. For his part the demon appeared superficially contrite. He was on his knees, head bowed, but I saw the sly smile that twitched at the corner of his mouth. *Now. It has to be now.* I gripped Volund's blade, took strength from the living steel's hunger for blood, swung my sword, and apported.

When I appeared behind Shallunsard, the blade was already whistling through the air. Using all the expert knowledge I'd gained over years of practicing the fatal arts I'd estimated where the bastard's head was before I made my move. If I'd got it wrong, if the strike was too low, it would slice into his back. Too high, and I might miss entirely, which would have been a deeply embarrassing last act before Rowan blew me to pieces. But underneath it all, and despite leaking a gallon of claret, I was still a Guild Blade and I was good at my job.

The Wild magic blade, forged by gods of another world, was eager to slake its thirst and sang as it snipped the bud from the stem. Shallunsard's body pitched forward. His noggin hit the ground and rolled away, light blazing from his dying eyes. It pleased me to see a look of horror dawn on Rowan's face just before the world became bright, hot, and extremely loud.

Chapter Twenty-One

"Wake up." Mother sounded less sharp than normal, not gentle; just happy drunk or perhaps high on pel. I rolled over and opened my eyes. In that half-doped state between waking and sleeping, I'd briefly assumed that I was in my bed in the *Mouse's Nest*.

I wasn't. I was lying on the edge of a crater with three-quarters of a corpse draped across me like we were bosom friends. I assumed it had been an ogren, but as the head and half the torso were missing that was just a guess. It could have been human for all I knew as some of those coves are equally hairy. It took a few minutes to squirm from under the dead weight, but eventually after much cursing managed to roll it off me. It flopped into the pit. Hungry critters were feeding on the banquet I'd provided scattered as it tumbled into the hole, their claws rasping on the clinker.

I rested for a couple of minutes before trying to sit up. The ghost of Mother's voice still echoed in my head. It was night and even though my eyesight wasn't as good as it used to be, I could sense the weight of thousands of dead surrounding the crater. There was no sign of Shallunsard's body or Rowan, the Hammer, or any of the Mage Lords. They had either been utterly destroyed or they'd fucked off, leaving me and their minions to rot. I pushed myself up. My right hand was blistered and burnt. Pain woke in charred nerves and the imprint of Volund's sword hilt was burned into my palm. The blade itself was sticking out of the ground beside me, entirely unscathed.

"I did it," I said, incredulous.

I'd killed Shallunsard. I'd also killed a few thousand humans, infernals, and warspawn, but nobody's perfect. Ash clouds drifted across the face of the moon. In the space between shadows, I looked at my hands. The right one was a mess of burns; the left was scorched but mostly unscathed. The demon mark and Rowan's sigil were gone.

"Well, what do you know." I retrieved my sword and climbed to my knees like a geriatric half-thoasa who'd been stabbed in the guts and then blown up.

Using my sword for support, I got to my feet. I was so very tired, but despite changing the course of history, I still had a few loose ends to tie up. A red scarf drifted past. I picked it up. It smelled of cinnamon and star steel at once familiar and also strange.

I set off for the gate. It was going to be a long, slow, painful walk back to the city but at least there was no one around to see my pathetic progress. Night tempered the ugliness of the crow fields and the hard ruins of Old Valen became a romantic impression of a city at peace; a sketch drawn in smoke and firelight scattered across the rind of the world.

***

The battlefield didn't so much end as peter out. The infernals had taken the fight into the already battered city before Shallunsard fell. The stink of schism magic hung in the air, underscoring the pungent aroma of death and burning. Nothing of this place smelled clean or wholesome, and the sooner I was away the better. The angle gate stood on its mound surrounded by rubble, but the Hammer's body had yet to be placed upon the stones. Perhaps now it wouldn't, perhaps he would really be laid to rest in the Hall of Heroes where he truly belonged. Whatever fate awaited his mortal remains, I imagined that somewhere in this vast tumble, prayers were being said for him and every cull who fancied themselves a poet would be striving to out eulogize their fellows.

If thoasa had an afterlife, I hoped the Hammer had found his way there. Even though he'd suffered from a fatal case of the heroics, he seemed a nice enough cove. Lightheaded, I stumbled and noticed that I was leaving quite the trail of claret behind me as I searched for the keystone. Darkness born inside my skull chewed at the edges of my vision. I gritted my teeth and fought through the pain until I found the monolith that would wake its fellows and take me to the last place I wanted to go.

There was something different about this trip through the gate. This time I knew where I was and where I wanted to go. It was as though I could see the route written in the scattered stars. I was in control; the captain of my ship, navigating these, most treacherous waters. A pity then that this was probably the last time I would do this.

When I stepped from the stones and into the Gate tower, I was ready for the Eldest. She would undoubtedly know that her favorite was dead. I was betting my life that she would want to know how he'd died rather than slot me out of hand. I needed that to be the case because her forbearance would give me the chance to do to her what I'd done to her boy or die trying.

It therefore came as a surprise when I arrived to find the chamber was empty. The bodies were gone, and the rubble had been cleared. While I tried to fathom what had happened, unfamiliar footsteps approached the door. I hid behind a monolith as glowstones woke. Dragon shadows passed overhead as Rowan's shadow crawled across the floor. She stood in the doorway, her silhouette outlined in blue. I smelled blood. "I didn't expect you to return," she said.

"I'll bet."

She entered the chamber, dragging her left leg. When she stepped into the light I saw that her clothes were torn and drenched in claret, and that half her face had been torn down to the bone.

"And I thought I looked bad." I went over, mindful that I'd just slain her kin.

"You do." Her white hair was streaked with scarlet. Blood oozed from a dozen deep gashes in her chest and stomach, and black veins of corruption were spreading across her snow pale skin. "Shallunsard is dead, isn't he?"

I expected the Eldest to appear then; to charge into the room, furious and vengeful, but only a thin breeze dogged Rowan's footsteps. "He is. Those bastard Mage Lords got him. I'm sorry. Funny thing: you were there too. You don't remember?"

She gave a lopsided smile. "Mage Lords, eh?" Darkness invaded the whites of her eyes. She stumbled. I reached out to help her. "Don't touch me!" she snarled, as she fought to master the sickness spreading through her battered body. A moment passed before she looked up at me and smiled. "For your own sake, stay away from me." The black veins reminded me of when Ozbert's demon had attacked Malin.

"What happened here?"

"She went insane when he was killed." Rowan's poisoned gaze turned to the sky, black tears ran down her cheek. Sensing the end was near, the dragons hammered the mountains with their savage cries. "I did what had to be done, what should have been done millennia ago."

"You slotted the Eldest?"

She turned her gaze upon me. "She didn't leave me any choice. *You* didn't leave me any choice."

I raised my hands. "Hold on there, fustilugs, this has nothing to do with me. I'm just a pawn in Fate's game. I've been roughly swived. I'm naught but a—"

"Shut up, Breed. For once in your life just shut up." She swayed, almost fell. This time I didn't try to help her. When she recovered her eyes fell on Volund's blade. "Is that the sword you used to slay my brother?"

I nodded.

"It must be a powerful weapon. Show me." Black veins crawled further up her neck. She closed her eyes and for a moment I thought she'd succumbed to the undeath plague, but then silver shone through her skin and the darkness retreated a handspan. I drew the blade, left-handed because my right was fucked. She took a step toward me. I took a step back. "I was there too, you say, at the end?"

I nodded. "Aye. You looked like an angel, gave a fine, moving speech, people cried. How is it you don't remember?"

"Because this place is out of time now, and I am anchored to this existence by the slenderest thread." She smiled. "You've broken reality, Breed." Silence opened like the Void. "Let's not pretend you don't have to do this."

"I wasn't going to."

She smiled again. "I am the last of my kind."

"Good. No offense."

"None taken. The ward above will fade when I am gone, so if you don't want to meet the neighbors I suggest you leave quickly and don't stop to rob the place."

"As if I would do such a...all right, point taken."

She stepped forward, took hold of my hand, and guided the point of the blade to her chest. "Goodbye, Breed." She tipped me the nod and I drove the thirsting blade through her heart.

"Goodbye, Rowan." Light died in her eyes. I stepped back, freeing the blade. As she began to fall I took her head with a single blow. Cut white hair flew like feathers and dark blood fountained. I staggered drunkenly until I could ground the blade and regain my balance. The ground shook, cracks raced up the walls, lumps of plaster fell and finally the last, live angle gate cracked and fell apart.

"Bollocks."

I slumped against a fallen monolith and put my sword across my knees. The icy touch of death settled upon me like a blanket of snow. I cannot say I'd had a good life, but it had certainly been eventful. I wasn't rich, I didn't have twenty children holding a vigil and weeping at my bedside, and no one would raise a statue to me, or write a ballad in my honor, but for all that I was more or less content. A pair of dragons landed on the ward and glared at me. I closed my eyes and waited for death.

***

An hour later, I still wasn't dead.

Bored, I opened my eyes. The dragons were still there, staring at me through a veil of drifting snow. The tips of their claws had begun to pierce the ward as the magic began to fade, but that was less disturbing than Rowan's corpse. In death there was no deception. The once graceful godling's flesh had turned deepest blue. Her red, glazed eyes stared fiercely at eternity and razor fangs protruded from her ragged maw.

"Got to say, you've looked better, Rowan."

One of the dragons pushed another claw through the ward, threw back its head, and gave a throaty, hissing growl, which I knew to be laughter having spent quite some time as a dragon. I also knew that I was dying and that I didn't want to be eaten by the grinning coves sitting above me. I could walk out and die in the snow. I could apport down the mountain and be eaten by something else. I could crawl away and die in a corner but that just seemed a bit shit after everything I'd been through.

Given a choice, I would have liked to die in Arduin. It had been my home for longer than anywhere else, and barring dying, being resurrected as a restless dead, and having to fight a necromantic dragon, it had been fun. But there was no going back. My home was a world away, and I had no means of…

"Oi," I shouted at the dragons. Neither responded. One was dozing and the other was licking its nethers. "Oi!" I shouted again and spiced my words with a hint of compulsion. Two pairs of eyes swiveled in my direction.

"You want in, and I want out, am I right?" Just as I could project a mortal voice when I was a dragon, I could do the reverse in my thoasan bone bag.

"You speak our tongue?" said the one with a dark scar running across his ice-white snout.

"I do. I was a dragon on and off for almost forty years. I shan't bore you with the details because, well, they're boring, so back to my question. You want in, right?"

It puffed out its chest, massive muscles swelled; its wings creaked. "We want what is ours. We want to see this place destroyed and our ancestral roost returned to us."

"Help me and it's yours."

They both laughed at that. Scar crouched, pressed the tip of his snout through the ward, and breathed a cloud of ice into the chamber. "It will be ours soon enough, smalling."

I focused on the ward and pushed a little magic into it, reinforced the pattern that already existed— a task made easier by the fact I was sitting on a mountain of star steel. The claws and the snout were pushed back. Both creatures snarled and slashed at the dome. "I'm stuck here unless you help me, and I can do this," I gestured to the ward, "for a very long time."

The second dragon spread its wings and slammed its horn-tipped flight fingers into the dome. It sparked but remained solid. "I fucking hate sorcerers," it snarled.

"Aye, me too. So, do we have a deal?"

They looked at each other, searching for an answer to the question in each other's eyes. After a long pause, Scar turned to me. "Deal."

Chapter Twenty-Two

After we had thrashed out the details amid much cursing and growling, they flew off to find what I thought I could use to fashion a new angle gate.

I felt instinctively that none of the stones in here would do. They were burned out, and would never wake again, at least, not in any way that I could fathom. I needed new monoliths to imbue. And that eyeless self-abuser, Doc, had mentioned something about dragon bones being used to make a gate, which struck a chord with me; if anything aside of enchanted stone could hold the power of the Void, it was dragon bone.

If I was wrong, I'd fail, and the dragons would have the last laugh. To die by ice dragon would be a poetic, if unpleasantly crunchy end after escaping years ago had set me on this, wild road in the first place. I sat down while I waited and pondered my potentially grim fate. It was a struggle to keep my eyes open. I was more tired than I'd been in a long time, and by tired, I mean, 'dying'.

"Smalling." Scar's bone-rattling voice woke me from my daze. "We have returned."

I didn't stand up. "Yes. I noticed. Did you bring what I asked for?"

His muzzle drew back, half smile, half snarl, displaying an almost perfect set of teeth. "We did. Drop the ward."

I drained the power from the ward and unpicked the bones of the spell. When I'd finished, I felt as light-headed as if I'd smoked a sack of pel. Scar spread his wings and roared. Snow began to fall inside the tower. The dragon's call was answered by a dozen more. High above the keep, wings snapped and drove the air in spinning torrents as the dragons came to reclaim their home.

Scar dropped into the chamber. He smelled of ice and granite. I noted that he was smaller than I had been in my elemental form but that his tail was twice as long as his body and had fluttering, sail-like fins running along its length. He prowled towards me, his great claws tearing lumps out of the bloodstained floor. He sniffed Rowan's carcass, withdrew sharply as though stung by the scent of decay.

"These creatures are a scourge. They do not belong here."

"Be of good cheer then, for that was the last of them."

He swung his head round to face me, narrowed his eyes. "Your guts are leaking."

"Yes."

"You will die soon."

"Yes, all right, no need to rub it in, for fuck's sake. It's why I want to go home."

He flicked Rowan's corpse into the dark well over which the platforms had been suspended. "I understand, smalling." He gave a long, wailing cry and one of the spiraling dragons stooped to a dive. When it was about a hundred feet above us it spread its wings and beat them to slow its tail-first descent. Clutched in its claws was the rib bone of a dragon.

"Tell her to drop it," I said to Scar, because I didn't have the strength to shout. He wailed again, and the dragon released the bone and banked away. I guided it down and embedded it into the floor of the chamber. Another eleven followed to complete my very own angle gate.

"You'd best not stand too close in case this goes awry," I said to Scar, who was hanging around to keep an eye on me just in case I tried to renege on our deal. Likewise I didn't give a shit about his safety, I just didn't want him within biting range while I was busy. I took a step back. "This looks good. And why shouldn't it? I mean, all the other gates were made by someone, why shouldn't it look right?"

"I do not care, smalling. Please, just leave now."

"I wasn't talking to you. Now if you wouldn't mind."

The dragon hopped onto a broken-toothed edge of wall and furled his wings. This time I didn't have to find the keystone to unlock the gate, I had to make one. I'd expected to feel nervous as this moment approached, fearful even, but I didn't. I felt balanced, secure in my abilities, and rooted in the moment. Time and place were irrelevant; strength and power were irrelevant. I could no more force the spell than I could turn the suns in the sky. I just had to do what needed to be done to wake my gate and open a path to home.

I put my hands on the grey bone. It was pitted, honeycombed with age and weathering. My bloody handprints were my sigils. I focused my power through them into the bone. The gate woke. I took a moment; put my head against the newly anointed pillar. "Please, take me home." I turned it to just the right angle to open a rift in the world, felt the pull of the Void as the angle locked. The air within the ring grew cold.

The dragon yawned and scratched his nethers, ruining the moment. I glared at him.

"Sorry, do carry on." He grinned.

"Wanker," I muttered and quickly stepped into the breach. As usual, I felt myself being stretched between worlds, felt every fiber of my being ironed flat before being picked over by fire ants. And then it was over, and I was home.

In Appleton.

I stumbled out of a shimmering ghost gate, which vanished like morning mist, leaving nothing to show it had ever been there. I was behind the corner where Tanner's Row met Slaughter Lane, just down from the meat market. Nothing had ever been built here on account of it being the perfect place for run-off from butchery and tanning to drain into the Silverlight marshes. The bones of a small boat languished in the shallows some ten feet from where I appeared, but other than that there was nothing but the mosquitos, garbage and me.

"When I said, 'home' I meant my nice, fucking palace in Arduin, the one with servants, comfy beds, and bastarding plumbing. Not this...shithole." I raged at the gods, but they deigned not to answer. Two suns shone behind the towering smokestacks rising from the calthracite burners.

I took a step, slipped in the mud and fell. "This isn't the home I meant," I said to my mud puddle reflection.

"What have we got here, Dirk?" To add to my joy, a pair of grubby culls emerged from a shaded alley leading from Tannery Row. The questioner, a broad-shouldered fellow with a booze battered face, put down a sack. It whimpered and rolled around until he put his foot on the rope that fastened it. Dirk was taller, thinner, and carrying a large rock. He wore the mournful expression of someone Fate had not favored; an expression I knew all too well.

"Looks like someone's lost their way, Anders." They exchanged a knowing look.

"Might we help you, friend?" said Anders. Whatever was in the sack struggled sufficiently to earn a swift kick. It yelped. Anders' hand strayed behind his back to where I presumed he kept his blade.

Tempting though it was to just lie there, I got up. "Look lads, I'm having a bit of a day so why don't you just fuck off and drown your dog somewhere else, eh?" Whatever was in the sack struggled violently. "It's not a dog, is it?"

Dirk blanched. "Get it." He chinned at me.

I drew my sword. "You sure you want to do this?"

"You get it," said Anders, ignoring my question.

"You're closer." The other miscreant countered.

"I'm holding the…goods."

I sheathed my blade. "How have you two survived to adulthood?" They looked at me, confused. "Don't answer; the sound of your mewling piss-dribble offends me. The pair of you: hie thee hence to the nearest temple and swear yourselves to five, no— *ten* years, lay servitude as penance for your undoubted lives of crime. Don't kill anyone, don't rob anyone, and don't rape anyone for the rest of your naturals." The compulsion spell made them wince but otherwise I encountered no resistance. Their eyes momentarily glazed before they trotted off without comment to the next, less murdersome chapter of their miserable lives. "Got to say, compulsion does have its uses." I hobbled over and untied the sack.

Inside was a spawn of some kind. It was small and skinny and looked young but could have been a fully grown adult for all I knew. It had coal black eyes, a large head, and was covered in wispy, grey down. It was bound and gagged but once out of the sack it wriggled free of its bonds and unfurled a pair of gossamer wings. "Urgh, that's better." It rolled its tiny shoulders. "I am in your debt, stranger," it said.

"No, you're not." I headed off in the direction of Tanner's. It darted after me.

"Wait, you saved me."

"And?"

It cocked its head. "Well, don't you want to know who you saved and from what?"

"No. I don't want or need to know either, now…" A sharp pain lanced through my stomach. "I have somewhere to go—"

"Johann." He offered brightly.

"Johann, whatever. Go find your people and secure yourself some attire, lest the greenshanks arrest you."

"What's a 'greenshanks'? Do you mean, city guard?"

"Aye, maybe. I don't know any more, things have changed since I was last here."

"I don't suppose you could lend me some coin, could you? I'll pay you back. I've got a system you see, I just need a stake…" He smiled sweetly.

I laughed. It hurt, but I laughed. I suppose there was something comforting about the familiarity of this home. "Nice try, Johann, but I'm all out."

"Ah. Pity. Thanks anyway…?"

"Breed." I waved and left Johann to his business. Using Volund's sword as a cane I limped over to the alley behind Blookmann's grindery. Because I was leaking I kept to the side streets and backways and hid in doorways when I caught sight of any greenshanks. To my surprise and pleasure the city guard I spied were not all humans. I mean, they were still city guards and therefore scum, but now they were equal opportunity scum and the city although still a shithole, didn't look like it had been attacked by demons.

Beneath Blookmann's grindery is a cellar. In the corner of the cellar is a stack of shelves that are rarely used and never moved, for behind them is a door that leads to the fief of the Queen of the Midnight Court, or Mother as I liked to think of her. I was relieved to find that some things hadn't changed, and the door was still there albeit rusty.

Mother. Now there was a cove I really wanted to talk to. I made my way slowly and painfully down to the sewers. This was not the 'home' I'd wanted to die in, but it was undoubtedly my home. I'd drawn my first breath down here, so I suppose it was a fitting place to draw my last.

I conjured a ball of light which scattered the dog rats that had been stalking me, enticed by the trail of blood I was leaving behind me. I stumbled towards the *Mouse's Nest,* an inn and the headquarters of the finest guild of murderers and thieves in Appleton…at the time…probably.

"Here be monsters," I said when I reached the door. Above the door was a skull in a cage. The skull had been gnawed open and lying snug within was a desiccated mouse that had died the death all craved; in its bed, fast asleep.

I pushed the door which groaned on rusted hinges. Even though my sense of smell had told me otherwise I was still disappointed by what I found. I'd smelled the musk of abandonment, but it would have been nice to open the door as I'd done a thousand times and be greeted by the babble of conversation, guarded looks, and the smell of pel and ale so strong it could knock my teeth out. The common room was swathed in darkness. The chairs were upended on the tables, the hearth was cold, and cloths hung over dusty barrel taps.

Small rats scattered at my approach, their claws splashed through the runoff dripping down the walls that had pooled where rushes used to be strewn. I sheathed my blade and made my way to the back room, which was likewise deserted. *The Mouse's Nest* had been closed for a long time if the depth of dust was anything to go by. Although there was a sliver of light shining from under the old tapestry of a knight that was hanging over the doorway leading down to Mother's chambers.

The light was accompanied by the sound of voices. I dispelled the ball of light, pulled the hanging aside and headed quietly down the stairs to Mother's audience chamber. Conversation stopped as I opened the door.

The room was lit by a dozen candles. Mother was standing by the Rat Bone Throne. She looked much like the day I'd last seen her in here, only today she was wearing a travelling cloak over her egg yellow gown. Crouched nearby was Ludo. One half of which was swigging from a bottle of wine while the other was enjoying a pipe of pel. All his eye stalks swiveled in my direction. Mother looked up slowly from behind her long dark curls an odd look of relieve crossed with sorrow on her face. I went over to greet her, mindful not to walk over the grate in the floor in case any dog rats were waiting for their dinner. I tugged the now blood-soaked scarf from my maille.

"Hello, Mother. You dropped this I think." I handed her the scarf.

***

"You're hurt," Mother observed.

"Well, yes, I mean, what do you expect after I find out that I've been lied to all my life? It's a betrayal."

"No, I mean you're bleeding. Let me see."

I slapped her hand away. "It's nothing. And don't try to change the subject."

"I didn't lie to you. Will you at least sit down if you won't let me look at that?"

I sat on the Rat Bone Throne. "You say you didn't lie, but you never mentioned you were an immortal Mage Lord either, or was that more of an 'omission'?"

"It was neither. I didn't know, not really. I, that is, Mother Blake was a shard, a piece of my persona. She was ruled by rage; simple, mortal cunning and a desire for wealth guided her— *my* actions. It had to be that way."

"I'd like to believe you, I really would." I really did. She sagged and walked away, shaking her head.

Ludo watched, intent, quiet, but I kept my eye on the old scoundrel. "You moved out then?"

"Yes, there came a point when you vanished that I realized it was time to get out of the gang boss business. Pork Chop and I came to an amicable arrangement. He gets Appleton and I went to Valen with a chest of his gold. I've been there ten years now."

"What happened to the Blades?"

"Every noblewoman needs retainers." She smiled. "I suppose you want me to explain myself?" Mother held out her hand to Ludo, who gave her the bottle of wine. She handed it to me.

"I think I can work most of it out, but there is something I want you to confirm, despite it being impossible."

"Only one?"

"Was the Hammer my father?"

Mother, *Halda,* took the bottle back and had a long swig. "Can't you work it out?"

Ludo tutted. "Tell the child, dear friend."

"Yes of course the Hammer is your father, I didn't have a thing for thoasa, you know?"

I'd suspected, but even now hearing her admit it, the truth was hard to swallow. "Er, right. Sorry only you know with him dying seven hundred years before I was born it wasn't quite as obvious as you might think. Oh, the Annurashi are all dead."

"All of them?"

"As far as I'm aware."

She raised the bottle to her thin lips. "I'll drink to that."

Ludo slapped a tentacle against its giant lobster claw. "They smelled of knives and fish heads. I was never keen." His, her or its eye stalks twitched.

"So, what did happen?"

"I thought you could work it out?"

"Don't be funny. And how is it that I look older than you?"

She gave a little smile. "Blame your father. Thoasa don't age well." She paced the dusty chamber, her skirts rustled like a saw blade. "Like I said, I had to split myself into pieces. I left shards of myself scattered through times, hoping that you might find some of them. But this isn't the place to start." She rubbed her eyes. She seemed weary and for the first time in our association, a little fragile. "After the battle when…" Her jaw tightened. "After they took that fucker Shallunsard away, I knew they would come for us next, because they'd seen how strong we were. I knew they would try to shackle our power. So, some of us fled."

"By 'they', you mean the Annurashi?"

"Who the fuck do you think I mean?" she snapped. "Ludorius and I fled through a gate." She gestured to Ludo. "If I'd stayed I'd have killed them or died trying, and I couldn't risk losing you too."

"Losing…? How long were you pregnant?"

"Shut up and let me finish. They wanted me to lie about your father. I couldn't stand it. The Annurashi came for us, Ludo helped me escape." She turned away, unable to continue. I looked to Ludo.

"Dear friend went into labor between worlds. We," it gestured to both halves of itself. "We held the universe at bay until you were born." It held its claw protectively. "It was quite the spell, but it…*changed* us."

"Fuck," I said. "I mean, thanks. I suppose that explains why I have an affinity for the angle gates."

"Oh, you think?" Mother snapped.

"You're really rude, you know that, don't you?"

"It has been said."

"I wonder what happened to my friends. I mean, if I slotted Shallunsard then they can't have been killed when Valen fell— Valen didn't fall, did it?"

"You just answered your own question. A Valen fell somewhere, but not *this* Valen."

"If you say so. Hey, have ye heard of House Vulsones?"

"Who hasn't?"

"Do you know Tobias Vulsones?"

"Only by reputation. Senator Tobias Vulsones is apparently a bit of a prick, although whatever it is he does with that tentacle of his has apparently made him a favorite with the Empirifex's eldest daughter." She winked.

I winced as another stabbing pain gripped me. It didn't sound like my Tobias, but then, this wasn't my Tobias. Even so, I was pleased he was doing well and that he was whole. "So after I was born, what then?"

"Ludo and I came here. It was a good place to hide and wait to see if the seeds I'd planted before I left took root. It wasn't easy; my powers were much diminished. Ludorius almost destroyed himself to save us and I had a child to raise and protect." She laughed. "But it wasn't all bad. We had some fun building the Guild. That part of me could forget most of what had happened and concentrate on the mundane until one day every trace of you vanished, and then not long after, I became myself or as much of myself as remained. That's when I knew you'd succeeded, that the demon would never return."

"So is that all I was, just a tool?"

"No, child. You are my strange, wonderful gift from him. You are unique."

"That's nice. Most people think I'm a bit of a cunt."

"Those who matter know you for who you truly are, but yes you can also be a bit of a cunt."

"Thanks?"

She shrugged. "It hasn't been easy for me either. Coming back to this craphole every year, waiting, hoping for a sign."

Ludo gestured to its selves. "It has been slightly harder for us, dear friend. In case you hadn't noticed."

"Don't start this again, Ludo…"

I snagged the bottle of wine and took a long swig. Bone weary, I lay my head against the throne while they bickered. A selfish part of me regretted that my ghosts were no longer ghosts. I could do with a friend right now, just someone who I didn't want to strangle, to be with me when I died. "Too much to ask, I suppose." I chuckled. The sweet iron taste of blood filled my mouth. I wasn't afraid. I felt weightless, at peace. The aches I'd carried for years, physical and emotional, vanished. It was time, and I was ready. I closed my eyes. The bottle slipped from my hand.

"What the…?" said Mother. "Oh, no you fucking don't."

END

VOLUND'S FORGE

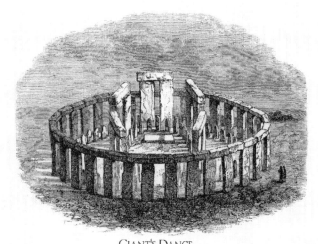

GIANT'S DANCE

The Spider and The Fly

It's been a long journey, but sadly we have come to the end of The Chronicles of Breed. I hope you enjoyed reading this series.

Don't worry. My next series, set in Edolis, will be released in 2019….

Keep your eyes peeled for the two deadliest assassins this side of Appleton in, **The Spider and The Fly.**

Free Books

If you haven't already read them; I would love to offer you two free *Chronicles of Breed* prequel novellas!

I love telling the stories of Breed's exploits; *The Best Laid Plans* and *A Fistful Of Rubies* are available for free if you just type the link below into your web browser.

http://kdavies.net/nltac

Author's Note

I would like to ask that you consider leaving me a review because they really help. Obviously, it would be awesome if you tell everyone how much you liked it, but even if you didn't it's always great to get feedback from my readers. Typing this link into your internet browser will make it really easy for you: http://kdavies.net/rtsw

It would be great if you could.

Thanks

K.T.

About The Author

When I'm not writing books, I work the day job, wrangle my kids, four dogs, and a grouchy, old cat. I play computer games, ride horses, practice medieval martial arts, grow vegetables, throw axes, and read, not at the same time, that could get messy.

I have a website here http://kdavies.net

And a Facebook page here: https://www.facebook.com/KTScribbles where we can hang out, have a couple of brewskis, and talk about the good old days.

You can also find me on Twitter @KTScribbles.

Once again, thank you so much for going on a ride with me and Breed. I hope I see you again soon.

All the best,

K.T.

Printed in Great Britain
by Amazon